Taken

DI Grant

A P Bateman

Facebook: @authorapbateman

www.apbateman.com

Rockhopper Publishing

Also by A P Bateman

The Town
The Island
Stone Cold

The DI Grant Series
Vice
Taken

Standalone Novel
Never Go Back
(A Big Dave story from the Alex King series)

Short Stories
The Perfect Murder?
Atonement

Find out more at:
www.apbateman.com

Dedication

For my wife and children,

because that is what everything is for…

Chapter One

There is a great sadness to be found in the eyes of the dead. A certain knowledge, too. They hold a secret you will not discover until it is your time, and in turn, it will be too late for you to share.

Grant bent down, catching his own reflection in the glossy eyes. There was a thick sheen of dried tears and they reminded him of his sister's dolls as a child. Inanimate. Inhuman. He thought back to when he had last looked into those same eyes – warm, loving and accepting. He had lost himself within the depths of her. Been drawn in. She had given him all he had wanted; all he had asked of her and more. They had shared passion and tenderness.

"No motive yet. But given her association, it's not a stretch of the imagination to say it was retribution," the Chief Superintendent said. "That or the bitch just knew too much…"

Grant fought the urge to smooth a hand across her face and stood back up. He took a breath, his heart pounding. "Any clue to how it was done?"

The senior officer looked at him. "There's a shit-load of

cocaine in the next room. Credit card and a rolled fifty-pound note. There's coke in her nose and mouth, traces around her nipples, even..." he trailed off. "Seems she had some fun with someone, and they snorted it off each other, but it all went too far. Accidental overdose, I'd say..."

"Bullshit!" Grant snapped. "She never did cocaine."

"And you would know? How would you know a thing like that? My, you really *did* get undercover, didn't you?"

"I know a frame-up when I see it. Someone pumped her full of some bad shit and staged a scene."

"Well obviously. But, who? Roper has half a dozen rival dealers, but most of them wouldn't have the balls to do something like this." He paused. "If someone wanted to get to Roper, then they could find a better way. Out-bid him or undercut him. This is too hands-on for international arms dealers. No, the woman's death is a statement."

Grant watched as the SOCO leader instructed the forensic officers to get the body into a body bag. He smarted as the woman's skirt was ridden up around her thighs in the process. He was familiar with the underwear, the cut of the material and the shape of the outline it covered. One of the officers respectfully pulled the skirt back down and together they heaved and wriggled the bag under her buttocks. He knew there was a small tattoo on the right cheek. She had apparently had it done for a dare when she was just eighteen. It was the only tattoo she had, and it was an outline of a dove holding an olive branch in its beak. She said she had been big on peace back then. Ironic, given who she had ended up marrying.

"Are you okay, DCI Grant?"

"Fine."

"What in God's name is a DCI doing in undercover work, anyway?"

"Experience."

"Perhaps somebody enjoys setting you up to fail?" The Chief Superintendent smirked. "Commander Maitland is no longer here to look after you."

"I know. I sent flowers to his widow."

"Maybe it was all that guff down in Cornwall last summer..." He smiled, relishing in scrutinising Grant's career. That was what happened to maverick police officers, they were built up, then torn back down. "Did a lot of damage to the police service down there. Made a few enemies, no doubt. Perhaps that's why someone sent you in undercover?"

Grant looked at the man. They had been at Hendon together. Right now, he felt like punching him, but instead he said, "I go where I'm sent. That tends to be how the chain of command works."

"You're blown, by the way."

"Blown?"

"Like a candle," the Chief Superintendent replied. "You're out. Finished. That's why I brought you here. Let you see what sloppy work does, what it means for people. The consequences it meant for her, and the waste of time and resources put in by your colleagues." He paused; his smirk was unnerving. The man was enjoying this. "Everyone knows you're a bit of a ladies' man. Maybe they knew it was only a matter of time before the lines became blurred and you fucked it all up..."

"What...?"

"Because you were fucking her," he said calmly. "The target's wife. Reckless, to say the least. Selfish, too, considering the hours of work others have put into this operation."

Grant flushed. He looked at the unit commander and

said, "So, you thought you'd teach me a lesson by bringing me here to see here body?"

"Roper did this to show you something. To show you that nobody betrays his trust. He's sent you a message. I thought you should see it, too. This operation is blown, and you're compromised. I'm not going after Roper for this because you were sleeping with the man's wife in the middle of an operation. Not only will the Crown Prosecution Service hesitate in bringing the case before a judge, but you have brought shame on my department, the entire Metropolitan Police Service, even. A simple verdict of misadventure, of her humping and snorting cocaine with an unknown and it not working out so well for her will give us an easy ride..." He paused, glaring at him. "One of our observation teams saw you and intercepted a call you made to her. And then you were seen again. And it's likely - no, damned obvious - that her husband saw you, too. Three years' work, two blown undercover officers preceding yourself, six million pounds of our budget and we're back to square one because you couldn't keep your dick in your bloody pants..."

"Get fucked, Malcolm..." Grant glared at him.

"No, but you bloody well did! Ever wondered why you are terminal at Chief Inspector? Why the doors of promotion have been closing in your face for some time now, ever since your demotion? Why career officers who came up with you are now heading up specialist units or have big shiny plaques on their office doors? Christ, you and I were at Hendon together!" He paused. "And I'll see you busted down to Inspector at the very least for this! Shit, you'll be in traffic as a PC when I've finished with you!"

"You're not a copper. You're a bloody politician, Malcolm..."

"Chief Superintendent Boyce to you," he corrected him. "And don't you ever forget it." Grant ignored him and took a final look at the woman's body as the two forensic technicians zippered up the bag and stole her from view. They ignored the two police officers bickering as they lifted her onto a gurney. Office politics. They had seen and heard it all before. "You take too many chances, Grant. Too many gut feelings, too many hunches. And then you suck those around you into your arrogance and they pay the price. Deborah, Chloe... you lost them through drinking and gambling and fucking around!"

"Don't ever talk about them," Grant glared at him. "Marriages break down. *Most* police marriages hit bumps in the road."

"It's not a damned bump in the road! You're divorced and you get to see Chloe one weekend in two, and then you manage to miss most of those..."

Grant watched the two men manoeuvre the gurney out of the bathroom and into the hotel room. He followed, turning his back on his superior. The technicians wheeled the gurney around the scattered furniture and broken glass. She had put up a struggle, at least. He thought back to the last time he had seen her in the hotel room. They had showered together, explored each other tentatively before heading to the bedroom in the suite she had paid for. They had been passionate and rough, then talked, sipped champagne and made love more delicately and intimately throughout the night. He had never once thought to ask how she had paid for the room, whether she had used a credit or debit card or a bank account that Roper would have known about. But the man surely had.

Grant didn't bother correcting his boss, although his observations had stung. He had missed enough weekends and contact time with Chloe because of the workload that the man had constantly piled upon him. And with the past six months spent in deep cover, he had purposely severed his ties with the outside world. Save for a few calls to his fifteen-year-old daughter from public phone boxes. They had met a few times, but he had spent their entire time together looking over his shoulder.

"What now?"

Chief Superintendent Boyce sneered. "That's it? You shagged an arms dealer's wife and get her killed, screwed up a four-year operation and ask *what now*?" He shook his head. "How do you sleep at night? Apart from in a shitty little flat, because Deborah got the house after all your philandering..."

"I told you not to mention my wife and child."

"For Christ's sake! Deborah and Chloe, Chloe and Deborah! What are you going to do? You're washed out, Grant. You're done. You're still drinking, aren't you? You won't even get your pension when I've finished my report..."

Grant looked at him, saw the arrogance and daring in the man's eyes. He'd swung the punch before thinking it through, but then, as the man was always reminding him, that's the sort of thing he did. Boyce reeled backwards and recoiled into the wall. Shit, it was done now. Just as well get hung for a sheep, as a lamb... Grant followed it up with a short, sharp two-punch combination and the man went out like a light.

Or a candle.

Chapter Two
Amsterdam, Holland

The office suite was modern and spacious and constructed entirely from silk white painted walls and smoked glass or mirrors. There were two female receptionists at a smoked glass desk each working at a MacBook with the wires plumbed straight to the floor in chrome pipes to hide them from unsightly view. All printing – not that the company committed more than was necessary to paper – was done at an unseen suite via wireless connection.

Richardson enjoyed the view. Not of the two canals visible below and the cafés on each side of the waterways, but of the upskirt view that he was occasionally afforded by one of the women as she moved in her seat taking calls on her headset. He could see she used a tanning bed or spray tan and had exquisite taste in underwear. He glanced away when he caught her eye, and somewhat self-consciously, she crossed her slender bronze legs and closed the proverbial door on him completely.

"Mister Van Cleef will see you now," the other receptionist said, stepping out from around the glass desk and walking towards him. She stood still, gestured gently with a hand to follow her. "He apologises for the wait..."

"It's not a problem," he replied. He caught sight of himself in some of the glass as they walked and was bought rapidly back down to earth. His appearance never somehow went with the way he felt and the confidence he exuded. He felt the king shit, but he looked like a sack of it. Balding, slightly hunched at the shoulders, fifty pounds heavier than he wanted to be and a good foot shorter than the elegant beauty who was now leading the way down the corridor. He knew he could never be in a relationship with a woman like this, but he could possibly rent one for an hour or so at a thousand euros after the meeting. It depended how the meeting went. He was thinking champagne and the full girlfriend experience if it went well, and possibly some sadomasochism if it went poorly. Take out a little frustration on somebody he could humiliate and would never see again.

The woman knocked on a glass door, where a thin, gaunt man with a flame of red hair sat behind a similar glass desk to those in the reception suite. Richardson stepped inside and the woman closed the door and walked back down the corridor as if it were a Milan catwalk.

The man did not stand, but he extended his hand towards him. Richardson reached, but there was still a void between them, and he had to do an awkward half-step shuffle to take hold of the man's soft, clammy hand.

"It's for the bugs," the man said, sweeping his hand in front of his surroundings. "Listening devices, cameras and the like. Glass defeats my enemies, whether they are my fellow competition, or the intelligence services of many nations that find my work... uncomfortable."

"That makes sense," Richardson mused.

"Indeed," said Van Cleef. "We can't be bugged, simply

because we would see any device that was planted. And parabolic microphones are thwarted by a pulse of white noise played constantly from speakers positioned around the outside of the building. Each pane of glass is ballistic resistant to three consecutive strikes from point fifty calibre bullets and although the glass appears clear from this side, a constant varying smoked tint alternates with the brightness of the sun, which plays havoc with cameras and makes them constantly adjust to compensate for the light." He paused, rather pleased with himself. "What security precautions do you take, your organisation, that is?" Richardson smirked at the man's question knowingly. The impertinence of it. Bad news travelled fast and far. The Dutchman grinned and added, "I hear you have had a little trouble..."

Richardson shrugged. "Sorted now," he said. "Well, almost." He made a note to tell Roper of the man's emboldened manner. It would be dealt with one day.

"I'll give him his dues; Roper doesn't fuck about, in his ham-fisted manner, at least. How long were they married?"

"Four years."

"Children? I know he has two by previous relationships."

"No."

"Well, that makes it easier, I suppose," he said, shutting the matter down entirely. "Now, Mister Richardson. How may I help you?"

"It's a delicate matter."

"Everything within these glass walls is a *delicate* matter."

"Even so..." Richardson shrugged. "Mister Roper wants a task undertaken."

The man looked at him, smoothed a hand through his

red hair and nodded thoughtfully. "You want to send a message to her lover."

"Yes."

"I must say, I am a little uncomfortable with your presence. You draw attention to my own organisation, so soon after your own was infiltrated."

"I wasn't followed."

"So sure?"

"Yes. And I'm sure your man can confirm it."

"My man?"

"You had me followed from the airport. I saw him."

"A pity you didn't see London's finest when they were following everybody in your own organisation."

"We did. We just played them, that's all."

Van Cleef nodded. "And Roper's wife? You knew all along she was fucking the undercover officer in question?"

Richardson smiled, then shrugged. "They were clever. It went unnoticed for a while. But once discovered, it was acted upon swiftly."

"Agreed." Van Cleef paused. "So, you want a job done, but you don't want the usual suspects shaken down afterwards?"

"No, that is correct."

"Well, Roper employs enough ex-soldiers as his hired muscle, surely someone has the skills?"

"They have the skills, but it's a big ask."

"Who took care of the wife?"

Richardson shook his head. "You know better than to ask that, Mister Van Cleef." He smiled. "That was a tragic *accident*, after all. A *misadventure*, I believe the coroner recorded as his verdict at the inquest. Besides, this is altogether more... specialist. The target is more than capable. A policeman for twenty years, six of those years spent in firearms units, three years in criminal intelligence, five years in anti-terrorism and after a hiatus after being injured in the line of duty, six months as an undercover officer in the Met's now neutered four-year operation to infiltrate Mister Roper's organisation. The man can blend in and mix with the people he's investigating. He fooled me, fooled Roper, too. And that doesn't happen, well, ever..."

"Description?"

"Around the six-foot mark, and about thirteen stone. He did some amateur boxing in his youth and was an international water polo player and freestyle swimmer. He's pretty handy in a fight. He sorted out a couple of blokes in short order one night outside a club while he was spying on us. He's played some rugby in his time, too and keeps himself fit with free weights and swimming. No distinguishing marks to speak of, not especially noticeable in clothing from what I remember of him. Tends to wear suits with an open collar and no tie, or jeans and a T-shirt or rugby jumper when he's off duty."

"Accent?"

"Neutral, English. Maybe a bit of London in there sometimes."

"Hair?"

"Short, fair to brown, a little greying at the temples."

"Anything else?"

"He's an alcoholic. Or recovering, I suppose. He's been known to fall epically off the wagon at times. Hides it well within the police force." Richardson paused. "We know he has an ex-wife and child, but we haven't been able to find out the details. Yet..."

Van Cleef nodded. He took a piece of paper from his inside jacket pocket and produced a Mont Blanc ballpoint pen. He slid both across the table to Richardson and said,

"Write down his name, if you please. We will never personally speak of his name..." He paused. "My associates will find out the rest, and then we will make contact via email to seek your confirmation and present our fee." Richardson wrote the name down and slid the paper across the table, where Van Cleef folded it without looking and slipped it back into his pocket. He took out a business card and slid it across the table. Richardson studied it. Just a web address and what appeared to be a password. He frowned. Van Cleef smiled. "That is an email account homepage. Don't worry, my cards are all individual. Look for my email in saved drafts. We will communicate via this draft email. Save it each time. And for god's sake, don't send it by accident. This way, we can log in and communicate with one another without a single communication being sent electronically. Nobody on the planet will discover us that way. Absolutely no trace." He paused. "We have many accounts, with many clients. To date, not a soul has intercepted our communications using this method. The CIA, FBI, Mossad, GCHQ, the NSA and both MI5 and MI6 are all in the dark."

"Clever."

"Well, Mister Richardson, that's what earns us the big bucks." The man paused, adjusting his wire rimmed spectacles and looking at Richardson intently. "Speaking of which, you will need to transfer half the funds, or this meeting is concluded." He slid another card across the table as Richardson took out his mobile phone. "This is a different account to when we conducted our last transaction."

"Got to keep moving, eh?" Richardson typed in the details and held the smartphone up to his eye for retina identification. It was an app with a discreet Swiss bank and the minimum opening balance had to be no less than five million US dollars. Richardson's face illuminated as the two bars of light scrolled up and down the screen simultaneously, meeting in the middle in the centre of his eye. He tried not to blink, and when he had managed three seconds without moving or blinking, the bars parted, and the transaction was confirmed by a large green tick. "The first half has been paid," he said. "As we agreed."

Van Cleef nodded and stood up extending his right hand to him across the desk indicating that the meeting was over. "Then all you and Mister Roper have to do is sit back and await our confirmation." He paused. "I don't have to remind you of the penalty clause for late or unforthcoming completion of payment, do I?"

Richardson smiled, but inside he was nervous. The reputation of this secretive outfit was known within the tight circles he operated in. After all, that was why he was here. He just hoped that Roper would not try and renege on the deal once the job had been completed. Roper was a chancer, but if he tried chancing his way out of paying Van Cleef and his organisation, Richardson knew that the man would be signing both their death warrants. "No, Mister Van Cleef, you do not."

Chapter Three
Three Months Later, Cornwall

"I just turned my back for a moment, and when I looked round, she was gone..."

How many parents would dread to utter those words? How many had, and are forever haunted by the hollowness of the sentence? Those words were the end of the sentence. The end of the line. *We got up, had breakfast... I walked her to school, and she chatted about the fun we had at the weekend... I met her at the school gates, she told me about her day... I put the laundry on to dry, she went out into the garden to play...* each of those sentences led on to another, but the final sentence was what would live with her for an eternity. *I just turned my back for a moment, and when I looked round, she was gone...* No parent would get past that last statement. There would always be the echo of doubt, uncertainty, remorse. Had she told her to go tidy her room, to feed the rabbit, to help her sort the washing, those words would never have had to leave her lips, and Grant would not have had to look into the distraught, pleading eyes of a mother and make promises he feared he could not fulfil.

It was a bleak spot. And Cornwall had a few. More than its fair share. The cottage was constructed from granite, huge squares each probably weighing half a ton. There were fourteen of them wide and nine high. The windows were small and let in little light. The roof was finished with slate, but most of the tiles were broken, and some were missing altogether. Grant was aware that on a good day, with the golden light and blue sky, the sea blue and calm beyond the cliffs, the cottage would have looked picture perfect. But this was late May and summer was proving to be shy to say the least. The light was grey, the sky was low and oppressive, and the sea raged, grey and foreboding, pounding the rocks below and unleashing relentless spumes of white spray up the cliffs. It was just after eight-AM, and it did not feel as if dawn would ever finish breaking. He watched the cottage, the windscreen of his car smeared with grease and salt. He flicked on the wipers, but it only made it worse. The cottage looked even darker.

Lilly Trefusis was eleven years old. She was a parent's delight. The sort of eleven-year-old who liked to climb trees, ride her bike and smash a tennis ball against the side of the house. She wasn't into *Snapchat, Twitter* or *Instagram*. Many of her friends were, and had set up false IDs, email accounts and lied about their ages. Many of her friends already had boyfriends or had lied about it, wanting what they were not yet ready to have. Lilly cared for none of these things and still carried around her teddy bear when she felt sad or nervous. This was viewed as immature by many of her peers, but to her mother, she was just an eleven-year-old girl.

It was unusual, unheard of even, for her to go off without informing her mother. But she was eleven. It wasn't inconceivable. There was a first time for everything. Friends passing by her back gate, the fear of social rejection if she didn't agree to come with them at that precise moment, the embarrassment at having to ask her mother's permission when many of her friends seemed to have roamed free from the age of nine. There was always a first time for 'out of character' behaviour. That's why kids got grounded. Her mother hoped this was it, but deep down she knew. Mothers always do.

Darkness had fallen, and inevitably desperation and worry had soared. There was an inevitability about darkness, the prospect of finding her ebbed with every minute. Lilly was not out playing with friends. A quick and desperate phone around showed that all her friends were in fact home, safe and well. Some of the mothers who seemed to allow their children to roam around free-range, seemed somewhat incredulous at the prospect that she did not know her own daughter's whereabouts. The police had been called, *Facebook* posts made and shared to local sites and businesses and a rudimentary, panicked and wholly ineffective search had taken place. The police had ramped it up and because of their search and rescue skills, personnel and equipment, the coastguard and RNLI had been called to search Gulruan, the coastline and the surrounding area some two miles inland from the coast. The search and rescue helicopter, now out of the Royal Navy's hands and privately contracted by a search and rescue company, had been called in and the area had been swept with a thermal imaging camera. Grant had to concede, that for his first major official incident since relocating to Cornwall, the response had been both swift and professional. He wasn't here to turn the force around. Far from it. He was a man who had used up all his warnings and credit. A man who had punched his boss and been suspended pending further investigation. Thankfully, he had a friend somewhere in the police service. Someone higher up the ladder than Chief Superintendent Malcolm Boyce, somebody who had pulled some strings at his tribunal and organised a transfer after his suspension. That transfer had taken him to the Devon and Cornwall Constabulary. Somewhere for him to start afresh and no doubt make the same mistakes, but at least he wasn't the Met's problem any longer. It came, however, with a caveat. His DCI rank had been stripped and he was now a Detective Inspector. High enough up the ranks to warrant an office and some seniority at the station, but still far enough down the scale to be tasked with investigations no self-respecting DCI would want. It wasn't all bad, though. Grant enjoyed the thrill of investigating crimes, and despite both the pay and status cut, he clocked up far fewer desk hours than what was becoming normal for ranks above inspector in the police service, and he could not remember the last time he'd known a DCI out asking questions of the public, rather than micro-managing their team.

Since the relocation and posting, he had a lot to prove to his new team. And this wasn't looking good since he had made a misjudged promise to a distraught mother and had a sinking feeling that already, Lilly Trefusis was going to be a body recovery at best. Because sometimes finding a body is easier to live with than the purgatory of a life-time cold case. For both the family and police officers alike.

Grant switched off the vehicle's engine and stepped out onto the shale track. There were old mine workings nearby, the remains of an engine house some fifty-metres distant. The shale was a mixture of red, orange and yellow rocks compressed to form a road. It was waste from the mine workings some two-hundred years or so previous. Wheal Penance had closed a century before, living up to its name, the copper and tin it produced had not been enough to pay for the costs in running the mine, and some saw it as a bad omen, penance for something in the miners' past. He slammed the Alfa Romeo's door, and it made a grinding creak as it folded closed on its hinges. That was new. The car was more than ten-years old with higher-than-average mileage, and the poor condition of the Cornish roads and the constant salt in the air near the coast had practically pensioned it off after just a couple of weeks. He doubted it would last another six months.

He made his way across the rough ground and saw the door ahead of him, bowed and worn, open slowly and the man appear, hovering on the doorstep. Grant readied himself as the man turned his head. The burns looked terrible in the photograph on file, and they looked a damned sight worse in the flesh. Pitted and layered, textured and shiny. The heat had made the man's right eye droop as well, like the socket had melted along with the flesh. The man also looked gaunt and hadn't aged well. Grant couldn't care less about the man's health, but he made a mental note to update his file. He'd most likely get the chance soon; a new photograph to go with his imminent arrest and charge.

"I was wondering how long it would take."

"Well, we wouldn't want to disappoint you," Grant said. He showed his warrant card and said, "DCI..." he stopped himself, force of habit. "DI Grant, CID." He tried not to stare at the right side of the man's face. A burn so deep and rippled that it reminded Grant of corpses he had seen after six months decomposition exposed to the sun and elements. Where the skin had tightened, and the flesh had rotted and shrunk underneath.

The man ignored the warrant card, looked not to have heard. "My name is already plastered all over Facebook," he protested. "On those tatty, buy and resell sites, and they're the worst. Like a fucking lynch mob, they are. Uneducated and opinionated, never considering the ramifications of the hate they incite."

"You're not permitted the use of a computer..." Grant paused. "So, how have you seen what people have posted online?"

"They never said anything about a smartphone in my probation interview."

"No internet access," Grant corrected him. "And you don't have a Facebook account. I checked. Which means, you are peeping at peoples' lives with a false user account. A false identity. Just like perverts and groomers do. For that you need an email account to sign up with social media. You're not permitted an email account, either."

"Prove it!" he snapped. "It's just what I 'erd, any rate. I never said I *saw* it..."

"That's what I do," Grant replied. "I prove things."

"I just use a good signal. I browse sometimes," the man said with a shrug. "I wasn't sure of my terms regarding a phone. You know as well as I do, that the terms won't last long. I'm out because the forensics boys and girls didn't do their jobs properly. I'm innocent, it's only a matter of time before my name is cleared officially and the government give me a handsome pay-out. Some money for a life in the sun. Well away from here."

Grant walked right up to him. At around six-feet-tall, he was at eye level, although the man was standing on a six-inch granite doorstep. "Mister Vigus, you're more aware of your terms than your barrister. You're a barrack room lawyer. Don't play games with me. I think it's obvious to anyone that you're out because of somebody's mistake. Enjoy the ride, because it won't last long." He stared at him, his eyes cold, but there was something else, too. Almost a sadness, a lack of emotion. "You've seen the social media posts; you know what's going on. I want to know what the hell you've done with that little girl."

"It wasn't me."

"Got an alibi?"

"Not this time," he said. "But it's early days. These things have a habit of working out well for me."

Grant peered past him; looked inside the dark and gloomy cottage as far as he could. "The guilty only have false alibis, but we tend to see through them eventually."

The man smiled. "Well, in that case, I don't have one or need one."

"What *do* you know?"

"Nothing," Vigus said, twisting his torso and blocking Grant's view of the inside of the cottage.

"You know that your name has been mentioned."

Vigus shrugged, ran a hand through his long, greasy dark hair. "Just that they think I'm involved..."

Grant nodded. "I've seen the chatter, too," he said. "Had any visitors yet?"

"No."

"That surprises me."

"Not as much as it does me," he replied. He looked past Grant and shrugged again. "But it's early days, looks like things are going to change soon enough..."

Grant turned and looked at the approaching vehicles. A small, red hatchback, a works van and a battered single cab pickup loaded with crab or lobster pots, coils of rope and flags pulled across the rough ground and parked on the hard-standing next to his Alfa Romeo. A blonde woman got out of the hatchback. Grant recognised her as Lisa Trefusis. The girl's mother. He'd spent most of the previous evening with her taking her statement, liaising with the SOCO teams and female family liaison officer. He hadn't been to sleep yet as he had organised a search on the moor. It didn't look like the woman had had any sleep either. Or brushed her hair. Or changed her clothes. He noted the fact. Genuine grief stripped people of inhibition. Hair, clothing and hygiene no longer mattered.

Lisa Trefusis glanced at the four men who got out of the two works vehicles. They hesitated, but then the largest of them surged forward and ran down the path.

"Where is she you dirty bastard?" he shouted. He was six-four and about half as wide. His hands looked like shovels. One of them reached out and a sausage-sized finger pointed at Vigus accusingly. The other men were braver now and followed suit, standing beside the big man. "Tell us now, you bloody freak!"

"You know what you've done!" Lisa Trefusis screamed. "Tell me where she is and what you've done with her!"

Grant squared up to the lead man. There was some volume in size difference. He took his warrant card out and held it steady. His right hand was holding the asp, a telescopic weighted metal baton. It was out of sight behind his right hip.

"Back off, mate..." the bigger man said through gritted pale, yellow teeth. At least two were missing in the front row. "None of your business..."

"I'm DI Grant," he said. "This is a police matter, and we are dealing with it. Now, turn around and take yourselves out of here."

"Then why else would you be here if you didn't suspect him?" Lisa Trefusis asked. "You suspect him too, don't you? Don't you!" She looked at Vigus. "Where is she? Where's my daughter?"

Vigus held up his hands. "I don't know. I have nothing to do with it."

"Liar!" she wailed.

"Maybe you should have taken better care of her, there's a lot of nutters out there," Vigus smirked. "A Carveth, pretty girl like that, out playing on her own. Who knows what someone might want to do with her...?"

The second man back lunged forwards and rushed past the largest man. Grant whipped out the asp and it extended on its way towards the man's kneecap. It hit with a sickening crunch and the man grunted and fell to the side. Grant dropped his warrant card and slapped him across the cheek with the palm of his hand, sending him off the doorstep and down onto the granite-chipped pathway.

"You can't do that!" the larger man shouted, but he was standing stock-still and didn't look like he would try his luck.

"The next one will be across the side of your head," Grant assured him coldly. "There'll be no vigilantism on my watch."

"Police brutality!" one of the men shouted.

"You haven't seen anything yet..." Grant said. "Now, pick up your friend and get the hell out of here."

The felled man was scrabbling to his feet. "I'll have your bloody job for that," he said.

"Then write a letter," Grant said coldly. "Only, do Miss Trefusis and her missing daughter a favour and don't send it for a week. I would prefer to spend my time finding Lilly, not wasting it fighting a complaint because some tosspot thought he'd try his hand at vigilante justice and got stopped by a police officer using acceptable force. You waste my time, and you jeopardise Lilly's life." He turned to Lisa

Trefusis. "Go home, please. I will come and see you later. And take your angry mob with you."

"Where is she?" she screamed one last time. She stared at Vigus, her lips quivering, and her face flushed. "Tell me you bastard!" She looked at Grant, tears in her eyes and her hands shaking as she wiped the tears away. "The bastard did it to me when I was a girl and, now he's done it to Lilly..."

Chapter Four

The mob drove away, and Grant remained on the doorstep. He had instructed Lisa Trefusis to go home and not to return to Vigus's cottage in any event. An air of calm came over the cottage, incident averted. He doubted the man would lodge a complaint, his ego was bruised more than his kneecap and his arm, which had broken the fall. The man was broad and toothless and looked like he'd taken a rugby tackle or two in his lifetime. Nothing compared to what Grant had done to him. He'd get over it after a few lunchtime pints. Grant had given him something to think about with his complaint and it wouldn't do anybody any good to hold up the investigation, especially in what was coined the 'first-forty-eight'. Forty-eight hours to find a missing person, or they probably never would. Perhaps that was true of American crime shows and docudramas, but in Grant's experience, it wasn't true. It was more like the first twenty-four. Which was why he hadn't slept last night and was running on coffee and adrenalin.

"I suggest you let me in," Grant said.

"You got a warrant?"

"I don't need one if I suspect you're in the process of committing a crime, or if a little girl's life is in danger," he replied. "First, no alibi. And now you want to see a warrant? If I have reason to suspect you are committing, or have committed a crime here, that's all I need."

Vigus opened the door wider. He looked to have changed his mind, but his expression was supercilious. "Tea?"

"Please." He followed the man inside. The room was a lounge-come-kitchen. Grant took one look at the collection of dirty dishes and carrier bags overflowing with rubbish and changed his mind. "Actually, I'm okay."

Vigus looked around. "I thought you'd say that." He ran a hand through his greasy hair again. Grant figured it was a habit. He wondered if it was a sign of lying. A tell. He noted to test him at some stage.

"Why?" Grant took in the sight. Dirty dishes, over-filled ashtray, the dustbin having long-since lost its battle with physics. Carrier bags too full of rubbish to be tied properly at the handles.

"It's a state, I know. My mother died recently. I have come down to sort out the house and sell it. It was a state when I moved in. I'm not getting on well with clearing up. It's like clearing *her* out..."

"You were close?" Grant asked. "Despite you living in Wales, that is."

"How did you..." he paused, seemed to realise quickly. "Never mind... Yes, I suppose," he said. "We're always close to our mothers, aren't we? Were you close to your mother, DI Grant?"

The detective ignored him. He'd been around long enough to know deflection techniques when he heard them. He never entered into a conversation with a suspect, especially when they were the ones to initiate it. He noted that the man had asked *were* instead of *are*. He thought it strange, wondered if the man had researched him. He obviously had internet access; it would not be difficult. But why? Perhaps it was a slip of the tongue. "You've skirted it all, haven't you," Grant stated.

"I don't know what you mean."

"There's no smoke without fire."

"Innocent until proven guilty."

"Bullshit!" Grant snapped. "Lisa Trefusis just dropped an allegation. Want to tell me about that?"

"No. You had better speak to her about that. And I had better be speaking with a solicitor."

"I imagine he's on a retainer," Grant quipped, but he wasn't smiling. He simply added, "I'm taking a look around."

"You are not!"

Grant looked at him. "Sit down and listen to me." Vigus looked at him defiantly for a moment, then his expression softened, and he perched on the arm of a worn, threadbare sofa. New in 1972. "Good. I'm going to bring you in. I'm going to have my time with you in an interview room. But not yet. I'm going to have a look around, get a feel for this place. A feel for you."

"But I haven't done anything!" Vigus snapped. He watched Grant's expression, became unnerved by his passiveness, his cold eyes. He had seen eyes like those before. There was little feeling in them. He had seen killers before, in prison. He doubted the policeman had killed anyone, perhaps it was a reflection at the evil he had seen during his career. Like there were no surprises left in life.

"You've done terrible things, Vigus."

"Prove it."

"I don't need to," said Grant. "Shit sticks, and it's stuck all over you now. Now you've done real time for your crimes. Or some of them. Looks like there's more to answer to."

"The evidence against me was refuted. Cast out as inaccurate. I resubmitted DNA samples and it showed it was one-hundred percent inaccurate. Not even ninety-five. Not even seventy. Not even close. A negative test."

"But I know you've done more. I know you've torn the hearts out of people in this community. What was it that Lisa Trefusis said? *He did it to me, now he's done it to my daughter...*"

"Bullshit!"

"She's lying?" Grant shook his head. "I'll be talking to her later. So, what about Maria Bright and Carrie-Ann Dixon? Are they both lying too?"

"They were three little bitches together! They all lied about me..." Vigus shook his head. "When it came down to it, I had reliable witnesses who gave me an alibi. The police didn't have to check too hard. It was a witch-hunt. All the girls involved in the allegations lied. They were playing a sick game and it went too far."

"So, Lisa Trefusis was among them? Did you do something to her? There were just two complaints made against you, two allegations. You just said *three* little bitches. Lisa Trefusis isn't on record as having ever made a complaint. So, something must have happened. Are you admitting to that?"

"I'm not admitting anything," Vigus sneered. "It was a long time ago. I left Gulruan and the idiots who live here, left Cornwall altogether."

"But you were caught in Wales. You had unlawful, under-aged sex with a minor. You raped her."

"I didn't rape her!" he protested. "Sure, she was

Carveth. But it wasn't like the prosecution painted it. I talked to her, that's all."

Grant clenched and unclenched his fists. He had a fifteen-year-old daughter. He hadn't seen her since he had relocated. He was divorced, Deborah had moved on, and he hadn't had the custody arrangement he'd hoped for. He hadn't wanted to be 'that guy' – the absent father who eventually loses contact with his children. But, unless he could sort out something soon, it was looking more and more likely to be the case. He had wanted to remain close, be a father if not part of a fractured, but amicable family. But he had gone through some bad times. Drunk through some bad times. He was a better man now, had tested himself and had barely touched a drink in the past two months, but the damage had been done. The drinking had caused him to make bad decisions and those decisions had a domino effect in both his marriage and his career.

He looked at the gaunt and tragic-looking man in front of him. He knew he would kill anyone who hurt his own daughter. He'd do it slowly and he'd bloody well enjoy it. He found it difficult not to beat Vigus at this moment. He needed to take a step back. He could handle another disciplinary, but it would not help Lilly Trefusis' case whatsoever.

"Vigus, you are a beast," he said. "And if you are involved in this, I'll see you get what's coming to you."

"Is that a threat, DI Grant?"

"No. It's a promise."

"And the difference is?"

Grant stared at him, took in his gaunt features, the grotesque burn taking up the whole side of his right cheek. "I guess you'll find out soon enough. But a threat is exactly that – the threat of an outcome. A promise is made by someone who will see it through..."

Vigus sneered, shook his head. "Those girls lied. The police saw that, otherwise I would have been charged. Those girls tarnished my name and good character, but those same lies never even got me into a courtroom. Not even close."

"No," Grant conceded. "Partly because fifteen-years ago the Devon and Cornwall Police had some pretty shitty officers in their CID. They had corrupt ones, too. But Stacy Hughes did get you into court in Wales. And you did time for what you did. DNA science and testing moved on since you upped sticks. And that DNA processing didn't lie, because it was inside a minor's vagina. A thirteen-year-old. Barely thirteen. Four days after her birthday. Are you still going to maintain you didn't do it? How did your semen get inside a thirteen-year-old girl, Vigus?"

"But it didn't," he sighed tiresomely. "I resubmitted a DNA sample after I was released and was cleared of the crime as a result. A full pardon. I was wrongly convicted, and it will stand as record, and I shall be vindicated and compensated accordingly. Like I said, I'm due a big pay out..." He paused. "This is harassment, DI Grant. I want to have legal representation before I say anything else. You're trampling all over my human and legal rights..."

Grant ignored him and said, "There's no smoke without fire," he glared. "Forensics made an error, a costly one. As a result, your verdict was overturned. However, they messed it up, you and I both know that you did it."

He smiled, his teeth yellow and rotten and broken. "But I'm innocent, DI Grant."

"You're nothing of the sort."

"My barrister will disagree. Perhaps I should contact him now and explain about this police harassment?"

"Do what you want."

"Oh, I generally do."

Grant nodded. "Me too," he paused. "I think you're in for a shit-storm. I think there are women around here who are going to make allegations and this time, they will be listened to."

"There's no DNA evidence for any of those women. It was fifteen years ago! Good luck making that stick."

"Girls," Grant corrected him. "They are women now, but they were girls at the time," he said. "Would there have been DNA evidence at the time of their allegations, I wonder?" He stared at Vigus, but the man looked down at the floor. "I know there would have been. You're a sick man."

"I'm just clearing up here, getting the house up for sale, then I'm gone." He looked exasperated. "I did someone else's time. I served with murderers and thieves. They don't like nonces. It wasn't an easy time for me inside."

"It's an easier time than what you gave those girls and their families," Grant said coldly. "So, this missing girl is a coincidence?"

"Of course!"

"That's a hell of a stretch," Grant said. "You turn up, stir up feelings once more, and then a girl around the same age as those who complained about you all those years ago goes missing. I don't buy it. You think you're untouchable. Well, we'll see about that." He walked past him and towards the closed and ill-fitting wooden door on the other side of the kitchen. It was painted in white gloss but had turned yellow with nicotine. The chips in the paint showed many layers of paint over the years. Who new how long? A hundred maybe. He worked the latch, brass and never treated. It had turned bronze in colour. "I'm taking a look around."

"You can't do that!" Vigus got to his feet but stopped when Grant turned and stared at him. "I mean, your warrant..."

"I don't need one," Grant said coldly. "Now, sit back down before I knock you down."

The stairs wound around in a tight spiral, carpeted and claustrophobic-inducing. The carpet pattern was worn on the tread, right down to the strands of threads. Grant found himself using his hands on the treads in front of him, climbing on all fours. When he reached the top, the low ceiling made it difficult for him to stand upright. The supporting beams were exposed oak and unstained. The ceiling was made from timber boards and glossed in the same manner as the door below. Like the paint downstairs, it was stained with nicotine. There were knick-knacks and trinkets in the recesses and photographs on the wall. Pictures of Daniel Jerimiah Vigus as a child. A sickly looking individual with the same greasy, swept back hair and a distant look in his eyes. The burn was prevalent in most of the pictures, no attempt to shield the deformation from view using a scarf or a change of camera angle. In fact, it was prevalent in each photograph, as if it had become his key feature. He certainly seemed an insipid and odd-looking child who underwent many changes. Styles, clothes and haircuts changed, and he seemed to fluctuate a great deal in weight, but the eyes remained sinister throughout. They were the images captured of a child that only a mother could love. Perhaps that had been his problem. It would have been hard to imagine the boy in the photographs having friends or relationships. There was no doubt that the boy had been an oddity, but he had carried it through into adulthood. A loner, longing for his past, the past he felt he should have had. A past where he kissed the girls, had a fondle, did the things adolescents did behind bike sheds or in the woods. Only when Daniel Vigus did these things for real, he had been a man of thirty and the girls had all been pre-teen. Not the same, not by a million miles and not in anyone's right mind. There had been complaints, historically. Enough to cast aspersions. Enough for people to suspect and enough for him to be handed a few beatings along the way. But not enough to go to court. Vigus wasn't a well-liked man, but he still had many witnesses to say he had been working in the fields at the time, or drinking in the local pubs. The allegations kept coming, as did the police force's inability to successfully charge him, and after a while he had taken his leave and his mother had spent the remaining years of her life as a social leper. Alone in the cottage on the cliff.

Daniel Jerimiah Vigus had offended again but this time he had been caught. A team of detectives and some undeniably incriminating DNA had sent him away for ten years. He had been living in North Wales at the time and had served his sentence in three different prisons around the country, but after unsuccessfully lobbying for a retest of DNA, he had paid for a private test upon his release and the results had come back showing no link. The Welsh police service retested, and the results were confirmed. No match. Devon and Cornwall police, who had filed Vigus's DNA after the last complaint against him, had been widely criticised for mixing up his DNA on file, and allowing a sex offender to go unpunished. Vigus was pardoned, but some temporary terms of parole had been set in place until his record could be struck off permanently and he could be taken off the sex-offender's register. Now he could look forward to a hefty compensation claim against the Home Office for a miscarriage of justice, as well as the prison service for the beatings he had received inside. Vigus had lobbied his parole officer to temporarily move from his relocation in Reading to prepare his family home for sale and move away to start a new life with the proceeds. There had been no charges brought against him for the historical allegations in Cornwall, so no objection had been made. The man would soon be out of the system. But three-weeks after arriving back in his hometown, Lilly Trefusis had gone missing.

Grant looked around upstairs. It didn't take long. There were only two bedrooms and a tiny bathroom. The décor hadn't been updated in forty-years. The smaller bedroom contained an iron bed with springs. It looked like a prison affair. Vigus should have felt right at home. There were books in a neatly stacked bookcase. Grant could see they had been arranged alphabetically. He squatted down and read some of the spines. Boy's adventure stories, horror offerings from King and Koontz, some dark fantasy and erotic titles from authors Grant did not recognise. It was easy to see that the man's tastes had changed as he had grown. Other than that, there was little to show for Vigus's possessions, but then Grant figured that the rest of the man's life would be in Reading, where he had recently been residing. All that remained here was the man's childhood. And that did not look to have been much.

The bathroom was naturally outdated. The bath was metal with potholed enamel paint. There were no panels, just a tub on legs, but before it was fashionable to have such things, and the finish was plain and had stained over the years. The tidemark had never been cleaned and the bath now had a two-tone effect. There was no shower, but a rubber hose contraption that looked like it could be used to give enemas was left dangling over the taps. The tiles were mildewed, and the grout was black. The floor was carpeted, and Grant reflected with some amusement that seventies Britain must have been the only era and country to carpet a bathroom. Just like the stairs, the carpet was threadbare. It was clear that no real income had come into the Vigus household for decades. Daniel Vigus' file had showed no employment records for his entire time in Gulruan, although it was noted he had done odd jobs and seasonal vegetable and flower picking. Certainly not enough income to improve the house as the years wore on.

DI Grant left the bathroom behind him and entered the larger bedroom. It smelled of damp and lavender and talcum powder. The bedroom of an old lady. He thought he could smell the stale odour of urine too. He looked at the bed and saw that the flowery sheets were stained. There was a form underneath the covers and Grant's heart raced, his face and neck flushed, and he felt a surge of anxiety in his stomach. He caught hold of the sheet and gently pulled it back. He was as prepared as he could be, but even so the sight shocked him. No child's body. Instead, he took in the bizarre form of pillows stuffed inside an old woman's night-dress. A limbless, headless figure in a flowery nightdress with what appeared to be semen stains all over it. Between the pillow 'body' and the headboard, a grainy photograph of Vigus's mother rested. It was a head and shoulders shot of a severe looking woman with hard eyes and a spiteful mouth. Grant found himself staring at the scene, mouth agape. He took a breath and tried to remain objective, not judgemental, but it was almost impossible to steady his emotions. He looked away, studied the empty side of the bed which looked to have been slept in. Creased and indented. Grant took out his mobile phone and took some pictures of the scene. He had seen many things in his long career as a police officer, but this was up there with the weirdest. And the sickest. He pocketed the phone and surveyed the rest of the room. Daniel Vigus's clothes were neatly folded on the bedside table, and he appeared to be living out of a suitcase. Grant walked over, glanced at the contents. He straightened up, surveyed the scene, the disturbing sight of the bed, the dead woman's nightdress clothing the pillows, the unwashed linen and bedspread. He hadn't been able to put Daniel Vigus in a box just yet, but he now knew that the man was completely disturbed.

Now he needed to unsettle him further.

Chapter Five

Grant left Daniel Vigus sitting in his lounge-come-kitchen, sobbing in embarrassment with his head in his hands, the slicked and greasy hair lolling in front of his face. Vigus had not wanted anyone to see the bedroom. He hadn't explained the scene to Grant, probably wouldn't have been able to. Who would? But Grant assumed it was a way of feeling close to his deceased mother, an effort to avoid letting go. But that didn't account for the semen stains. That threw a whole new meaning into the mix. One that Grant did not have the mental capacity to understand. Like Alfred Hitchcock's *Psycho* with bells on. He made a mental note to speak with a criminal psychologist about it but wasn't sure Cornwall would have one. Maybe there was someone in Exeter at Middlemoor, the police HQ he could speak to. Although from what he had just witnessed, he knew a private Harley Street phycologist who may well be able to shed some light on the matter and decided it would be a better route to take.

Grant looked at his watch, then over at Vigus's Land Rover Discovery. It was a sixteen-year-old model, dented and scuffed. He walked closer, took a small Swiss Army knife from his pocket and thumbed the knife blade open. He reached around and stabbed the inside wall of the driver's-side front tyre. He was momentarily out of view of the cottage, noted there were no windows on that side, only windows front and back and on the side facing the sea. Handy. But he figured nobody would have wanted a view of the working pump house and hundreds of years' worth of mining waste. He listened to the rush of air and had the knife folded and back in his pocket before he reached his own car. The puncture would buy him some time. He pulled out his mobile phone, cursed at the lack of signal and as he sat down into the driver's seat, he wedged it between his legs and started the engine. He glanced down at the screen several times on his way back to the main coast road, got a signal after a mile. He dialled, glancing between the road and the screen, then held it to his ear as the dialling tone rang. It wasn't the safest way to drive, but he reasoned he wasn't drunk. Not yet at least.

"*Hello, Boss.*" A woman's voice, warm and friendly.

"I've left Vigus' place. Get down there and for god's sake, be discreet."

"*It's pretty exposed,*" she paused. "*He's going to notice me following him.*"

"Then be better at what you do, DC Carveth."

"*That's easy for you to say. I have an idea though, just need to perform a short detour.*"

"Whatever. I'm going to visit the girl's mother again. Where the hell is the family liaison officer? I've just had the mother down at Vigus' cottage shouting the odds, making historical allegations and about to unleash a vigilante posse. Lisa Trefusis shouldn't have been able to leave her house without us knowing about it."

"I'll look into it."

"It's all about sussing out the family as much as providing support in times like these. It's about having someone on the inside," he said. He was angry. The officer in the role would have known the importance of this, would have done the relevant training. Probably knew the woman of old or was related. Everyone seemed to know everybody else down here. "What do we know about her?"

"Other than what we know from the briefing?"

"Yes."

"Nothing to add. Single mum, works part-time in a convenience shop in St. Ives, claims a few benefits and keeps her working hours down because of it..."

"For fuck's sake, Carveth..."

"What more do you want?"

"That's just the incidentals. I want her history. I want to know if she's got a past that we should know about. I want to know why today she accused Daniel Vigus of doing unthinkable things to her as a child, and none of which is on file. And that now everybody thinks he has done the same to her daughter."

"So that's three women accusing him of historical abuse?"

"I think there will be more."

"The slimy shit..."

"Stay objective, DC Carveth. Now get over to his place and see what he gets up to."

"I'm twenty-minutes away..."

He thought about the puncture, the huge off-road tyres and the rocky terrain. The spare wheel on a sixteen-year-old vehicle bolted underneath the rear axle. Corrosion, mud and difficult to reach. If the spare hadn't been used in a few years, then the man might well be there until the AA came and did it for him. "It's okay, I've slowed him down a bit." He hung up the phone and speeded up. The roads were narrow and winding. He skirted Gulruan, a large village with a single pub, a newsagents and convenience shop, and a large council estate. It made no sense to put the people in need of social housing and access to seek employment in a community slap-bang in the middle of the moors with few jobs and little in the way of transport links. But then, perhaps that had been the reasoning behind it. It kept them in one place and out of thriving tourist towns like St. Ives. Gulruan was a desolate place, but as Grant was quickly learning, it held a great deal of secrets and a sordid past.

DI Grant had taken up temporary office in Penzance. He worked out of the Camborne and Bodmin stations, Cornwall's CID being a fluid unit basing itself wherever the investigation ran on the ground. The counties of Devon and Cornwall were the largest geographical policing area in the country with one of the smallest forces and the largest seasonal influx of tourists anywhere in the UK. The constabulary had recently taken on much of Dorset's admin work as well, stretching it even further. Eleven-million people visited the two counties throughout the summer months. Statistically, to commit a crime in Cornwall in the summer was to all but get away with it. Grant had come to the county a month ago. Many had been wary at the transfer and sensed the reasoning behind the move hadn't entirely been Grant's decision. Others were dubious of a detective inspector arriving, meaning a local's promotion from detective sergeant had been overlooked, but were at least thankful the outgoing DI had risen to the rank of DCI and now headed CID in Bodmin. Grant had been told that he could have applied for that role, despite his recent demotion. However, as much as Chief Superintendent Boyce's influence had cost him his rank, he soon realised that career wise, he was where he wanted to be. Life as a DCI would mean much of his working week behind a desk, directing an investigation and seldom working in the field. Grant had found that with the role of DI he could shadow a good and promising detective constable or sergeant and keep his finger on the pulse. He had been a DCI once, and he had fought against it the whole time, it being a relief when he had been demoted. The charges had been dubious, but he hadn't fought the allegations too rigorously.

As with most rural locations the arrival of someone from the 'bright lights' had both alienated him and garnered support in equal measures. Many saw him as a big-shot and despised his presence, while others saw him as an officer with his finger on the pulse and an officer with experience which simply could not be replicated within the extremities of the country. Grant, however, had done his homework and was in awe of the constabulary's remit. Rated third for homicides, second for weapons offences, second for drug offences and fifth for burglaries in the latest national crime statistics, coupled with a police HQ over a hundred miles away in Exeter and the eastern-most edge of its borders closer to London than the furthest most extremity of its jurisdiction, Grant could see the police service had its work cut out and he would learn as much as he would lend in experience. The posting that had at first angered him and made him feel like he was being put out to grass, was likely to be as big a challenge as he had ever faced. For those wanting to know more about the new DI, his record was out there in the public domain. He had once singlehandedly taken on a terrorist on Westminster Bridge. After both entering the Thames, Grant had failed to save the terrorist and there were speculations that he had in fact drowned the terrorist when both men had gone under the surface. Grant had been awarded the George Cross medal for his bravery on the bridge, an accolade that garnered much condemnation from those same people who made accusations about his failure to save the terrorist.

Lisa Trefusis' house was on the edge of the council estate. A private residence that would have been part of a more exclusive setting ten-years ago, but expansion had taken away its exclusivity, and neighbours from different walks of life now merged as one. The house was a dormer-bungalow, extended upwards and outwards some twenty-years previous. Grant had checked and it was owned by a landlord who rented out similar properties in desperate need of refurbishment to council tenants. The garden was basic, merely a patchy lawn and a few bushes that Grant would not be able to identify. The garden backed onto a pathway that led down past the estate to the park and a network of lanes beyond. It would have been easy to attract the girl's attention and whisk her away. Once into those lanes, nobody would have seen a thing. And nobody had.

Grant had barely managed to close the car door before Lisa Trefusis confronted him.

"Protecting known rapists now, are you?" she seethed. She was an attractive thirty-something with blonde hair and good features, but those features were twisted in anger right now, her eyes moist from crying, her sockets dark from lack of sleep. She was wired, perhaps on coffee, perhaps on more. Grant felt for her, but he could see she was as tough as it gets.

"No. But we have nothing on him but historical allegations and showing up and shouting the odds with a group of vigilantes is not going to get Lilly back," he said calmly. And now it was tough love time. "In fact, if he is guilty of this, he now knows that the world and their dog is onto him, so if he is holding Lilly somewhere, you've as good as scared him away..."

She held a pair of shaking hands to her quivering lips and tears started up again. "Oh, no..."

"So, from this moment on, you cooperate with me. You tell me everything, you do as I say, and you don't try any shit like that again. Understand?" She nodded meekly. "Say it."

"What?"

"Say you understand."

"I understand," she said. Her expression softened. "What has he done with her?" She started to sob. "How can he get away with it?"

Grant watched a community police vehicle pull up and park. It was a Vauxhall Corsa painted in police livery, but without the blues and twos on top. He saw the uniformed policewoman pull a face when she saw he was watching. She got out of the car holding a carrier bag. Grant stared at her expectantly. She took the hint and shrugged.

"We needed tea and milk," she said lamely. "There's a lot of tea being drunk today."

"How long does that take? There's a newsagent in the village..."

"I needed some time alone," Lisa interrupted. "Tamsin, I mean, PC Gould said she'd get the milk and sugar and give me a few minutes alone. I shouldn't have taken off like I did."

"Tea," Grant said. "PC Gould said, tea and milk. No mention of sugar." He turned to the officer. "Get that tea on. I'll have a coffee if there is one. Black, double strong, one sugar." She nodded and walked past, and he added, "We'll talk about this later, PC Gould."

She shrugged dejectedly. "I'm sorry, Sir."

Grant wouldn't. He seldom went over things with someone he had already admonished. The threat was usually enough. Right now, PC Tamsin Gould would spend the next eight hours waiting for a bollocking. Whether or not it came, she wouldn't leave her post again. He turned back to Lisa Trefusis. Her eyes were red and sore-looking. But there were no tears. He figured she was all cried-out. "Who were the men out at Daniel Vigus's cottage?" He felt his phone vibrate and took it out of his pocket. It was his daughter Chloe. He hesitated, his thumb hovering over the answer icon.

"Locals."

"Obviously," he replied distractedly. He was struggling to multitask. Deborah had always said he had trouble with the easiest of tasks if someone was talking to him. Or arguing with him, which was the case for most of the final year in their marriage.

"The big one was my cousin. The one that you knocked down was a local farmworker. The others weren't Gulruan boys, they were from Sennen Cove further down the coast. They're fishermen, work out of Newlyn."

"Farmers and fishermen," Grant mused, still unsure whether to answer the phone. He'd never not answered a call from his daughter before. "Tough blokes..."

"Got to be. Farmers, fishermen, daffodil pickers, miners, benefit claimers," she paused. "They've done most of it. Most have, around here."

"Did you organise them, get the posse together?" The call went to answerphone. He cursed quietly, slipped the phone back into his pocket.

"No."

"Really?"

"Yes, really! I went down there, and the others turned up. I didn't organise anything."

"Well, I will advise you to go absolutely nowhere near him, okay?"

"Okay."

Grant looked at her. Her eyes had dried, the shakes had stopped, and she looked a little more in control of her emotions. "There is no record of a complaint from you on file. Nothing to correspond with your allegation down at Vigus' home. Are you lying about that?"

"No!" she snapped.

"Then tell me what happened."

She had started to shake. She wiped the corner of her eyes. They were moist with tears. She shrugged. "There were a few girls who said Vigus touched them. There were two girls whose parents tried to have the police charge him, but both cases were thrown out. A few other girls spoke about him touching them up. But you know what girls are like, don't you? They love to have a good story, gossip worse than old ladies. Vigus cornered me in a lane near the beach. The lane goes right up the valley to Gulruan and to the left it runs all the way down to the cove. He pressed me down..." She paused, wiped her eyes again and breathed a long steadying breath. "... Down in the grass and tore off my pants. He put his fingers inside me... looking down at me and smiling the whole time... that hideous fucking burn of his... it was vile... and so painful..."

"Who did you tell about this?" Grant asked quietly, as sensitively as he could.

"Nobody," she said. "I was too embarrassed, horrified, ashamed. I couldn't tell my parents. My mother never even told me about periods. I couldn't tell her about where he put his fingers, the sneer on his face..." she sighed, but looked resolute. "I saw what the other girls went through, how people provided an alibi for Vigus, how the girls were painted as little hussies because they had to be lying. I didn't want to go through all of that. I know the girls weren't lying, but the alibis for him were all from solid citizens."

Grant said nothing. What could he say? He looked up as the female police officer walked out of the house and down the two steps into the garden. He was thankful for the interruption. PC Gould carried two mugs, handed the black coffee to Grant. She still looked sheepish. "Thanks," he said as he took the mug. "So, you two know each other?" he asked, moving things on.

"We went to the same school," PC Gould said.

"I've seen her around a few times lately," Lisa Trefusis said. It wasn't a particularly cold day, but she was warming her hands on the mug of tea. "Nice to catch up, eh?"

"If only it could have been under better circumstances," PC Gould said quickly. She looked back at Grant. "I'll be inside, if you want that chat, Sir."

Grant nodded and she walked back up the path. He looked back at Lisa, sipped the coffee, felt a little guilty at taking a break in the middle of the investigation. He wondered if the missing girl's mother would be thinking the same. There was an intensity, a desperation in her eyes. He believed she had been telling the truth, but he knew his instincts. And those instincts told him that Vigus had been surprised by her claim. The man had been shocked. He would have bet all he owned that Daniel Vigus had never laid a hand on her all those years ago. And then there was Chloe. Why had she called? He just hoped that she was ok, and he would call her back as soon as he could. His phone vibrated twice, and he knew he had a voicemail. He'd check it in a moment but didn't want a distraught mother thinking he was distracted.

She bowed her head. "I'm sorry. I let myself down, let Lilly down. I shouldn't have gone down there shouting the odds..."

"Lisa! Lisa!" Both Grant and Lisa Trefusis looked around at the shouting coming from behind them in the street. "Lisa!" The woman was slim, tall and brunette. She struggled with the gate, managed to get it open, then left it swinging as she made her way up the path. "Jesus, girl. I came as soon as I heard. I mean, I heard about a missing girl, saw the things on social media, saw that bastard Vigus was up to his old tricks, but I never knew it was Lilly..." she said tearfully, flinging her arms around Lisa Trefusis and hugging her close. "Jesus Christ, are you okay? Silly question, I mean, how are you? Oh, that's just as stupid... come here, babe," she said and hugged her again. "Don't worry, Maria's here for you..." Grant watched. He knew that the woman would need friends at a time like this. Lisa Trefusis certainly looked relieved. He drank down his coffee, it was too hot to chug, but he ended up doing so, nonetheless.

"This is Inspector Grant. He's in charge of the investigation," Lisa told her.

"Not doing a lot, is he? Your lot want to get down to that evil bastard Daniel Vigus' place and arrest him!" she snapped. "It's all very well hanging about here drinking coffee, but you need to take some bloody action!" She paused, releasing Lisa from her embrace and squaring up to Grant. "It's all bloody *dreckly* down here!"

Grant had heard the expression a few times since he had been in Cornwall. One for 'in a minute'. It was a time-honoured Cornish tradition. *'I'll do it dreckly...'* In most cases it wouldn't get done at all.

"You're not from around here, then?"

She scoffed. "I was. Moved away for a few years, came back a couple of months ago." She looked at Lisa, wrapped an arm around her. "And a bloody good job I did. That monster needs someone to smash two bricks together with his cock and balls in the middle," she said. "Perhaps we should do it?"

"I wouldn't recommend that," said Grant. He turned to Lisa. "I need to have a word with my officer," he said and walked up the path and into the house. He paused, turning to look back at them. "Not, Maria Bright, madam?" he asked.

"Oh, you've actually done your homework, then," she stated flatly. "That bastard Vigus has it coming. You bastards never listened to us, never took our complaints seriously, now look what's happened!"

Grant watched the woman turn her back on him and put her arm around Lisa Trefusis' shoulders. She leaned in and the two women started to talk. He thought it looked as if they were conspiring, but he realised Maria Bright was comforting her, or more likely slating the police.

PC Tamsin Gould was washing a cup in the sink and looking at the two women through the net curtains. She turned around and looked at Grant. "I'm sorry I left my assignment, Sir."

"Family liaison is an important facet to any investigation. Not only do the family get to know what happens during an investigation or have a point of contact if they remember something important, but it gives us eyes and ears if the family are disingenuous." He paused. "Lisa Trefusis led a posse down to Daniel Vigus' property and they were out for blood. If I hadn't been there, then it will have escalated for sure. You would have been responsible."

"I'm sorry, Sir."

Grant shrugged. "Will you do it again?"

"Never, Sir!"

"Then it's dealt with," he said and walked over to her. She backed up against the sink, looked for a moment like she was undecided whether to say something else to him or step out of the way. She stepped out of the way and sighed as he leaned against the sink and stared out through the net curtains at the two women in the garden. "Relax, PC Gould. Ms Trefusis has a visitor."

"I noticed."

"You did more than notice," he said. "You were practically spying on them."

"I was not!"

Grant shrugged. "Who is she?"

Gould sighed. "She was a year or two older than me."

"And still is..."

"I meant, she was a year or two ahead of me in school."

"Which school?"

"Humphry Davy."

"Christ, now that place sounds *Cornish*."

"As Cornish as it gets," she smiled. "The guy invented the safety light that could be used around flammable gases. Changed mining forever."

"No shit."

"He discovered sodium and potassium and some other stuff, too."

"Amazing. What about something relevant to the case?"

"Sorry, Sir." She paused, a little flustered. "Maria Bright. Not that bright, if I'm honest. Made up for it by having a D-cup at thirteen. A bit of a goer in school. Had all the boys, all the friends too. Not averse to showing her fanny for a few sweets. Maybe let the boys do more when she was older."

"And a mean girl?"

"Horrid. If you weren't in her group, then you were nothing."

"Have you seen her since?"

She nodded. "Well, everybody knows everybody on Facebook, don't they?"

Grant shrugged. He didn't have anything more technical than a banking app and an iPhone, and certainly no social media. When he needed to view a suspect's profile, he used one of the hundreds of ghost accounts created by the police service for that purpose. "Have you seen her since she relocated back to Cornwall?"

"No. But I obviously recognised her from her social media account, just then."

"It may be hard, in fact, it's going to be extremely difficult. But stick around here for a few hours." He looked at his watch. "Make that until clock-off time tonight. Keep your eyes and ears open. That will be it for family liaison duty. There's another PC coming around unannounced tonight. Report back to me in the morning at Penzance station." He swilled his mug out under the tap and placed it in the sink, then walked back outside. He nodded a farewell to Lisa and said, "I'll contact you with any developments."

"You sure will," Maria Bright interrupted. "Round the clock updates and no less. I know people, Inspector Grant. Sit on this and I'll be making some calls."

Grant said nothing as he walked back to his Alfa Romeo. He could tell when people were telling the truth. Most of the time, at least. So, if Lisa Trefusis hadn't called the vigilante posse, then who had? He didn't think he'd get good odds betting against Maria Bright. She seemed embedded in this case now – justice by proxy.

He sat down heavily in the seat and took out his mobile phone. There were two messages from DC Heather Carveth. One saying she was in position and that Vigus still hadn't moved and the other asking where he was. He ignored them both; he'd be there soon enough. He thought briefly about how Heather looked, and her gentle, warm manner, then almost as quickly, he put the thought aside. He was a detective inspector, and she was a detective constable. Two ranks between and a gulf apart. Besides, after what he had experienced down here at the end of last summer, he was off women for the moment. Especially women he worked with. He dialled his voicemail and listened to Chloe's message.

"Hi Dad! Why won't you pick up? Look, I've fallen out with Simon. He's a dick... I'm on my way down on the train and I get in at Penzance around seven. Can you come meet me? I'll try again, but I don't have much battery left and all the charging ports are in use. Miss you... Bye..."

Grant groaned. He couldn't wait to see her, but her timing couldn't have been worse. A missing child and what could soon turn into a media-fest and the daunting possibility that this could still become a murder case. Not the ideal circumstances to have his daughter come down and stay with him. He hadn't even made up the spare room yet and doubted if there was anything edible in the house. He'd told Chloe he was working out of Penzance, but he didn't live there. His movements were to be fluid, so he'd stuck a pin in a map and had rented a house at a small coastal village called Portreath on the north coast, which he thought would centralise him a little more. It hadn't been a bad plan and he had taken to walking the cliffs and nearby woodland to clear his head, rather than stare at the bottom of a bottle.

And then there was Deborah. Should he text or call? A call would be the mature thing to do. He had wanted an amicable relationship, post-divorce. So far, he hadn't seen any signs of that, so he gave up on mature and started to type out a text. Chloe was fifteen. Surely, she could catch a train. Shit, school... He explained that he would have her for a few days, that it couldn't hurt and that he'd drive her back to London when he could get some cover. He hit send and instantly regretted it. Another shitstorm on the forecast. Still, this time he couldn't lose her, so for the first time in a long while he thought fuck it and put the phone back in his pocket and looked forward to seeing his daughter, whatever the consequence.

Chapter Six
The New Forest, Hampshire

At first the silence had been eerily quiet. He had heard nothing. But he knew the importance of tuning into his surroundings and with the vehicle's engine ticking itself cool and with his window open, he had begun to pick out the woodland sounds around him. Birds cackled and cooed, spring was here, and birds got it on early. There were buds on the trees, and a few remaining snowdrops and tiny daffodils added colour to the forest floor and the green shoots of bluebells had broken through the debris and would carpet the forest in blue in another couple of months.

He had found the spot using *Google Earth* and could see that he was at the end of a track a whole mile from the quiet road, and that the nearest agricultural land was more than a mile away on all sides. There would always be the possibility of ramblers or dog walkers, but he reasoned that people tended to veer away from gunfire, not stride towards it. Not civilians, anyway.

He opened the door and got out, breathing in the damp odour of the forest. As he walked around to the boot of the car, he could hear his own footsteps cracking last year's seed pods and fallen leaves until he stopped, and silence enveloped him once more.

The boot popped and a bird took to the wing, cackling as it flew out of the clearing. And then silence once more.

He put on a pair of thin leather gloves and reached inside and unfolded the blanket. The AK47 was old and well-used and as far as he could ascertain, had been brought into the country via Syria. Migrants, maybe. You couldn't blame someone for carrying some protection as they fled their former lives in a war-torn country or oppressive regime. Or perhaps it had come to these shores by way of a Russian gang. He had stripped the weapon down and cleaned it thoroughly, then carefully reassembled it with well-practised familiarity and precision. The weapon had not come with ammunition from the cache he had collected it from. Ammunition worked like a fingerprint, so he wouldn't have used it anyway. He always loaded his own ammunition and despite the UK having some of the most stringent firearm laws with quantities of ammunition authorised to be purchased and held stipulated on an individual's firearms licence, bullet heads, nitro-powder, primers and shell casings could all be purchased individually. The crazy loophole meant he could use his own press to manufacture almost any bullet for any gun. For this weapon, he had pressed ninety-rounds of 7.62x39mm full metal jacketed ammunition using popular hunting .308 brass cases that he had cut and re-necked to size to test fire, and then moulded thirty .30 calibre soft-nosed hunting tips which would form into the shape of a mushroom upon impact and quadruple the size of the exit wound. The man loaded one of the three, thirty-round curved magazines with the full metal jacketed ammunition, then set about loading just ten of the soft-nosed bullets into the other. He had wiped every case after making them and now using the gloves he could rest assure that he would leave no fingerprints or DNA on them. He rested the magazines beside the rifle and took out the pistol. A 9mm Browning Hi-Power. It had MOD markings and looked to be well-used. It had most probably had a chequered history, and would no doubt be known to various police forces around the country but would almost certainly have been smuggled out of a British military base at some time. Again, no ammunition had been supplied, but he had pressed out thirty hollow-points and loaded one of the two, thirteen-round magazines. He loaded the pistol, worked the slide and applied the safety catch before tucking it into his waistband and picking up the AK47 and the magazines, along with a carrier bag full of tinned food he had purchased earlier at a Spar convenience shop.

The man walked through the clearing following an animal trail through a cluster of trees and out into another clearing. The New Forest was a sporadic woodland interspersed by farms, villages and acres of grassy common, as well as roads and tracks, but from what he could see on *Google Earth* he was in a thick area of forest uninterrupted for at least a hundred acres. The forest floor was damp underfoot and twigs of dead wood crumbled as he stepped on them, and he stopped walking every twenty metres or so to listen, watch for movement and take stock of his surroundings. After a few hundred metres he walked into another clearing and looked all around him. He started to set out the tins of food on the ground in clusters. When he had finished and walked back to the fringe of the forest, he had targets set at approximately fifteen, thirty and seventy metres distant.

He placed the rifle on the ground and took out the

pistol, flicking off the safety with his thumb as he took in the neatly stacked cans of beans. He aimed at the centre of the top can at fifteen metres and the bullet clipped the top of the can and it split wide open on the other side and baked beans splattered out on the ground behind the tower of tins and the tin dropped off the stack. He noted the bullet would still be on the rise leaving the barrel, so he aimed lower on the next tin, choosing the one on the left. The bullet hit dead centre, the tin split wide open again and the tin spun backwards onto the ground. He fired at the remaining tin, then fired three rapid shots at the three on the ground, missing one but firing instantly and hitting it. He aimed out to thirty metres and fired, striking the first three tins dead centre. He stopped with two rounds remaining, applied the safety and tucked the pistol back into his waistband as he picked up the rifle and dropped the selector down two clicks from 'safe' through 'auto' and onto 'single fire'. The pistol's report had been sharp and loud, but the AK47 would be on another level. He looked around him. Nothing. Nobody to be seen and no sounds other than the ringing in his ears and the silence of the forest, the nearby wildlife having evacuated upon the first shot. He shouldered the rifle and aimed at the remaining tins in the thirty-metre pile and fired. The bullet struck dead centre and he fired and hit the second tin as he had the first. The simple vee and pin sights were easy to use and were adjustable to both windage and elevation, but the weapon seemed well set up. He aimed and fired ten rounds at the destroyed tin cans, and they spun high in the air. He switched magazines to the soft nosed bullets and aimed out to the pile at seventy metres. He missed a couple but generally hit and destroyed every-thing with the first shot. He cycled a few rounds through on fully automatic, then switched magazines and fired short bursts into the tins. He knew that he would hit them but was just trying out the weapon and checking that both types of ammunition fed through smoothly. The weapon handled well, and he did not bother picking up the empty cases both weapons had ejected because he was confident there was not a single trace of DNA or fingerprints on them.

He cradled the rifle over the crook of his elbow, securing it in place with his forearm and walked back the way he had come. There were no sounds of birds or creatures in the undergrowth. The gunshots would have driven everything in the area for cover. And yet, he could hear movement. Certainly not a deer. It did not take much to spook a deer and stalking them was a real skill. Likewise, foxes took off at the slightest sound. He suspected a wild boar would be less timid and they were prone to charge at people and barge through obstructions when threatened, and he knew the New Forest to have a feral wild boar problem. Many of the picturesque villages in the area had gardens and village greens devastated by the beasts.

The man had used all the ammunition for the AK47, so with the prospect of a wild boar sharing his path in mind, he drew the 9mm Browning and vigilantly continued.

"I say!" There was no warning, and the woman strode out from a thicket of holly and continued towards him. "There are rules for shooting!" The man stopped in his tracks and looked at her. "You can't just blast away with that thing! You've terrified Jessie!" She struggled to control an excited golden retriever that appeared more excited to see someone on her walk than cowering at its experience with the gunfire. "Machine guns are illegal, anyway. What are you doing with that?" She fumbled with her mobile phone and added, "I'm calling the police, you know..." Her voice was cultured, and she exuded an arrogance the man would have associated with the British class system. Upper middle class, maybe gentry even. He was Swiss, or at least he was by repatriation, so knew a little of his own class system, which he figured was similar, but more income related as opposed to status and values, but she reminded him of a character from an Agatha Christie television adaptation. Quite at home in a country house hosting a black-tie dinner. He also knew that she was a 'Karen'. A white, middle-aged, middle-class woman who for whatever reason, was so frustrated with her life that she needed to attack others at the slightest, or in often case, no provocation.

He looked at her, saw she was close to finishing dialling and aimed the pistol at her. "Stop dialling," he said. She looked up, her thumb hovering over the keypad. He suspected she had dialled but had not yet pressed the dial icon. "Put the phone away..."

"How dare you point that thing at me," she said contemptuously. "*You* put that away at once!"

The man had to admire her tenacity, but he could see there was no talking her down. She simply couldn't help herself. Some people simply couldn't see further than their own nose. She stood less than twenty feet from him, which was the optimum distance for using a pistol during combat. They could certainly hit targets further away, but in a close quarter combat scenario twenty feet was more realistic. He centred the sights on her forehead, then remembering the rise from a 9mm, he lowered it so that the sights aimed at her top lip and then he squeezed the trigger. The bullet hit her dead centre on the bridge of her nose and the back of the woman's head blew out in a pink mist and she dropped onto her knees. She was still staring at him, her eyes seeming to question what he had done, her mouth moving but no sound was forthcoming. The dog had flinched, startled by the noise, and was pulling at the retractable leash still clasped in the woman's hand. Then the body fell forwards and rested still on the forest floor and the dog whimpered and sniffed at its owner, before licking at the blood on the body's neck and shoulders. The man watched as the dog did what came natural to it and rather than allow the dog to eat out the remnants of the brain cavity created by the hollow-point bullet, he shot the dog in the back of the head then moved closer to inspect his handiwork. He had trimmed far more lead from the bullet than he normally would have, making a thin rim to the hollow-point and yet still retaining the structural integrity with the copper coated jacket on the outer edge. He had fluted the rim of the bullet cavity as well, which he had drilled out slowly with a 6mm drill bit, and that had certainly been an improvement over his previous attempts, expanding more than he could have imagined. He smiled at the result and headed back down the path towards his vehicle without pausing to look back. The tools of his trade were working perfectly. It was time for him to go to work.

Chapter Seven
The River House, London

The meeting was in a conference room on the second floor of MI6's unique looking headquarters that looked like a Lego Aztec pyramid. The room was a soulless box with electric sockets, USB charging points and conference call facilities. It was swept daily for listening devices by the security team who then placed a seal over the door handle to be broken by whoever had requested the room that day. Even hot-desking, low ranking personnel could see if the room was clean or soiled and could make their choices based entirely on the yellow and red plastic seal. It wasn't a room where priority meetings generally took place – those were generally a few floors higher - and Hill had chosen it for that reason. Even within the walls of the Secret Intelligence Service, or what was commonly called MI6, this conversation was not a comfortable one.

John Hill was in the chair and to his left sat Michelle Jordan, an operations officer and to his right, Paul Manyon, who worked in procurements. Although nobody really knew what the man did on a day-to-day basis.

"It's a cunning way to communicate clandestinely. Does GCHQ know?" asked Hill. He was section chief of organised crime, domestic division.

"I imagine so," Manyon replied. "Can't let them know yet, obviously."

"Can't sit on it too long either," commented Jordan. "If communication via something as simple as a saved and unsent email draft with mutual access can defeat our intercepting capabilities, then the boffins in Cheltenham need to get onto it pretty bloody quick smart."

"Agreed," replied Hill. "But we need to get this matter sorted first."

"It's not too high a price, considering." Manyon paused. "Not that we'd do it ourselves, but considering that it's already in play, all we have to do is sit back and allow it to happen. I can't see a problem with that. I've certainly been expected to do a lot worse in my time here."

"It's still a man's life," said Michelle Jordan sharply. "And a police officer at that."

"Oh, come on, Michelle." Manyon paused. "A chequered history. He's been promoted and demoted more times than anybody I've come across in the police service. He was even investigated for corruption once..."

"And found innocent!"

"Shit generally sticks, Michelle. No smoke without fire. Besides, his last job went to hell in a handcart. Big time. He was shagging the asset's wife and got the woman killed as a result. The operation was compromised, and the Met lost its advantage and Roper tightened his security as a result. The operation to infiltrate Roper's organisation has since been shelved."

"Which is handy for us because it takes the heat off the asset we have in place in Roper's organisation. But we can't let a police officer die just to keep our man in play!" she protested.

"We turn a blind eye, that's all. It's one bloody flatfoot. And not a particularly good one at that," said Manyon. "Honestly, Michelle are you even cut out for this line of work?"

"Now, now," Hill interjected, holding his hands up like a boxing referee. "Let's just agree. It's a sensitive matter. But John Roper has undercut Russian backed bids supplying General Kartum and the Yemini forces with weapons and that means we can finally get a foothold out there. If we can help Richardson maintain his cover, and aid him in his tasks with some of the more sensitive issues, the red tape and the customs paperwork and transportation checks, then he has agreed to negotiate our influence with General Kartum and we can steer the political direction of the Yemen and that means the Saudis will be left out in the cold after their efforts leading the campaign against the insurgents and the Americans will have no presence whatsoever. And with the US President publicly distancing his administration from Middle East relations, we have a chance to be front and centre and hold valuable Red Sea influences like we used to in Aden under our administration until nineteen-sixty-seven. We may even be able to forge the way for a base of some sort out there, a handy stop off for India and China, or a looming and probably inevitable future conflict with Iran."

"Richardson has Roper in the palm of his hand. Roper trusts him, and now that the Met have been caught with their pants down, and their operation is blown, all the heat is off Richardson. We are getting first class intelligence from him, but he is paving the way for Roper to succeed in the Yemen, and with that, getting us a foothold in that shitty little country we deem to be so important for Middle East security." Manyon smiled. "We could be the most important people out there since Lawrence of Arabia helped carve up the Middle East."

Michelle Jordan looked at him incredulously. She was related to TE Lawrence and knew more about the man than Manyon ever would. And she had studied the Ottoman Empire and First World War history at Oxford. "And a police officer's life is worth that?"

"My dear Michelle," Manyon said condescendingly. "It's the bigger picture. A sacrificial lamb. One hit, a washed-up copper and an assassin who will likely get it done and disappear without trace. *SecureTech* are Holland based and run by a Dutch national. And with Brexit, we have no worries about such a matter."

"Richardson has given us this intelligence as much to test our belief in him as to wipe some of the blood onto our hands. If we report this, then Richardson will pull out of the deal. We will be no closer to turning Roper, and with the upcoming Yemen deal, we will be left out in the cold. It's a question of trust and belief." Hill raised his hand to pre-empt Michelle Jordan's objection. "The information he gave us will tell him if he can trust us. We can still work together and achieve much for Britain's interests."

"And what about Box?" she asked.

"MI5 haven't even got a clue we're looking into Roper's affairs, much less about the hit he's got planned for DI Grant, or that we have an asset in Roper's organisation." Manyon paused, glancing at Hill. "We need to move on this. Show Richardson he can trust us and get ourselves embedded in Yemen. Fuck what he has in mind for one lowly copper down in the West Country."

"I'm inclined to agree," said Hill. "Michelle?"

Michelle Jordan gnawed at the inside of her cheek. She couldn't bring herself to agree, but she knew how important getting an intelligence foothold into the Yemen was, not to mention a political and military angle. Her father had been stationed in Aden in sixty-two. He had often spoken of the stability British troops and police had maintained before a weak labour government and a change in political direction had lost it. And then the fundamentalists had gotten their foothold and kept the country in the stone ages. One man. That's all it was. And all they had to do was turn a blind eye.

"Alright," she said finally, and the two men at the table breathed a sigh of relief and shook hands excitedly, and before she knew it she was involved in their celebration and they were making plans for Roper's first arms shipment to clear through the Suez Canal and a man's life had been valued as less worth than some signatures on a sheet of paper.

Chapter Eight

Grant pulled in front of the plain grey Ford Focus and switched off the engine. He got out and walked towards it, both front doors opening in unison and the two detectives stepping out. One was an attractive brunette, slim, medium build and around thirty years of age. Grant couldn't remember having ever been so attracted to a woman, and to his dismay he'd had an instant rapport with her, too. He could see it in her eyes; she felt the same way. Awkward. However, he still felt a pang of rawness and pictured the last woman he had been intimate with lying dead on a hotel floor. It wasn't something he was sure he'd ever get over. Drink, recklessness and regret had made him play the field since his divorce, seeking solace in the comforting arms of women. Any women, but mainly the wrong kind of women. He had only just realised that he wanted more than bedroom conquests. So much more, and he could see everything he craved in the eyes of Heather Carveth. But he knew it would not be practical to find the right woman within his work. The gulf in rank between them made the situation unworkable as there was always the chance that people would view that a subordinate may have felt pressured to accept a date, or in fact could even accept one to accelerate their career. Not that he thought Heather Carveth would do such a thing, but these things were always viewed negatively by colleagues and the more senior ranks. This didn't help him in the early hours when he lay awake thinking of her, the one person he thought could make him happy. The one person he desired near constantly and yearned to be with. As a result, he had adopted a gruff, over-compensatory manner with DC Heather Carveth. Mostly, he would call her by her surname and snapped at her more than was necessary. And it all seemed to work to his detriment. She looked at him with more warmth than the other officers. She jumped to his command but wasn't afraid to question him. In a workplace full of detectives, their colleagues had deduced the attraction from the start. Now Grant knew his affections could work against the woman, as he had already signed off on putting an officer with less ability and promise through to their sergeant's exam, leaving her stagnated as a detective constable for another year. By rights, Carveth should have objected, put in for a transfer, but the fact she had not had spoken volumes of her feelings towards Grant. Like most workplace attractions, it was a mess and had all the potential to become messier.

Grant looked at the tall, slim, blonde-haired man closing the passenger door. He was too young to be a police officer, let alone a detective. He even had spots. The observation made Grant feel his age. A man's forties was such a conundrum – not young by any means, but still he saw himself as twenty-five. He referred to people in their fifties as 'old men', but it he was so close to knocking on that door that he would get a shock when he used his own date of birth.

Small victories were taken in comparing the amount of hair he had or the grey that was showing at the sides to someone he knew to be a similar age. He still managed to keep himself fit and could hit his physical goals as he always had, but perhaps felt it the next day a little more. But the 'boy' before him gave him no wriggle room, and he knew that in his eyes, Grant would be viewed as an old timer. For this reason, he played the experience card and used sarcasm and his rank to compensate. It was never his proudest moment. He nodded at DC David Jones. The man shouldn't have been a detective either. He should have earned a billion in stock options at some Silicon Valley development cooperation by now. He was a genius. But like most naturally gifted people, he was heavily flawed. He lacked self-belief, and Grant was waiting for the opportunity to pull the rug from under him and see how he coped. He wasn't malicious in his intent, but he reckoned the man's potential would never be realised until he was truly tested.

"What have you got, Carveth?" he asked, his manner typically gruff, his feelings for her, far softer. "Who's keeping an eye on the target?"

"Telekinetic hover..." the young man answered for her.

"For Christ's sake, Jones," Grant rolled his eyes. "In English, if you please."

"It's a drone. But it uses AI." He paused. "That's artificial intelligence."

Devon and Cornwall police had been pioneers in the use of drones to view, search and film, partly because of the terrain, and partly because an hour in the police helicopter cost a thousand pounds and the force had been pared to the bone through funding cuts. If a person went missing on Bodmin Moor, or a hiker fell down a gully a couple of drones with wide-angle cameras flying at a thousand feet could find them when a search party of a hundred officers could take days. The drones had turned potential body-recovery operations into life-saving ones.

"So, what's artificial intelligence? Thinking computers, isn't it?" Grant was already on unfamiliar territory, and he hated the fact he was about to learn it through the indecently young police officer. "Robots?"

"Exactomundo..." DC Jones said.

"Remind me why you're single again?"

"I don't get out much," Jones said. He wasn't retorting to Grant's sarcasm; like most geniuses he had a foot on a rung reasonably high up the autism ladder. "The drone operates much like the ones the police service have employed, but there are a few interesting additions."

"You've pimped your ride," Grant commented, instantly regretting it. Now he was sounding old, too. Down with the kids...

"No, a ground up build. Mine has a solar panel along the outriggers, that's eight in total. Adding approximately twenty-seven percent to its operating time."

"Approximately? There's nothing approximate about that," Grant interjected.

David Jones ignored the interruption. "Twenty-seven-point-three-two-six to be precise. The rotors generate a small dynamo to give a further twenty-five percent."

"Approximately?"

"Exactly," the young man paused. "The unit is half the size of the force's drones, but it's the camera and processor that makes the difference. I have flown it over Vigus's cottage and sighted him leaving."

"He's not there?"

"Relax, boss," DC Heather Carveth interjected. "Listen to David."

Grant stared at her. Her hair was scraped back in a ponytail, and she wore little makeup. He was quite sure she was the most beautiful woman alive.

"The software maps-out Vigus' gait, height, body mass, hair colour and facial recognition. Now, if Vigus stood in a crowd, it would focus only on him. No lookalikes. I have also allowed the software to read the vehicle's number plate, shape, size, colour and so forth. The targets are set, the vehicle and the person. At present, the drone is in a controlled hover, searching for the primary target."

"Daniel Vigus," Grant mused. "Have you patented any of this tech? It could be worth a fortune to the MOD."

"I'd rather the military don't benefit from my imaginings." Jones shrugged. "The police service can have it for free, though. It's experimental, but it works."

Grant shook his head, incredulous. He turned to Carveth. "So, what did Vigus do after he left?"

She took out a receipt, handed it to Grant. "He drove out of Gulruan and joined the A30 at Penzance. He drove to Pool and stopped at the B&Q and bought some tools. Some heavy rope, a shovel and a pickaxe. When he left, I showed the cashier my warrant card and then the manager gave me a copy of his receipt. It turns out he paid cash and refused the offer of a receipt."

Grant stared at the receipt, worked his way down the list of tools, or their abbreviations. The receipt showed the method of payment and both the time and date of purchase. "So, it looks like our man is going to do some digging..."

Chapter Nine

Grant had left DC David Jones to return to a suitable vantage-point and continue the observation on Vigus with his old-fashioned camera. In this case a digital model with a wireless roaming capability to upload photographs and video to a secure storage cloud. The lens was a hugely powerful telephoto zoom and Jones would choose a laying up point some five-hundred metres from the cottage with the unmarked Ford parked out of sight on the road. But first, he had been instructed to recall the drone and recharge both the battery and the handset controller using the auxiliary charging points in the vehicle.

Both DC Carveth and DI Grant had travelled in his Alfa Romeo to the town of Hayle, where a young woman was about to have her world rocked once more. Or at least, her day marginally ruined by a visit from the police at her home. It all depended on whether she had been telling the truth the first-time around.

Grant had typed the address into the satnav and was following the route out of Hayle and towards Hayle Towans and the village of Phillack. They passed a pub called the Bucket of Blood. "Sounds appealing," he commented.

Carveth laughed. "Sounds like a pasties and cider place, or scampi and chips in a basket," she said and shrugged. "Having said that, it probably has a Michelin Star for all I know. You never can tell down here."

"Are you from Cornwall?" he asked. He'd daydreamed about dating her and more and couldn't believe he knew next to nothing about her. It hadn't really seemed either relevant or wise to find out more. "You don't sound like you are."

"I am," she said. "Well, I moved down with my family from Northumberland when I was three, so I suppose it doesn't count as being from Cornwall, but I only think about Cornwall as my home. I lived in Truro, then went to university in Hampshire for three years. I couldn't think what to do with my degree and decided that the police force, or *service* as it's called now, would be a good idea. I thought at least I could return to Cornwall and be on a national wage. Salaries are shocking down here, compared to the cost of living. You're best off in public service roles."

"Didn't you think about fast-tracking with a degree?"

"I was," she said. "I got into CID quickly, should have done my sergeant's exam by now..."

Grant felt a pang of regret at having held her back. He was worried she had seen through him. And if she had, then others would, too. Perhaps he should organise a transfer for her. Set her free.

"You're a good copper," he said. "I'd like for you to work with me more. I will get you where you want to go." He paused, his heart racing. He was abusing his position of power and trust. He looked at her; her warm eyes, her soft skin, her glossy hair, and he didn't care. "You need to be patient," he said. "Now that Wilson has the exam under his belt, he will apply for the soonest sergeant's position that becomes available and he'll most likely switch to traffic to get it. It's like a game of chess. You can't move too soon. There are two detective sergeants in Cornwall who are both coming up for retirement in eighteen-months to two years' time. We'll have you qualified and a shoo-in for the position. You don't want to rush it and transfer to an easier position to fill, that you won't get out of again, and be cleaning up the mangled bodies of motorcyclists and putting out bollards in the early hours, do you? Visiting relatives to tell them their child was spread all over the road by a drunk driver who merely sustained a few bruises?"

"I suppose not," she said. "CID is where I want to be. Amongst other things..." she blushed, but Grant didn't notice. "I want to stay right here," she added.

Grant didn't seem to hear as he pulled the car into a rutted layby and looked at the cottage. It would have been the quintessential Cornish cottage, had several poorly executed concrete block and roughly rendered single-storey extensions not completely ruined its aesthetics. It was ripe for development, but from the look of it, the owner lacked the funds, and the cottage would be staying as it was.

Grant led the way across the road and through the broken front gate. It was off the hinges and hanging halfway across the pathway. A robust-looking woman of around thirty was pegging out washing in the rear garden. The sky was blue and clear, the wind was powerful, sweeping in from the ocean a mile distant. Grant could smell the sea - the salt and seaweed and shellfish more associated with harbours. The woman looked up, frowned, but finished pegging out a pair of ripped men's jeans. Ripped more by work and retained through budget rather than a specific purchase or alteration.

"Carrie-Ann Dixon?" Grant asked.

"Nope."

"I have her down as living at this address," he said. He took out his warrant card and opened it as he neared. There was a baby in a pushchair beside her sucking its thumb. A bag of clothes pegs hung over the handle. The garden was littered with plastic toys and building waste from around five-years back, judging from the build-up of moss on the side of the extension.

"Carrie-Ann Dixon," she corrected him. "I got married three years ago."

Grant shrugged. He'd got her details off the electoral roll. There were no citations, charges or cautions for Carrie-Ann Dixon on the police database. Other than her historical complaint. He would check again under her married name later.

"My name is Detective Inspector Grant and I'd like to ask you a few questions."

"You want to talk about Daniel Vigus," she said curtly.

"What makes you say that?" he asked.

"Pretty obvious, really." She dropped a sweater into the basket and tossed the pegs on top before looking at him. The baby started to cry, and she ignored it. Impassive. She looked weary, like a crying baby was the least of her worries and she could ignore it for however long it took. "It's all over Facebook about that girl. The talk is that Daniel Vigus has been back just three-weeks and then a girl goes missing yesterday."

"So why should it be obvious that the police want to talk to you?" Carveth interjected.

Carrie-Ann stared at her, then directed her reply to

Grant. "Because of my allegations."

"Allegations?" Grant asked. "You mean complaints, surely?"

She shrugged. "Same difference."

"No," he said. "They're a world apart. An allegation is a word somebody would use had they not be substantiated. Like the police, for instance. We'd say allegations. His defence lawyer would say allegations. But an innocent party who had been wronged would say *complaints...*"

"They weren't substantiated!" she said sharply. "He didn't even go to court!"

"I know. But in your eyes, you haven't made allegations. The term is too neutral. You made complaints about him. About things he did to you."

She stared at him, still ignoring her child's screams. She didn't look the most maternal of mothers. The crying was on a downwards spiral. Grant knew these things only got worse until they were picked up and comforted, or all cried out. This child was hours away from crying itself out. It just needed a cuddle, changing or some milk.

"Complaints, then," she said as she bent down and snatched the sweater out of the basket, slung it over the line and clamped a peg on it. It wasn't neatly pegged out like the rest of the washing. She took out a packet of cigarettes and fumbled one out. "I don't want to talk about it," she said. She flicked the wheel of a disposable lighter, waved the flame around the tip of the cigarette and took a deep drag. She exhaled the smoke as she spoke. "Look, it was a dark time. Things have moved on. I don't want to think about it, and I don't want to think about that shit Vigus..."

Grant nodded. "Why do you think the police didn't charge Vigus?"

"Bunch of useless coppers down here," she said, looking

at them awkwardly and shrugged. "At that time, at least."

"Where is your husband?"

"At work."

"Does he know about what Daniel Vigus did to you?"

"No."

"Really?"

"He knows I was touched up by a pervert..." She paused. "That was the talk, but it went further than that. Vigus raped me..."

"There was no mention of DNA testing in the file."

She hesitated, then said, "I'd had a bath by the time I got the courage to make a complaint..." She drew on the cigarette, blew out a long plume of smoke and shuddered. "The fucking bastard..."

Grant nodded. The baby was still crying, and he squatted down and made a silly face. He could see it was in fact a girl and that she was clawing at a snotty and worn teddy bear on the ground. He picked it up and walked it up the girl's leg until it got close enough for her to clasp onto. He thought briefly of Chloe and how quickly those early years had gone. Blink and you miss it. He straightened up. The baby had stopped crying and was snuggling the soft toy. "What was it like growing up in Gulruan?" he asked, taking Carrie-Ann away from the memory of being raped.

She seemed surprised by the question. The change in tack. She shrugged, glanced at her watch. She looked worried, suddenly hurried. "Boring. Small village, smaller back then. I couldn't wait to get out."

"Friends?"

"A few."

"Like whom?"

She shrugged. "Loads."

"Too many to mention..." Grant paused. "Were you

friends with Maria Bright?"

"Yes. You know I was." Again, she glanced at her watch.

"She made allegations, too."

"You mean complaints."

"No, I mean allegations. This is coming from me." Grant looked at her. "Are you late for something? Are we taking up too much of your time?"

"No," she said hastily. "My husband will be home soon. I don't want to be talking about this when he's here."

"But he knows something happened," Carveth said quietly.

Carrie-Ann looked perplexed. "I know! I just don't want it all dragging up in front of him."

"He doesn't know, does he?" Grant said. "Or rather, it didn't happen," he stated flatly.

"Of course, it did!"

"What about Maria Bright? Did it happen to her?"

"I was raped by that monster! We both were!" she screamed, tears in her eyes and her face turning violet.

"Boss..." DC Carveth stepped forward, concerned. She looked unsure what to do next.

"I think he is a monster," Grant said. "I think he did unspeakable things to many girls. But I don't think he did those things to you. I don't think the police were useless, I just think there wasn't enough evidence... because it never happened."

"Fuck off!" she snapped and stormed off into the house.

Grant looked at the baby. She had started crying again. He turned to Carveth and nodded towards it. "Give that a push around, will you?"

"What Carrie-Ann Dixon just said..." she paused. "Right back at you, boss. You want me to wheel a pushchair around because I'm a woman?"

"No. I want you to wheel a pushchair around because I'm lead officer and want to interview somebody..." Grant swore under his breath. She had a point, and they weren't social services. He was sure the child was used to it. He nodded for Carveth to follow him, and the sound of the baby crying faded out as they stepped inside. "Mrs Dixon, I apologise for my bluntness," he called.

She appeared from a doorway and wiped her eyes. Again, she looked at her watch. "I was twelve, almost thirteen," she said. "Vigus was a real perv, used to make himself present when the bus dropped us off from school, or when we were playing at the beach. I think he loved the summertime. All the girls in bikinis or knickers and no tops on the beach. He would be down there for hours. All day even. And he never removed his coat. As we got older, we all knew what he was doing underneath it."

A van pulled up outside and the driver was talking animatedly on a mobile phone. Carrie-Ann looked scared.

"Is that your husband?" Carveth asked.

"Yes," she said. "Look, you've got to go."

Grant shook his head. "Tell us what happened."

"Please!"

"What happened, Mrs Dixon?" he persisted.

"Boss..."

"Quiet, DC Carveth," he said coldly. "What happened? Tell me and we'll leave out the back way."

"Look..." she said, ducking her head to watch her husband out of the window. He was still talking on his phone. "He touched up my friend. Touched her breast, rubbed her thigh. My friend was curious. Actually, she quite enjoyed it on a weird level. Never been touched before, but he turned and looked at her, that horrible burn the whole side of his face... She asked for him to stop, but he carried on, arousing himself I suppose, and then he forced himself on her."

"Raped her?"

"Yes. Sort of. It was a fumble; she was very confused."

"And this would have been Maria Bright?" She hesitated, then nodded. "But there were no samples of semen ever taken. And she hadn't lost her virginity during the alleged assault, that was what confused the investigators."

"Look, it's gross, but Maria fiddled about with herself. Jesus, we all experiment... but she bled badly and took her own virginity, if you get my drift, six months before." She shuddered. "Vigus did penetrate her, but he knew what he was doing, and he finished himself off. Outside of her." She shuddered at the thought. "She said that was the worst part. Horribly sordid. She'd heard what he was like and was scared the police wouldn't believe her. He had done the same with another girl, but she was rumoured to have only been eleven."

"Who?"

"I don't know, just rumours. I'm not even sure if they were true, but Maria Bright was my friend. She told her teacher what happened, and her teacher called the police and her parents. Maria made it sound worse than it was. I know that doesn't sound possible, but she intentionally left out the part about the initial fondling, which she admitted to enjoying. It kind of snowballed for her. Then she told them he did it to me too when they didn't believe her. She got to me before the police did and we worked out what to say. He'd done it to her, and the other girl who we didn't know, so it didn't feel so bad to lie. I was just making her case more solid."

"Or jeopardising it, because the police saw straight through you and discounted her story because your story cast doubt upon her own." Grant could have felt sanctimonious, but he'd been there. He had once omitted evidence to consolidate his case. A terrorist had walked free from charges of terrorist related offences, only to successfully carry out another plot and kill innocent shoppers at a Christmas market. Grant had been demoted to Detective Sergeant and transferred to an undercover unit. He had won back his rank but had lost his marriage and a whole lot more besides. He figured it had been karma.

"It wasn't just *my* lame story that ruined the chances of charging him. Two witnesses came forward to say they knew where Daniel Vigus was. He had a solid alibi. But it was bullshit. He was abusing and raping my friend at the time, the alibis were nothing but lies!" Carrie-Ann could see her husband dialling another number, but he had opened the door of his van and had a leg hanging out. "Look, he didn't go down, so I never retracted my statement. Please go now, my husband knows nothing of this. I didn't tell him anything about it..."

"Because there was nothing to tell," Carveth said incredulously.

"Don't judge me, you fucking privileged middle-class bitch!" she snapped.

Grant nodded. "No. You can do that yourself."

"Sanctimonious prick!" she snapped. "I won't lose any sleep over Daniel Vigus. He's a dirty, filthy bastard. He's done terrible things to other girls. My lie was nothing but a way to help lock him up!" She paused. "I was just twelve-years-old and didn't know any better! And you want to get out there looking for that little girl, not dragging up the past. Vigus will have had something to do with her disappearance, you mark my words!"

Chapter Ten

Grant carried on driving towards the coast. He stopped the car and stared at the sea. He needed to think. In London he had several places where he would sit and work through the order of things. Usually, high up on a roof terrace or one of the many bars in tall buildings with a beer in hand. The London skyline would do the rest. Or perhaps it had been the beer. But those days were behind him. He had battled with drink and had started to think he might be winning. There did not have to be a specific view, just a place to stare distantly at and reorder what he had learned. Now that he was in Cornwall, the sea had become the catalyst of choice. The north coast provided rough Atlantic seas, craggy cliffs and distant views across to bays pounded by the surf. To the south, at the head of the English Channel, he could be afforded infinite horizons and calm, glassy waters. He stared out across the bay towards St. Ives where he could see colourful boats and matching buildings built in terraces and appearing to be stacked together before planning had been a thing. It was the view depicted in many artistic works, and he found his mind clearing as many an artist would have before creating their masterpiece.

"Boss?"

"Yes."

"I asked whether we should be getting on with finding Lilly?"

Grant shook his head. "Sorry, I was miles away..."

"But Lilly?" she asked, looking at him with concern.

"Of course." He paused, opened his door. "You can drive," he said gruffly and walked around the car. DC Carveth slid over and adjusted the seat. Grant found himself marvelling at her flexibility, then shook the thought out of his head. As with every time since her death, when he thought about another woman, he pictured Anastasia Roper lying dead on a hotel floor. "I need to think," he said as he dropped down into the seat. It seemed warmer than his own and he could smell a faint fragrance of perfume around him. "Drive us back to Gulruan. I want to see how the search is going."

"Okay," she replied and swung the Alfa Romeo around in a wide arc. "You know, we have pool cars that we can use."

"I know," he said.

"Then why don't you use one?"

"I'm trying to kill it."

"Why?"

"My ex-wife wants it. She obviously didn't get enough in the divorce, so has gone after the car because she paid the deposit when I bought it." He paused. "There. You think less of me now, don't you? Rather than give a Alfa Romeo back to my ex, I'd rather run it into the ground."

"Er..."

"There's loads I could tell you about me and if I did,

then the puppy dog eyes would dry-up and turn into a thou-sand-yard stare."

"Puppy dog eyes?" she hesitated a beat, then it dawned on her, "Fuck you, Sir..."

"DC Carveth..."

"Oh, don't worry," She paused. "I think the puppy dog thing is already long-gone!"

"I'm sorry, I didn't mean..."

"I'm with the ex-wife," she said, her face flushed with embarrassment. "Now, if you don't mind, I'll just shut up and drive so you can do some precious thinking."

Grant looked out of the window. He needed the day to end. And he needed a drink. But he still had a missing twelve-year-old girl to find. And on top of that he had his own daughter arriving by train and bringing a big load of drama and problems with her; neither of which did he feel equipped to deal with. Drama and problems had been Deborah's department, and now he felt wholly unequipped.

"What are you thinking about, anyway?" Carveth asked as she threaded the agile Alfa Romeo through a series of S-bends.

"A game of chess."

She nodded. "Like, whether we should keep Vigus under surveillance, or whether we should make a move?"

Grant shook his head. "Nope. Just a game of chess I had at university."

"A game *you* had?"

He nodded. "Yes."

"And the significance?"

"I'm not entirely sure, but it feels familiar..." He paused. "And there's another case I keep coming back to."

"One of yours?"

"No. But it was quite significant and in the public eye."

"Madeleine McCann?"

"No. Almost the opposite, if that's possible. But Lord only knows what went on there." He paused. "But, at the moment it's more about a game of chess and a tournament that was turned upside down. I can't really elaborate until I work it through in my own head."

"Well, better not take too long," she said. "It looks like things are ramping up here..."

Chapter Eleven

He had driven out from the New Forest and joined the A35 all the way to Honiton in Devon. It had been a slow but scenic route and he used the time to reflect on what had brought him to this point, and what he would do once he reached Cornwall. He was not familiar with the county, but he had already seen from studying the map that the county was cut off from the rest of the country. Like the extremity of a limb. Bordered by the sea and the River Tamar, the county was practically an island. Only two main roads fed in and out of the county. The A30 and the A38. Neither was solely dual carriageway, but the A30 looked to be the fastest route. There were no motorways in the county, which he thought to be odd considering its appeal to tourists. He had studied other roads by which to make his getaway, but they were like mere capillaries compared to the arterial A roads feeding the county.

He felt nothing for the woman he had killed that morning. He didn't set out to kill. He set out to make money from killing. But the woman had been the type not to back down, and he knew that when things started to go wrong, there was a finite time to sever the fuse. Escalation could not be avoided beyond a certain point. Had he ignored her she would have made the call. She could have given her location and would undoubtedly had taken a photo of him with her phone. Had she been able to describe or photograph his vehicle, then the police would soon find him by number plate recognition software from the thousands of road cameras working constantly in the south of England. No, he had done what needed to be done. And by shooting the dog he had spared her family the indignity of the family pet eating out what remained in the woman's skull. It was the pragmatic thing to do.

He held a Swiss passport, and considered himself to be Swiss, living in the foothills of the Alps and working throughout Europe, applying his deadly trade. But he had grown up in war torn Kosovo. He had lost his family, witnessed his mother and sisters being raped and sold for sex to Serbian soldiers. His grandmother had been raped in front of his family, then attached to two armoured personnel carriers and ripped in two. His father and brother had been forced to commit a sex act on each other and as a seven-year-old, he had been forced to watch. He did not understand what they were doing, but he understood the finality of the gunshots to their heads when they had finished. He had escaped into the forest and survived for a week by drinking from puddles and eating the mushrooms his grandmother had taught him to pick, and the berries his mother had shown him how to make into delicious juice. He had eaten the tips of fir trees, the bud at which the branches forked. They were sweet and sticky and filled his belly. He had been cold at night and had hidden under fallen trees, fearful of wolves, lynx and bears, but he had seen nothing more than a deer and some grouse hens. He had stumbled into a UN convoy and the soldiers had taken him to an aid station, where he had been taken to Italy and efforts had been made to find his family, but he knew they were all dead. Four months later, it had been discovered that he had not one single living relative. By then he was living in an Italian foster home and under the ever-looming promise to be repatriated in Kosovo when the conflict was resolved. It never materialised, and he was thankful, because he never wanted to step foot in that part of the world ever again. At sixteen, he was made a ward of the European court and allowed to travel to France and work the season on the Riviera. He had learned to be a man there, and a poor one at that. He had discovered women and he had discovered the thrill of drinking hard and fighting harder. Down on his luck, unemployed and desperate he had joined the French Foreign Legion and discovered true belonging, but only after the remnants of the man he had been, had been beaten out of him. He had then discovered camaraderie, self-worth and duty. Not to France, but to his band of brothers. Misfits from around the world, men on the run and professional soldiers from other nations on attachment to learn new skills. And he had learned all he would need to become an assassin, one of the most notable, notorious and successful in the Western world.

Chapter Twelve

"So where is Vigus now?"

Grant looked past DCI Nangiles at the scene on the moor. Uniformed police officers were leading civilian volunteers in line walks and from Grant's experience, when civilians helped, they had a whole host of reasons, and few ended solely at concern for the victim. He looked back at Nangiles. He was a few years younger than DI Grant at thirty-eight, and he had the look of a man with his sights set on a whole lot higher than detective chief inspector. "Vigus is under electronic surveillance."

"You have no such court warrant for that."

"It's fluid. The equipment being used isn't officially operational, so I'm only using it as a means to know where the man is," he said. "Not as evidence in court."

DCI Nangiles nodded sagely. "I'd heard that about you, Grant..."

"DI Grant," he corrected him.

"Of course, DI Grant. But until recently, you were a DS. Briefly a DI, and then even a DCI. Now you're back to a detective inspector. It would seem you play a bit of a yoyo game with rank, commensurate I would imagine, with your performance." He paused. "Must make for an interesting budget, financially? One would never know where they were or if they would indeed struggle with bills. That would be enough for a spouse to find difficult…"

"Is there something you want to say, DCI Nangiles? Man to man, unless that's a problem for you?"

"No thank you detective inspector."

"It's always better to get things out in the open."

Nangiles shook his head. "You're a canny fellow, Grant. Everyone knows what you did with that terrorist. And so do you. But you got a medal because of it. A celebrity police officer who knows how to get out of scrapes and dodge accusations."

"I was vindicated, DCI Nangiles," Grant replied coldly. "Do I need to see the federation rep and discuss your take on this?"

"Of course not," Nangiles replied defensively. "Nothing of the sort."

"I thought not."

Nangiles bristled, and said, "Well, I have minions to both utilise and organise before I go home to my wife and family for a homecooked dinner."

"Naturally," Grant commented. "Best be where your skills are of most use to the investigation." He turned to DC Carveth, who had looked awkward throughout the verbal to and fro. "I'll show you how to organise this. I doubt you get many searches like this down here. This isn't my first rodeo."

"I already have organised this," DCI Nangiles said defensively.

"Yes, Sir, but if you don't mind me commenting, purely for the sake of the investigation and the wellbeing of a twelve-year-old girl, things have moved on a bit in the discipline of searches. Most probably hasn't filtered down to the sticks just yet." He paused. "I can take over here and you can get home to your shepherd's pie, or I can type up my comments and send to Middlemoor to put it on record, if you'd prefer?"

DCI Nangiles looked at Grant for a moment. Grant simply stared back. He had played enough poker in his time to give nothing away and was far from intimidated by the man in front of him. He had taken down larger men, with higher ranks than that of DCI. Nangiles nodded and walked to his car. Grant hadn't made a friend there, but he didn't care. He'd seen Nangiles's kind before, and they always came unstuck.

"Wow," said DC Carveth. "That was interesting. Did I say interesting? I meant bloody awkward."

"Not for me," he replied. He turned to her and said, "Get an update from DC Jones. Find out what Vigus has been up to. I'm going to talk to whoever has set this up."

"And tell them it's all wrong?" she laughed. "That will win you friends and favour."

"I've got you in my corner, Heather. I don't need any more than that..." He walked up the slope and onto the moor. He regretted saying it almost at once, but it had felt good. He only wished he had seen her face. She could have looked pleased, outraged or indifferent, but he would never know. He cursed, satisfied he was out of earshot.

He found the uniformed inspector and nodded a greeting. "DI Grant," he said.

The man was in his late forties and had grey hair under his peaked hat. He nodded. "Inspector Hocking," he replied. They shook hands and Hocking spoke briefly into his radio mic and ticked an area off a chart he had fastened to a clipboard. "Not come across you before," he said.

"Moved down from the Met about a month ago."

Hocking nodded. "How are you finding it?"

"Wide open spaces," Grant replied. "A big area with bugger-all resources."

"Welcome to the constabulary!" He nodded down to the waste ground and the vehicles parked on it. "You've met the new DCI, then?"

"On and off over the past couple of months."

"He's a dickhead. But I expect you already know that."

"I *had* noticed."

Hocking smiled. "So, are we doing it all wrong? City copper, down from the Met..."

"No. Looks good, but I confess, I told DCI Nangiles it may have been a bit old hat."

The inspector shrugged. "I've made a few changes to his orders, DI Grant. I keep abreast of the latest developments in crime and forensics," he said without hostility. "But if it finds a little girl safe and sound, I'll change whatever you suggest. I'm not in it for medals and commendations."

Grant nodded. "No, Inspector Hocking, it all looks good to me."

"Call me Gavin," he replied.

"Grant."

The inspector nodded and answered his radio again. He made another note on his clipboard and said, "I'd better be getting back to it."

"Good luck."

Grant made his way back down the moorland slope and waved at DC Heather Carveth. She walked over; her face ashen. "What is it?"

"DC David Jones called. He's lost Vigus..."

Chapter Thirteen

"Look, boss, it's not as bad as all that," DC David Jones ventured. "I have Vigus back in position. Maybe it was a glitch in the system?" he said despondently. "I just don't know. But right now..." He showed Grant the monitor. "Vigus is walking the cliffs north of Gulruan, south of St. Ives."

Grant watched the man's gait, his profile as Jones zoomed in. Vigus seemed blissfully unaware that several hundred feet above his head, a tiny drone followed slowly, its software identifying him over anybody else. Not that the cliffs of West Cornwall were particularly dense with walkers at this time of year.

"Where did he go?"

"I lost him in St. Ives."

Grant nodded. "For how long?"

"An hour." He paused. "I don't get it. It's like he simply vanished, then reappeared an hour later."

"And the vehicle?"

"Short stay carpark. The drone latched on and

followed. At speed the drone gains height to maintain contact, then drops in altitude as the vehicle slows. The drone can hit seventy miles per hour, but most vehicles average a great deal less on a journey. Usually half that speed on a short journey. The height gained means the drone can go point to point, rather than follow the road. I lost Vigus at Hayle. I went manual on the controls, but he had left the vehicle and... well, as I said... it must have been a glitch because it locked back onto the vehicle. I lost him again..." He shrugged, his face flushing with embarrassment. "But the drone latched back on the vehicle, and he parked at an empty carpark near the cliff path and went for his walk. The drone has locked on and been with him ever since." He paused. "I'm sorry, DI Grant, the system obviously isn't ready to be deployed. It's my fault entirely."

Grant nodded thoughtfully. "So, where is he now?"

"Approximately a mile away. He will be about level with the search at Gulruan Moor, but a mile further west."

"And his vehicle?"

"Two hundred metres down the road in a layby-come-carpark."

Grant nodded and looked at DC Heather Carveth. "Right, come with me. We're going to search the man's vehicle."

Carveth protested but Grant didn't listen. They drove in silence with Jones in the backseat monitoring Vigus's progress on his monitor. Grant stopped beside the Land Rover Discovery and said, "You two stay here, I don't want you incriminated."

"Bugger that!" Carveth got out and walked around the Alfa Romeo. "So, do you have a special tool, or skills for this sort of thing?"

Grant looked around him, then stooped and picked up a sizeable rock. He hefted it for weight in his hand, then smashed it through the rear window. "Something like that..." he said, almost laughing at the astonishment on Carveth's face. "Okay, gloves on, evidence bags out and swab like there's no tomorrow." Grant reached in and opened the door. The alarm sounded using the vehicle's horn and a high-pitched wail and both its headlights and hazard lights flashed in unison.

Carveth swabbed the rear seats and footwells, while Grant worked his swabs over the front seats and cabin. Carveth reached over the rear seats and swabbed around the boot space. As the swabs were used on both ends, they were sealed in sandwich style bags and numbered.

"This will all be inadmissible in a court of law."

"I just want to find Lilly Trefusis safe and well."

"But Vigus needs to go down!" Carveth paused. "We can't jeopardise a case like this."

"I can, and I will, if it means finding and saving a little girl," said Grant. "Until this becomes a murder enquiry, I'll do what it takes."

"Even if it means crossing the line?"

"I'll trample all over the line and take a disciplinary if it saves her life."

Carveth stared at him, but she wasn't judging him. She was in awe of him, and he could tell she had warmed to him once more. He enjoyed knowing that, even though it would be simpler all round if she hadn't.

"We'd better get out of here," she said quietly. The Land Rover's lights were still flashing, but the horn and siren had stopped. It was a battery saving feature. Grant had always found that people ignored alarms anyway.

"I'll confirm that," DC David Jones said, appearing at

the broken window. "He's running back and covering ground quite quickly."

"He can't have heard the alarm... wait," Grant said and ran his hands over the dashboard. He pulled out a button camera and a length of wire. "The bastard..." He pulled the camera out further, then used his Swiss army knife to cut the wire. The wires flashed, but the rubberised handle stopped Grant from getting a nasty shock. "Ok, let's get the hell out of here!"

Carveth gathered the evidence bags and walked back to the Alfa Romeo. Jones was already in the back, his eyes on the screen of the monitor. He confirmed that Vigus was just six-hundred metres distant. Grant sat down heavily and started the car. He tucked the camera and length of wire into his door pocket. He waited. Engine running.

"My god, don't goad him!" Carveth exclaimed. "He could have us for an illegal search. DCI Nangiles won't exactly back you up, given that you've already crossed swords!"

Grant smiled and put the Alfa Romeo in reverse. He backed out of the carpark and changed gear, speeding back down the road just two-hundred metres to where Jones had parked the Ford Focus. "Stay on him, Jones," he said and nodded towards the door to indicate he should leave. Jones left without a word, still smarting at his failure with the drone. Grant turned to DC Carveth. "I have something for you to do," he said. "First I'll drop you back at Penzance station and you can arrange for a car to use. Then, after you make some enquiries for me, you can meet back up with me."

"Where?"

"That depends on what you find out."

"Boss, I'm worried about how this is progressing," she said quietly.

"How so?"

"It doesn't seem to be, that's all." She paused. "And all we're doing is breaking the law."

Grant concentrated on the road. The corners were sharp, and the white lines broke occasionally so there was not enough room for two vehicles to pass. They dropped down a steep hill, surrounded by damp, bare woods. He imagined they would look more inviting in the summer months, but right now they appeared unwelcoming and eerie. "But we've learned so much," he said.

"We have?"

"You don't think so?"

"I..." she shrugged. "We're still no closer to finding Lilly Trefusis."

"We're so much closer than we were a few hours ago." He smiled and glanced at his wristwatch. "My daughter is travelling down from London on the train. I have to collect her from the station and take her home. It's not exactly convenient, given the circumstances..."

"Oh," DC Heather Carveth said quietly.

"I don't get to see her as often as I'd like," he paused. "Scrap that, I barely get to see her at all. I could only really hang onto my career if I clasped hold of the straw someone handed me. Cornwall wouldn't have been my first choice and especially not when factoring in custody and visitation."

"How old is she?"

"Fifteen."

"Wow, that's an age," she said. "I suspect I was bad enough, but I remember my sisters. One three years older, the other two years younger. Fifteen was a horrible time for my parents. Hell, I found my sisters difficult enough."

"Fuelled by hormones?"

"Pretty much." She smiled. "Except today parents have all the extra worries of constant social media drip-feeding their kids with expectations, peer pressure hitting them from all directions via so many mediums... you've got *Snapchat, Instagram, Facebook, Messenger*, group chats and round-robin texts. Then they've got to worry about their responses and if someone has screen shot their comments to send to other people. That can be social suicide. And when they step outside the virtual world and meet their peers, everyone is so damned opinionated these days."

"You're not making this any easier, Heather."

"Heather? That's the second time you haven't called me *Carveth*."

"Sorry, DC Carveth," Grant said, rather stiffly.

"No, it's okay, Sir." She paused. "It's rather nice, actually."

Grant did not respond. They had reached Penzance and they drove in silence the rest of the way. When they stopped, he reached for his notebook, made a few notes and carefully listed some names. "All you can get on these," he said as he scribbled with his pencil. He was old school. Pencils could be sharpened using the pavement. They worked at all angles and in the rain, too. Of which he had discovered Cornwall to offer up in equal quantities to dry weather. More so, even. He tore out the two pages and handed them to DC Carveth. "Start with the boyfriends, partners or husbands. Any link you can get to our suspect. Then work through the women. The answer will be there somewhere."

"DI Grant!" the shout came from across the carpark.

"Wait there!" Grant looked past Carveth and watched as DCI Nangiles stormed across the carpark. He was talking on his mobile phone and nodding animatedly. When he reached them, he had placed the phone back inside his pocket and was standing with his hands on his hips. He bent down and stared in through the window. "DI Grant, do you want to tell me why we have an incident room with a whiteboard that has nothing written on it?"

Grant turned to Carveth and said, "Get on with what I said, DC Carveth. And look at the partners first, remember?" She nodded, got out and hurried across the carpark. DI Grant watched her go then opened his door. Nangiles didn't budge, so he gave it a decent shove and once he got his foot out, he kicked the door open as if he did not know the man was there, and DCI Nangiles stumbled backwards.

Grant stood up straight, broader and taller than the DCI. He regarded him for a moment, then said, "DC Carveth is making background checks on the girls who made allegations on Daniel Vigus, and I have an officer engaged in surveillance on the main suspect, I have interviewed witnesses..."

"There are no witnesses!" Nangiles interrupted.

"There are *always* witnesses."

"But nobody saw Lilly Trefusis disappear. Daniel Vigus isn't even a person of interest. He's quite the opposite in fact, because he's already on a list with a big fucking red circle around his name saying – leave him the fuck alone because he's suing the Home Office for hundreds of thousands of pounds! Now, get up to Gulruan Moor and help with the search..."

Grant shook his head. "That's not a priority, trust me."

"A girl is missing!"

"Anything else?"

"What?"

"Before you break early for your cottage pie and a night in with the missus, that is." Grant paused. "Because I've got things to do." He got back in the car and started the engine before looking up at him. "I'm not big on boards and pinning up photographs. I prefer to get out in the field and investigate."

"I'm not impressed with your work so far, DI Grant. I'm going to make recommendations for your transfer," DCI Nangiles smirked.

"London would be nice."

"I'm serious!"

"On what grounds?"

"You seem to have a special interest in DC Carveth. She's somewhat younger than you, and a couple of ranks lower. Police officers need to be on their best behaviour these days, misogyny has been endemic in the police service, and it needs to change. I'm not sure any relationship would be viewed as appropriate, especially as her line manager, you could recommend her for any upcoming promotions, or pass her by to keep her near you..."

DI Grant watched the man walk back across the carpark to the building, with a sinking feeling in his gut. His fears had been confirmed and people had already seen through him. Her pass on promotion had not gone unnoticed. But that was an aside. No matter what his feelings for Heather Carveth and the fact he hadn't handled the situation well, he hadn't been ready to have his investigation skills brought into question. Daniel Vigus was a thoroughly vile individual, but he had served his time. And that time had been proven to be a miscarriage of justice. At this point there was no proof the man had done anything wrong. Nothing but historical allegations. And that was a separate case. A separate matter. Right now, a young girl was missing and that was the priority. But Grant had looked into Vigus' eyes, and he had been met with pure evil. He had seen the boy in the photographs and the bewildering scene in the bedroom. But more than that, he had seen the utter conviction in Lisa Trefusis' eyes as she recounted her experience as a child. After twenty years in the job, he had learned to read people. And that was what had scared him the most.

Chapter Fourteen

Grant pulled into a field gateway as he crested the hill. He switched off the engine and punched the centre of the steering wheel. For a moment he was relieved the airbag had not activated. And then he punched it again. He would gladly have exchanged the steering wheel column for the centre of DCI Nangiles' face. But there was still time.

With Penzance behind him and the moor of Gulruan leading down to the coast with glimpses of St. Ives in the distance, he checked his phone and chuckled when he saw he had a signal. He had no idea how long it would last, or whether it would fade as soon as he started to use the device, so he took the opportunity while it presented itself. The signal was quite sporadic around the county, and he had spoken with people using all networks, who often had the same story. He opened his mail provider icon and started to type out an email. He found the name he wanted, having used her before, and detailed what he had seen at Vigus's cottage. The shocking image of the towels and pillows dressed in his mother's nightgown came to him as he described his findings in detail. Then he attached the photographs. Lucy Milarini, arguably one of the most respected criminal psychologists in the country, would study the photographs and draw her own conclusions, but they were merely 2D and Grant's thorough description would enhance her own understanding of the scene. He was hoping she would look at them and give her interpretation as a favour – they had once worked together on a traumatic serial killer case – but he added that if she needed remuneration, then he would try to clear it with Middlemoor. He also added that an eleven-year-old girl was missing and that her opinion could be a vital aid to his investigation. He smiled as he typed that, she wouldn't be holding out on her findings for a fee anytime soon. He made a note to send her flowers, champagne and chocolates later. When things had been dire with his wife during their initial separation, he had made a move towards Lucy, but she was married and committed to her relationship, and he had been shot down in flames. He had been glad, in the end. Work matters and colleague relationships were always complicated by intimacy. His thoughts turned to Heather Carveth. His heart fluttered as a result. She was ten years his junior, but he was a fit man with a younger outlook than most. She wasn't in a relationship, he'd already checked subtly with DC David Jones, and had asked if she had any children while they had been investigating a neglect complaint a month previous. He hadn't risked a search on the PNC databases, as they always flagged the user, but informal coffee machine chat to his colleagues at various police stations had told him enough about her for him to realise she did not have too much baggage to make matters complicated. Only the already complicated matter of Grant's ex-wife, his long-distance relationship with his daughter, working together with a woman he was attracted to beyond reason and the gulf in rank between them.

Grant sent the email and checked his phone for messages. None from Chloe, but she was low on battery and may not have found a charging socket yet. It was always a free for all on the trains and once people were plugged in, they tended to hog the socket until their devices were charged to a hundred percent, or for the entirety of their journey. Whichever came first. He scrolled through, then checked his email in box. Nothing from Deborah. That was peculiar. He sent another message, then bit the bullet and rang. There was no reply. Deborah had recently given up her work, so there was no point trying the number he had for her. Simon was a dickhead, but he made forty-grand or so more a year than Grant, so she had given up her work as a dentist practice secretary and become a lady of leisure. He hadn't held out much hope, Deborah had always been too independent to be a kept woman and would soon tire of the gym, coffee shop catch ups and park runs. Or at least, that was what he had thought. He didn't know her now, just a distant and hazy version. More youthful and with more laughs, at least until the death nails towards the end.

He slipped the phone back into his pocket and checked his watch. It was an Omega Seamaster, and he had been awarded one, along with his team as an international water polo player. Grant had let his career get in the way of the Olympics, but it was a reminder that he had been a champion once. He had been a compulsive gambler and alcoholic, too. But he had got the watch back after he had pawned it during an exceptionally dark time and it now reminded him that he could defeat his battles, at least day by day.

Grant took in the view. The sea was dark blue with a

froth of white against the sand all the way up the coast as waves were unleased on the shore. Craggy headlands protruded into the blue and created a scene of staggered beaches all the way up to Pentire Point. He couldn't see past Newquay but caught sight of a stretch of golden sand at Watergate Bay. He hadn't been to any of those places. He had checked them out on a map, but since he had been transferred, he had hit the ground running. Maybe caught on the hop by events, perhaps trying to prove his worth, but he had been here for over a month and had barely taken a day off, let alone explored his surroundings. As he took in the beauty of the coastline, he made a promise to himself to change that.

He looked back down at the moor and saw a red flag being waved from side to side. He started the car and sped out of the gateway and drove quickly down the switchback road. He could no longer see glimpses of St. Ives or the beaches further up the coast. The sky was turning grey with low clouds, and he imagined the sea would soon mirror the colour. He had never experienced such a changeable climate as the microclimate of Cornwall. Regularly milder than the rest of the country, but with strong winds and driving rain. The rain. Horizontal, vertical, and 'mizzle'. Mizzle was the worst – the Cornish name for a cross between mist and drizzle that soaked through your clothes and chilled into the marrow of your bones.

Grant swung the Alfa Romeo into the area of waste ground constituting a carpark, the underside grounding out and the shock absorbers taking a pounding over the potholes. If Deborah wanted it so badly, she could have it. He switched off the ignition and got out. Inspector Hocking looked up from his command post, which consisted of a couple of folding tables, a laptop and some thermos flasks and paper cups. He was talking animatedly into the mic clipped to his lapel. He looked up as Grant walked towards him and waved him over.

"We have a significant discovery," he said. "Forensics are on the way over. A pair of girl's knickers..." He shuddered, correcting himself. "Sorry, pants."

Grant nodded. "Well, there'll be DNA on them for sure." He paused. "How long before any swabs can be checked against the hair strands taken from Lilly Trefusis' bedroom?"

"It's four hours to do the profile test."

"Same as in London," Grant interrupted.

"Yes, but no. We need to allow for travel time down here."

"Can we use the chopper?"

Inspector Hocking shrugged. "The helicopter is based at Exeter airport, so for it to come down here, collect and run them back will take an hour. We can have them there within an hour and twenty minutes if we have permission to run blues and twos. Add another thirty minutes if we are denied."

"Jesus..." Grant shook his head. A bureaucrat sitting in the Exeter headquarters would have the say, and after assessing the risks, would come back with a speed limit run and avoid a potential incident. "Okay, so let's just get it on the way. The helicopter option is a no brainer, but it isn't going to happen. But while someone's getting a semi over the saving on budget and risk, if we get the blues and twos, at least it's already mobile."

"Agreed. And if the chopper thing becomes reality, we can liaise and meet along the way." He looked up and watched a red quadbike coming down the moor, its engine whining and exhaust popping on the down change. The rider was a uniformed policeman wearing a white open-faced helmet. He switched off the quadbike, got off and opened a box fitted on the back. Hocking turned and waved at a vehicle pulling into the carpark. It was a police liveried BMW X5 and an officer got out and started to jog up the slope. "This is a good start, no waiting around."

Grant nodded. He took out his phone and said, "Let me take a picture of the evidence. I can get started with an identification from the mother."

"The likelihood is high." Inspector Hocking paused. "Don't you think?"

"A mother knows what underwear her child has. It could be a straight no way, and you can turn the car around before it gets as far as Bodmin."

Inspector Hocking shrugged. "Won't hurt, I suppose. But if they're similar and she says yes, and the DNA says no, then she has heartache for nothing."

"Her daughter's missing. It's a world of heartache. But a no keeps hope and saves resources and a yes gets her ready for a bigger blow."

He took the sealed plastic evidence bag off the uniformed officer and placed it on the table. He spread the pants out as best he could inside the bag and took some photographs, making sure he got a close-up of the label. He passed the bag to the officer and stood back for Inspector Hocking to give the order. Grant respected jurisdiction and Hocking was running this search. He wasn't running the investigation, but he had set out his stall and the officers would be looking to him until a more high-ranking officer arrived on the scene.

Grant watched the officer jog back down the hill. The officer on the quadbike seemed unsure what he should do next. He looked at Hocking and said, "It's just one find. The search needs to continue. Especially now that we may have something."

Hocking nodded and told the officer to take the quad-bike back and resume.

"Who found the underwear?"

"One of our promising young officers," he said.

"Always good for the career. To get noticed, that is."

"She's going places, I'm sure." Hocking paused. "You know her, I believe. She was your family liaison officer, yesterday and this morning until DCI Nangiles ordered her to assist in the search. PC Tamsin Gould."

Chapter Fifteen

He was viewing the footage on an iPad with 4G. He had downloaded a facial recognition app from a site he was subscribed to on the dark web using TOR network to bridge VPN addresses, often through Holland and Poland. Even the sites within the centre of the technological layers of the internet onion offered apps as well as software. They moved with the times just like everybody else. The software had cost him two-thousand US dollars, but he had made his money back on the first hit he had made afterwards. The same site, which now cost him two-hundred dollars a month, kept him informed on updates and had the latest surveillance technology and boasted that much of its technology had been acquired through CIA contacts. He had purchased wireless cameras to go with the software and they worked in much the same way as wildlife trail cameras. They were battery powered with three solar receptors on the casing and were magnetic but could be strapped to a solid fixing using cable ties through two eyelets. A small rubber-coated antenna sent the images to a dedicated server using 4G or Bluetooth and the iPad was permanently signed in. When the facial recognition software picked out DI Grant, an alarm would sound, which would also send a text to his mobile phone. The man smiled as he viewed the footage of the final installation. He had fixed a camera to a fence opposite police HQ at Middlemoor in Exeter, and he had fixed others at Bodmin, Truro, Camborne and Penzance police stations as he had travelled down the county. The likelihood of the target using other stations was slim, but even so, he had more cameras, and he would deploy them more tactically tomorrow. But he had heard about a missing girl in the area, and it wasn't a stretch of the imagination for the constabulary's newest recruit – an experienced detective inspector from the Metropolitan police – to be involved in the investigation. He settled back in the seat of his car and scrolled the internet on his mobile phone. Local Cornish Facebook sites, local buy and sell groups, local press websites, Radio Cornwall, West Country Television – it would not take him long to find out the name of the child, and it would take him less time to find out where she lived.

Chapter Sixteen

The road to the cliffs, like most of the roads in the area, was a winding track barely wide enough for two vehicles to pass and was hemmed in on either side by head-high hedges. Initially constructed from granite, the stacked rock hedges had filled with dust and debris and leaves over time, which had turned into soil from which plants and grass had rooted over the decades. The only visible patches of granite were from where vehicles had collided after their drivers had run out of either room or driving talent.

Grant had just experienced the 'kiss' of a Cornish hedge. He was crouched down on his haunches and assessing the damage. He figured it was his ex-wife's problem now. The nearside front wing was gouged, two great streaks of silver in the burgundy paint and a crumple on the rim of the wheel arch. He shrugged as he stood up, a Toyota pickup truck speeding through the narrow gap between his vehicle and the opposite hedge. He recognised the driver as the man from outside Vigus' cottage that morning. The man Lisa Trefusis had said was her cousin. The man looked focused. Enraged. Grant watched the battered pickup weaving through the narrow corners, lobster pots stacked and weaving from side to side in the rear bed. Lengths of bamboo with triangular shaped flags cut from coal or fertiliser or animal feed bags affixed rattled and swayed with the speed and momentum.

Grant recognised a man on a mission, and he got into the Alfa Romeo and took off after the pickup. The roads were difficult to drive at speed, and Grant was met with an oncoming car and then a tractor. When he got past the tractor, he had lost the pickup. However, there weren't too many destinations out here, and he dropped down to the coast road and headed out for Gulruan Head and the wind-swept bluff at the head of the old mining track that led to Daniel Vigus' cottage and the trail of disused 'Tin Mines' – or more accurately the pumping houses – beyond.

At the end of the road, in a turn-in frequented by dog walkers parking their cars before walking the headland, Grant saw DC David Jones fiddling with the remote control and monitor of the drone. Jones looked up as Grant shouted, "Have you seen an old silver pickup truck heading this way?"

Jones frowned but nodded. "Yes. Going like a bat out of hell!"

Grant nodded and floored the accelerator. The powerful 3.2 litre engine wailed, and the twin exhausts howled as Grant took the vehicle up to eighty on the rutted tarmac track. The severe righthand corner loomed, and he hammered on the brakes, ready for the sharp bend and the rough stone track leading out of the apex. Grant saw the pickup parked on the heather and the man cradling a double-barrelled shotgun. He was loading the two barrels as he looked up and watched Grant skid to a halt and send up a puff of dust and mud and grit.

DI Grant flung his door open, and the seat belt went the other way, the metal clip smacking against the rear door and the belt failing to retract. He stepped out onto the gravelly surface and pointed at the gun. "Do you have a licence for that?"

The man hesitated a moment, then said, "Of course…"

Grant paced over and the man seemed unsure what to do next. Grant grabbed the barrels and pulled the weapon out of the man's hands. He pulled out the two shotgun shells and put them in his pocket. "Are you sure?"

"Yes. I have a shotgun certificate. I was going rabbiting."

DI Grant stared at the man. He usually won in a staring contest. He had piercing eyes, but he had long ago learned to stare comfortably and knowingly into a suspect's eyes during interviews, and he seldom blinked first. He could spot a liar, too. "Driving erratically to within a hundred metres of a person you were told to avoid this morning? A person whom people suspect of a crime, and a series of historical crimes and who has stirred up a vigilante response in the area?" He paused, staring the man up and down. "I'm not a hunter myself, but I don't think faded blue jeans, a yellow fisherman's windcheater and yellow welly boots make for the best camouflage for creeping up on bunnies…"

"I only have to get fifty yards from one and the lead shot will do the rest. It's not like bloody deer stalking with a rifle."

"Do you own a rifle?"

"No."

"Any other guns?"

The man shook his head dejectedly. It appeared that

whatever blood and emotion had been stirred up earlier had well and truly dwindled. "I..."

"So, you're Lisa Trefusis' cousin, right?"

"That's not illegal, is it?"

"I guess marrying her would be." Grant paused and grinned. "That goes on down here, right?"

"No. Well, maybe in Camborne or when it's really dark in the evenings," he replied sarcastically. "But I think you'll find it's no different down here to anywhere else. Except for the lack of shopping centres and chain restaurants."

Grant stared at him. "What ammunition have you got on you?"

The man shrugged, took two more shells out of his pocket and handed them over.

DI Grant took them and looked at them. He frowned, looking back at the man. Whilst serving as a firearms officer he had trained with pump action shotguns using solid lead slugs and oo buck – nine lead balls, each approximately 8mm in diameter. He knew the applications of such ammunition and unless the man had murder in mind, it just didn't add up. "Buckshot? For rabbits? You'll have nothing left but the fur." He held the cartridges up to the dwindling light and the nine lead balls were clearly visible. "These are double-oh-buck. For foxes, or brick walls, or disabling vehicles, even..."

"I..."

"Don't interrupt me," snapped DI Grant. "You can pick this up from Penzance police station next week," he said. "Bring your shotgun certificate in to be checked and a gunslip to transport it safely home."

"That's it?"

He could see that the man had been acting in fury, and now in the cold light of day, his run-in with Grant had taken a somewhat sobering effect on him. Grant couldn't see the advantages in taking the man in. The community was suffering, there was no sense in burning bridges. "Well, you *were* just out rabbiting when a police officer in the area expressed concern with you shooting so close to the coastal footpath. You could have hit a rambler."

"Thanks." The man nodded, subdued. He was flushed with embarrassment, but he also appeared relieved. "It's just, with what happened to Lisa and all, and now Lilly..." He gritted his teeth at the thought of her anywhere near Daniel Vigus.

"I heard her allegation this morning. When did you find out?"

He shrugged. "Last night. She was hysterical. But it all makes sense, I knew all about what he had done to Maria Bright and there was always talk of a girl who had been too scared to come forward."

Grant nodded. He'd read the file. "Where was this?"

"At her house. We went around to console her."

"Who?"

"The missus and me."

Grant nodded. He hadn't read the log PC Gould should have compiled, but he made a mental note to and check for discrepancies in her report. Something hadn't seemed quite right the way she had left her alone.

"I'd best be getting off now..." he said sheepishly. He realised he had been saved from a terrible lack of judgement and the effect appeared to have affected his entire demeanour. "I'll pick up the gun when all of this has died down or has hopefully been resolved."

"Yeah, best do that," said Grant. "And do yourself a favour; stay out of the pub tonight. Drink tends to blur one's perspective. Get an early night. Things will look better tomorrow. Take my word for it."

Grant opened the boot of his car and wedged the shotgun against a sports bag he kept there. He had planned on going to the gym but hadn't made it yet. But he lived in hope. The bag was stuffed with trainers, kit, toiletries and a towel. It was heavy enough to hold the shotgun firmly in place. Grant tossed the four cartridges in a pocket recess that contained a first aid kit and some cabin and upholstery wet wipes he had once bought when he cared for the vehicle and hadn't been about to lose it through divorce and pettiness.

DI Grant had no doubt that he had prevented a murder. But it was a hollow victory. If Daniel Vigus had indeed done all suspected of him, then he should not be walking the earth. He looked up and searched the skies for the drone. After a minute of looking, he spotted it. High in what Jones had called a telekinetic hover. Whatever the hell that was. The stupid kid and his genius. Irony, right there. But it had been neither fool proof, nor proven. It had lost Vigus twice. And now Grant wondered what the man had got up to with his purchases from the hardware depot. There was nothing for it but to pay the man a visit and unsettle him once more.

Chapter Seventeen

"Show me your warrant." Vigus stood defiantly at the threshold. He was filming Grant on his smartphone. "Or go away and come back when you have one."

"I hope that's not on a live feed anywhere. Your release terms stipulate no internet access."

"I've since been cleared of any wrongdoing."

Grant shrugged. "But until the condition is lifted, and that means by a judge, then the terms remain the same. Whether or not you've been pardoned."

"What was that with the shotgun out there?" Vigus asked. "He was here for me, and you let him go, didn't you? You should have arrested him!"

Grant shook his head. "Just a guy hunting rabbits who should have stayed away from the footpath." He paused. "Besides, it's me you need to worry about." He took a step forward, but almost twisted his ankle on the loose stones. There were piles of rock everywhere. Some had been stacked, some piled loose. That's what you got for building a cottage on a load of mining waste. Grant kicked the stones away and took the first step. Eye level with Vigus.

"I'll have your job for this harassment."

"And I'd stick that phone right up your arsehole, if I didn't think you'd enjoy it so much..."

"Once more for the camera?"

Grant snatched the phone and tossed it over Vigus's shoulder and into the darkest recesses of the cottage.

"What the fuck?" Vigus snapped. "And I know it was you who punctured my tyre! What the hell were you playing at? And the camera in my car... I saw you searching it without a warrant! You destroyed my camera!"

"Got the footage?"

"You know I haven't."

"Then report it."

"I... I will..."

"Good luck finding my prints in your car."

"I *will* report it..."

"Will you really?" Grant stared at him and said, "It's all catching up with you, Vigus. Your past. Nobody can truly outrun it, least of all a weird little man like you. Because the crap you've done, however you've gotten away with it, it's too far out of the box for you to put the lid back on." He stepped up to the top step and Vigus was forced back over the threshold. He jabbed him in the chest with his forefinger and the man winced. "There is a little girl missing, and I want to know what the hell has happened to her..."

"I don't know!" He looked at Grant pleadingly. "I don't know anything about Lilly Trefusis!"

"But you know her mother, don't you..." Grant glared at him and Vigus failed to hold his stare. "There's a world of hurt heading your way, Vigus. And you're not getting out of it. Justice is heading your way."

"I've just beaten justice," Vigus smirked defiantly. "And I'm going to make a ton of money because of it."

"No, you've beaten the judiciary system." Grant paused. "Justice is coming, and it may be in the form of a pumped up local with a shotgun, or a shove over a cliff edge, but it's coming and I sure as hell won't stop it next time." He turned and took the three steps back down onto the loose chippings, then looked back at him. "And don't make too many plans to spend that money. You'll either be locked away or dead before long. Personally, I don't care which."

Chapter Eighteen

"I got it all on the camera," said DC Jones.

"What?"

"The man with the gun," he said. "John Crocker, Lisa Trefusis' cousin."

"You know him?"

"Well, everybody knows a Crocker down here. Load of bloody gippos..."

"Without the racial connotations, if you please, DC Jones?" Grant paused. "I believe travellers are the term we use these days."

"But down here, gippos aren't just gypsies and we use the term like you would with chavs in London. They don't need a pony and trap, or a caravan and a tarmac laying scam."

"Even still..."

Jones shrugged, apparently unperturbed. "Local character. Big drinker and brawler. He was something of a rugby star. Played for Penzance for years. He even played with the Pirates before his knee gave out. I think he was in their reserve team."

Grant nodded. "What about Vigus?"

"He's still there."

"Did you get me talking to him?"

"Yes."

"I suppose you got the footage of me tossing his phone back inside the house..." He didn't care about the man's mobile phone, but it wouldn't go down well at a disciplinary. And he'd had more than his fair share of those.

"There's been some data corruption," Jones replied without looking up from the monitor. Grant could see that the young man was smiling. "As I said, it's a prototype system. There have been more than a few glitches."

"I like you, David. Remind me to buy you a drink some time." Grant looked past him and watched the plain Vauxhall Corsa indicate and pull in behind his car.

DC Heather Carveth got out. She was juggling three coffees in takeaway cups and struggling to close the door. She frowned and pulled a face as neither man went to her aid. "I couldn't remember if you took sugar," she said to Grant. "I sugared one, so you'll have to fight over it."

"Urgh... I can't drink it without," said Jones with all the social grace of a thirteen-year-old boy.

DC Carveth passed Jones the sweetened cup and looked shocked when Grant intercepted it and took a sip through the mouthpiece. She grinned as Grant scalded himself and flinched. "Serve's you right, Sir!"

"Hey, I thought you were going to buy me a drink?" Jones protested.

Grant nodded. "Yes, but that doesn't extend to sacrificing a sugared coffee." He paused as they all took a sip and smiled when he saw DC Jones screwing his face up at the taste. "Carveth, I need you to come with me to speak to Lisa

Trefusis. See if you can read the woman and give me your take on her."

"Why?"

"You're a woman. And women are perceptive, especially of other women."

"No, I mean, why do you want me to read her? Is she a suspect now?"

"Everyone's a suspect," replied Grant. "And sadly, in these such cases, it often turns out to be true of the parents. But the woman made some allegations about Daniel Vigus this morning, and I want to press her more about what she's been hiding, if indeed she really has, for fifteen years."

"Okay, Sir." She paused to take another mouthful of coffee, then said, "Good news on the find up at the moor, eh?"

Grant shrugged. "I don't see anything good about finding a pair of child's pants in a missing person's case," he said.

"But surely we're a step closer?"

"To finding a body," he interrupted. "No, I can't think of anything good to come from the discovery. It's likely to be confirmation of something far more sinister, and undoubtedly permanent."

"Sorry," she said lamely.

"Don't be," he said. "I've just been around the block a little more and for a lot longer and have seen a few of these cases. The discovery of underwear matching the DNA to the wearer usually tells a story of sordid acts. At this stage, it signifies that Lilly Trefusis is at great risk, but is most likely already dead."

Carveth shook her head and Jones winced at the coffee again. Grant drank his down, the liquid hot enough to burn all the way down his throat, but just cool enough to avoid damaging himself. He enjoyed the sensation. For him, two degrees in temperature was the difference between enjoying a coffee and eventually leaving it.

"What should I do now, Sir?" Jones asked.

"Stay here for a while, I want to know where Vigus goes and what he does. Does that toy of yours have to be charged soon?"

"Yes. But it's a straightforward battery change. I have a new one ready." He paused. "And it's not a toy, Sir."

Grant nodded. "Okay. But make the change swift. I don't want you missing him again."

Chapter Nineteen

"Turn off here, boss."

Grant frowned, but he followed the instruction. He had a lot to learn about the area, but he was surprised DC Heather Carveth was so well versed with the roads, given the remit of CID.

"Where does this take us?"

"To Wheal Ruan."

"And why are we going to Wheal Ruan?"

"Just a hunch."

"I'm the DI. I'm the one supposed to get the hunches."

"In a TV drama maybe, but this is real life, boss," she said, smiling. "I have hunches, too. A complete mind of my own, in fact."

"So, what is at Wheal Ruan?" Grant slowed the vehicle for a particularly narrow section of road. It reminded him of roads he had driven in the Lake District with Deborah and Chloe when they had been together, and in happier times. All stone hedges with a collection of wing mirrors and vehicle parts on the road, crushed reminders to watch your speed and know your vehicle's width.

"Well, apart from the remnants of a tin mine pumping house and a mountain of mine waste, there's about a dozen cottages and a pub there called the Jolly Smuggler."

Grant looked at his watch. "It's not lunchtime, yet."

"The people I want to talk to are the type who get to the pub early and leave late, if you get what I mean."

"You know people down here?"

"No, but as I said, it's a hunch." She paused and pointed to a narrow road on their right. "I ended up down here once, walking and exploring with my ex."

Grant thought about her striding out across the moors and navigating narrow lanes with a faceless partner. No doubt tall, strapping and fit and ten years younger than himself. To his surprise and annoyance, he felt a pang of jealousy. "Sounds fun," he said with little conviction.

"We walked from St. Ives to Land's End one day and we ended up stopping at this pub for some lunch. It was incredibly basic, though. Pasty and a pint or ham, egg and chips, or a ploughman's. But there were some local barflies there and they seemed to know all there was to know about Gulruan. They didn't give off a friendly vibe to two unsuspecting *emmets* passing through."

"I've heard that word before," said Grant. "What does it mean?"

Carveth smiled. "It means outsider or incomer. But I've heard old Cornish people use the term for ants, as well. So, I guess when the word was first coined for incomers it was for tourists who came down in their droves and clogged everything up."

"That was mighty friendly of them." He paused. "What with all the spending they do."

She laughed. "It's the same the world over. Across the Tamar in Devon and the label *grockle* is used. I was travelling in Australia and had a woman blatantly shouted *tourist* at me in Sydney."

Grant shrugged. He hadn't taken many holidays over the years and regretted not having the wealth of family memories other people seemed to have. He wondered whether he would ever improve his custody issues and take Chloe away before she cringed at the thought of holidaying with her old man. For all he knew, she was already at that stage.

"My ex made some snide quip about the film *Strawdogs* and it all got a bit rowdy, they didn't take it well," she continued. "I hadn't seen the film, but I made a point to watch it afterwards and could see why they all got so offended. But to my ex's defence, and I haven't really got a good word to say about him these days, he was quite right, though. A step back in time and well and truly off the beaten track. Like a time-warp and full of the smallest minded people you could imagine. The area has changed over the years with incomers, or *emmets*, and technology, but there are still people in a triangle from St. Just to Penzance to Gulruan who have never been outside the county, let alone the country. People of a certain age with roots in farming and long-forgotten mining."

Grant had seen the film about a woman returning with her new husband to buy a property in the place she grew up, a story of jealousy, ignorance and probably the true essence of a closed-minded community hating incomers. Or *emmets*, for that matter. One of Dustin Hoffman's finest films. Filmed on a tiny budget and probably all the better for it. He guessed it was now considered one of those *cult* films, but he remembered enjoying it at the time. However, he reflected that at this moment and in view of both recent and historical events, the infamous rape scene wasn't sitting well with him. He imagined viewing it as a documentary of Daniel Vigus and his ilk.

Grant saw a weathered wooden sign that looked to have been painted many years ago. It depicted a smuggler who looked to have had too much rum. Red faced and beaming a toothless smile, a cutlass in one hand and a tankard in the other. Paint flaked and the colour had faded. The pub was square and grey and built from granite blocks hewn from the very hills between which it nestled. He could imagine the building unchanged from days when Redcoats and customs officers hunted down smugglers and wreckers handing out swift justice from the barrel of a Brown Bess and a sharp blade.

Outside, a blackboard advertised pasties daily from a bakery in Sennen and a euchre night every Wednesday.

"What the hell is euchre?" Grant asked.

"It's a card game. It's not Cornish, but it is popular with the older people in old fashioned pubs. The economy, smoking ban and general modernisation is making drinking dens like this extremely rare. Pubs need to be restaurants now and charge a fortune for a burger to stay afloat."

"I detect an air of cynicism, DC Carveth."

She shrugged. "It's just we're slowly losing our identity, as a county."

Grant shook his head. "You're not, though. It may seem like that, but you're just moving with the times. Back in London, my local used to do pie and mash and foam cups of jellied eels or whelks and there was a dartboard so well used that the darts fell out more often than they stuck in. Now the place does craft beers, has a wine list with three-hundred quid bottles of Merlot on it and a chef who aspires to get a Michelin Star. You can't eat there for under fifty quid a head, and you can book on their own app. It's just that times are changing, and down here, on this remote peninsular with only one county border, you probably find it more noticeable."

"I suppose." Carveth waited for Grant to park beside a battered Land Rover defender with two gundogs sitting patiently in the front seats. "But these people, the locals frequenting this pub, they see themselves as the last bastion of independence, the last true Cornishmen." She paused. "Right here is as *Old Cornwall* as it gets. It dilutes the further you go up. Except for Bodmin and St. Austell. It all starts again there," she said with a smile. "But down here, they see the people of Liskeard and Launceston as English, just because they're near the border."

"Jesus Christ," said Grant. "Where the hell have I been sent to?" He grinned and opened his door. One of the dogs in the Land Rover growled.

"See?" she said. "Even the bloody dog doesn't like emmets!"

Outside a simple galvanised steel bucket acted as a giant ashtray and was overflowing with cigarette butts and rainwater, infused and coloured with ash and nicotine, the colour of tannin. Even so, Grant could smell pipe smoke from within – despite the Europe-wide smoking ban - and when he opened the painted door, chipped and flaking, he was engulfed by smoke and the low hum of voices, which stopped as he walked in. Grant turned to Carveth, raised an eyebrow, then continued across the exposed wooden floorboards towards the bar.

He glanced at his watch. A little early, but in his experience bar staff never talked to a man in a suit who ordered a coffee. He perused the taps but could already see the pub had no affiliation with a brewery. He ordered a Guinness and waited for Carveth, who hesitated, unsure what the deal was. Drinking on duty was strictly forbidden, but when the detective inspector did so, she decided it would be ok to follow his lead. She opted for half a lager. It wasn't the time or occasion to go for wine or spirits, and she got that drinking tea or coffee might give them away.

"What business you got 'eer, pard?" a gravelly voice growled from somewhere behind the pipe smoke.

"Just having a drink. Didn't see a sign telling me I couldn't," replied Grant. He took a sip off the top and wiped his froth moustache away with the back of his hand.

"Teasy as an adder, aren't 'he?" the man said. He stood up and walked through the smoke. He was eighty if he was a day and bent over double. Grant guessed he wasn't getting challenged to a fight, but you never could tell. "Get it over with then, copper. Mine's a double."

"Who said I'm a copper?"

"Well, you sure as hell ain't here for the food," the man chuckled. "Or the ambience..." He looked at DC Carveth and said, "Won't find avocado on the menu 'ere, *maid*."

Grant shrugged. "I might be a salesman passing through. Don't know why you'd assume I was a policeman."

"Really? What *yer* selling then?" The man reached the bar and tapped his pipe on the countertop. He then swiped the unburned tobacco and ash onto the floor with his hand. The barman said nothing, turned back to a newspaper. Grant noticed it was a copy of the West Briton, the main local newspaper, although this copy was a few days old. "What's that smell?" he asked. He sniffed the air and said, "Dog...? pig...? horse...? No, I got it... it's *bullshit*..." He laughed raucously. "We thought someone would be along sooner or later." He turned around and said, "Didn't we, John?"

"Yep." The sound of a chair scraping slowly backwards

on the floor and a man as tall as a doorway and almost as wide, stepped out from behind an alcove. "Mine's a double, too," he told them. "You want to chat to *we*, then we's need greasing with a rum or three..."

Grant had never heard the word 'we' used to replace 'us', but assumed it was a Cornish thing. He nodded at the barman, and he started to pour out two large rums. He noticed the bottle came from underneath the bar and not from the optic measures above. The barman didn't use any measure cup, either. He had a customs and excise scam going. Not the first that the establishment would have seen over the years. Grant imagined the days when the king's men would drag inn keepers out and haul them off to Bodmin jail, torching illegal contraband and fighting running battles with smugglers and locals alike.

"So, what are we drinking to?" Grant asked when the two men had a drink in their hands.

"You tell us," said the older man. He tried to straighten as he refilled his pipe, but his spine wasn't having any of it.

"You know there's a smoking ban, right?"

"Yeah, I know there's a smoking ban, *me 'handsome*, just don't give a fuck, that's all..."

Grant nodded and sipped some more of his Guinness. He wasn't about to start quoting the law or statutory fines. But why the owner of such a quiet pub would risk a £2000 fine was anybody's guess. He was more worried that he hadn't thought twice about ordering an alcoholic drink when he had worked so hard to stay dry. But he thought a Guinness should be ok, or was he being naïve? Would it lead to something with more of a hit? Would he be looking at the inside of an empty whisky bottle in the early hours and feeling nothing but shame and despair?

"You want to talk about Vigus," said John. "He's a

wrong-un, that one. Just as well he buggered off then went to jail, the fucker would have been taken care of for sure. Still might be, if he stays around too long." He punched the flat of his left hand and twisted his fist, just in case Grant didn't understand.

"Okay, you got me. We're detectives," said Grant. "DI Grant and my assisting officer, DC Carveth."

"Not from 'round 'ere, though..."

"DC Carveth is from Cornwall, I'm from London."

"That make 'he an *emmet*, then."

"So, I hear."

"Got no problem with emmets, myself. Emmets are like haemorrhoids, see?"

Grant shrugged. "Not sure I do."

"Well, when they come down and go back up again, that's all right by me. It's when they come down and stay down, that's the *bleddy* problem..." He laughed raucously at his own joke and the barman, and the giant joined in. "That sick little fucker do it, then?" the old man growled, the humour suddenly leaving his eyes.

"I'm not at liberty to say, but he is a person of interest in our investigation."

"I thought he would be."

"Why?"

"Why d'yer think?"

Grant shrugged. "You tell me."

"Always was a little bastard. He touched those girls, did things a sight more than that, too. I know the talk. But the bastard had an alibi, apparently. Out in the fields working, not that he knew what hard work was, lazy little bastard. I blame Mavis. She was the sick little bastard's mother. Died a few weeks ago. Daft bitch..." He downed his rum and Grant nodded for the barman to refill his glass. The other man watched, downed his and put the glass on the bar. Grant made no offer of another drink - thought he'd see how much he would add to the conversation. "She created a little fucking monster if you ask me…"

Grant nodded and took the glass from the barman, handing it over to the old man. Good to remind him who was buying. "How so?"

"Well, she couldn't keep him in line for starters."

"No, she couldn't," agreed John.

Grant looked at the giant and asked, "Why?"

"Because he was a wrong-un," said the big man. "He was like a dog that just won't leave you alone. Dry humping your fucking leg, off looking for a bitch. The only way you can stop it is to cut his fucking balls off. That's what Vigus needed. Or what he needed was to take a fall down a fucking mine shaft. That's what he would have got if he stayed. There's plenty done wrong ended up down one of them…"

"I'll pretend I didn't hear that," said Grant. But he didn't doubt the man. He felt a chill down his spine and reached for his glass. "So, what else would you blame her for?"

"Drove her husband away," said the old man. "Harvey was as tough as they come, but he drank his wage and worked away a lot. Fisherman. Days at a time and then port-hopped his way around the country for a while. Starts off in Newlyn, and before you know it, he's in Aberdeen and on his tenth vessel and been away six months. Then he comes back and spends most of the time in the pubs. Brags that he gives the wife six months' worth of cock in a week and sends the young boy, barely much more than a toddler mind, out for long walks while he takes care of business. He didn't like old Mavis much, couldn't have. She was too close to that boy of hers. Harvey wasn't at all close to the boy, though. The numbers didn't match up, see? What with him being away sometimes months at a time. Not unless his cock stretched from the other side of the *bleddy* country!" He laughed raucously. "Born the wrong side of the blanket, I reckon. Anyway, old Harvey didn't have any qualms about it. He was on Mavis like a fucking rabbit. Wrong it was." He chuckled and shook his head. "Hate fucking, it was. All these bloody youngsters today think they know it all, have a term for everything. But that's what Harvey Vigus did to his missus."

"That would be rape, then," said Carveth.

"Can't rape your own wife, maid! *To have and to hold*, it's in the *bleddy* wedding vows..." the old man laughed, and the giant patted him on the back. "Then that woman shows up..."

"What woman?" asked Grant.

"Some bird from Padstow. Turns out Harvey Vigus was shacking up with a woman up there whenever he stopped into harbour. She turns up one day with a kid in tow, says it's Harvey Vigus'. Harvey ups and runs off. Never 'seen 'im again."

"And the woman?"

The old man shook his head. "Took off back to Padstow, I suppose. Either that or started up a new life with Harvey someplace. Good luck to her and the boy, because she'd need it with that wrong-un."

"So, that left Vigus alone with his mother," Grant commented.

"Yeah, but it was all wrong with Vigus and his mother, though," the giant added.

"In what way?" asked Carveth.

Neither man spoke, simply took another sip. The giant

seemed to remember his glass was empty and looked at Grant, who nodded to the barman. The barman poured. Grant tossed a twenty-pound note onto the bar and the barman slipped it into his pocket. No change. Grant shrugged and sipped some more of his Guinness. It was ok. He didn't feel a compelling urge to down it and look for another. Carveth followed suit and seemed to realise the men weren't going to talk to the monkey when they had the organ grinder getting them drunk.

"In what way?" Grant repeated Carveth's question.

"I reckon she still had him on the *bleddy* teat when he was old enough to do a day's work." The old man struck a match and lit his pipe, while the giant sipped more rum and nodded in agreement. "Of course, Harvey was gone long before then. Don't know where he went or what he did afterwards, he just plain disappeared. Him and that fancy woman and her little bastard..."

"And then there was that horrible burn," the giant said.

The old man nodded. "He was burned badly as a young lad, and nobody knew what happened. But there was talk of it happening again. All blistered up and raw. People wondered if the woman had done it to him on purpose. Some kind of punishment. That's the sort of woman she was, I'd imagine. Very godly. Old Testament, like."

"And social services or the police didn't get involved?" asked Grant, incredulously.

"The Vigus' flew under the radar," replied the old man. "With some families, that's the best way for everybody." He shook his empty glass and Grant rolled his eyes at the barman. Told him that John the Giant could have another, too. "That's 'handsome'," he said, sipping down a third of the glass. "Nobody cared about young Vigus. They just saw that face of his and walked the other way."

Grant listened. He couldn't help wondering what the catalyst for such a man had been. The overbearing mother, the absent and unloving father with a hatred of the woman he married and using sex as a release, a punishment even. That would certainly have a detrimental effect on a young child as he was forced to walk the cliffs, not knowing whether his mother was all right. Grant imagined a young Vigus walking back in. A meal suffered in silence before the man went to the pub and drank his pay away. Grant would bet the shirt on his back that Harvey Vigus came back inebriated and violent. And then the cycle would repeat itself until there was no money left and he had to crew a fishing boat again. His absence likely making life more bearable for the mother and son. So, where had Harvey Vigus gone? What had been the man's fate?

Grant finished his pint, wiped the foam from his lips and took out another twenty-pound note. "Keep them coming," he told the barman, as he dropped it on the countertop. "Gentlemen, you've been a great help."

The old man nodded. "And that's an end to it. We've said enough and won't repeat none of it again." He paused, finishing his glass. "Unless you happen to stop by and oil the cogs again. Can't give nothin' for free, can us?"

Grant nodded, noting the man's turn of phrase. Like Eric Morecambe had once said, *I'm playing all the right notes, but not necessarily in the right order...* He looked at Carveth to finish her drink, which she couldn't do quickly enough. "You've been a great help," he said. "But I'm not sure that I could afford another chat with either of you..."

Chapter Twenty

The road from the headland to Gulruan, like most of the roads in the area, was a switchback of sharp turns, short straights and hedges that offered no forgiveness to the uninitiated or unsuspecting. To get the line wrong at speed, was to meet with solid granite. Irresistible force versus immovable object. DI Grant had already learned the hard way. DC Heather Carveth drove them with well-practised precision. She weaved the big Alfa Romeo through the bends and when they were met with an oncoming vehicle, she barely touched the brakes as she went through the gaps with mere inches to spare.

Grant was seated in the passenger seat having reasoned that Heather's half pint was safer than his pint and that there wouldn't be an issue had he had some breakfast that morning, but for safety's sake he had decided not to drive. However, he was having his doubts now. He grabbed the door handle, his foot moving to invisible pedals on the passenger floor.

"Are you okay, boss?"

"Fine. I mean, terrified, but fine." He paused. "That was

an interesting insight into our main suspect. Only suspect, I suppose..."

She nodded, but the speed never dropped. "That is, if he's a suspect at all. I mean, there's allegations and doubt surrounding historical claims, but he can't just be a suspect in Lilly's disappearance because of that."

"You sound like DCI Nangiles."

"God forbid." She paused. "I think we learned a lot back there. About Vigus' character, that is. They were friendlier than when I was there with my ex," she said pointedly. "But he was a real dickhead, so maybe that was on him?" She laughed. "I couldn't find much on the women," she said. "Except for Maria Bright. Or rather by association, that is. She moved up to Eastleigh in Hampshire to be with someone she met online. While she was there, she had a run-in for drugs possession but was let off with a caution. And then she had a fight with another woman outside a night club in West Quay, Southampton. Both women were charged with affray. Fines and community service. But it's her partner that has rung a bell. Andy Beam, the man she met online, he did time for serious assault and theft, and he served three years in Parkhurst on the Isle of Wight."

"Where Vigus did three years of his ten-year sentence." Grant said thoughtfully. "Did their times overlap?"

"By two years."

"Shit..." he said. "So, Maria Bright would have been visiting him, communicating with him, all the while Daniel Vigus was in the same prison doing time for rape and sexual assault."

"It may not be significant. Don't sex offenders serve time in isolation to the rest of the cons?"

"Not always," replied Grant. "Trust me, it's significant.

Because there are one hundred and seventeen prisons in the UK and prisoners get moved about. The fact that Maria Bright's boyfriend did two years in the same prison as the man she accused of raping her puts a great big fairy on top of the Christmas tree..."

DC Carveth pulled into the side of the road and parked with the offside wheels on the grass verge. She switched off the engine and looked at the row of houses.

"Crazy how the council house tenants out here," she said. "Almost a mile from the local convenience shop, terrible bus routes and not many of them at that, and more than five miles to the nearest proper town or supermarket."

"Perhaps that's the point," he replied. "Out of sight; out of mind."

"It can't be."

"I imagine it is. I bet the families on this estate have been here for generations."

She nodded. "Yeah, they have at that." She paused. "Do you think that man is press?" She nodded towards a man sitting in a blue Ford Focus. "He looks the type to dig around in a story like this. Bloody vultures..."

"No, he looks more like a debt collector to me," Grant said. He studied the man in the Ford. He'd encountered many reporters waiting for scraps, snippets or quotes from an officer at a crime scene or a victim's family member. He preferred *firemen* or *ambulance* chasers. At least the journalists waiting outside a fire or ambulance station got to write a fresh story, often laced with heroism and hope, or tragedy and despair. It somehow made them seem less callous than the type who waits at a missing girl's home to report the comings and goings of family and friends - the suspects in the making, the speculative articles written to incite rage and sympathy and suspicion from readers who would later think their opinions to be their own, and not drip fed intent.

The man looked foreign somehow. Slavic. A prominent nose and strong jaw. But he looked damaged. Like the man had seen everything. And as Grant studied him, he could tell the man will have wished he had seen nothing. The man wore his soul on his face, and it was dark. There was pain in his eyes, a long-suffering pain that would always be present. Grant hesitated. The man seemed more interested in him than the house and the distraught woman inside. He got out of the car and took out his warrant card. DC Carveth followed suit. The man shifted in his seat. And as the two detectives walked towards him, he raised the pistol.

Grant had a choice. Left or right. Retreat and he'd take a bullet in the back. Advance and he'd merely swap his back for his front and be a closer target. To the left and the man's aim could only get better. His arm would sweep through an unobstructed arc of fire through one hundred and eighty degrees. Grant caught hold of Carveth's collar and yanked her with him as he darted to their right, and the bullet missed them both and went through the passenger door of the Alfa Romeo. They were already near the vehicle's bonnet and the man had to wrap his arm around the door pillar and aim at them through the windscreen. He fired twice and both shots missed, kicking up chunks of the worn tarmac surface of the road. The man pulled his arm back inside the vehicle and aimed through the windscreen, but he seemed to have second thoughts about shattering his own windscreen – it wasn't like he was taking return fire - and went for the door handle instead. He had assessed the situation and without a weapon being fired back at him, he had the luxury of time and better decision making. He didn't see DI Grant start his sprint, but he heard him leap onto the bonnet and looked up in time to see Grant kick the top of the door frame and smash the door against his legs. The man screamed in a holler of both pain and rage and watched as Grant landed on the road next to him. He brought the pistol up to aim, but Grant had hold of the door and started to slam the door against him, ripped it wide open and slammed it again. He took the brunt of the blow through his shins and against his chest as the door frame pounded him, forcing his body back inside the vehicle. He dropped the pistol on the fourth slam, and it clattered on the road surface. Grant turned around and went for the pistol and the man fell back into his seat and slammed the door closed. The tables had turned, and he wasted no time in starting the engine and stamping on the accelerator. The front wheels juddered and skipped as they tried to spin but were hampered by the traction control, which made for a getaway that was slow at first, then decidedly erratic when the car regained drive.

Grant picked up the weapon and aimed at the speeding vehicle. His finger took up a pound of pressure and he re-sighted. The pistol jumped in his hands. The slight shock which often came from the first shot was cancelled out as he fired three more times in quick succession and the rear windscreen of the Ford imploded inwards and the car careened across the road. But the man regained control and the Ford increased in speed and braked hard for the bend, then was gone. Grant's finger had hovered on the trigger, almost all the trigger tension used up. He had stopped short at firing a volley into the vehicle. He had his aim, felt comfortable with the weapon, even if he hadn't used one for a while. But he had enough control to know he would only be getting a one-way ticket to prison if he continued to fire. After all, he had no way of knowing if his attacker was armed, and any prosecuting barrister would tear him in two and argue that after gaining possession of the gun, he could safely assume the retreating driver was of no further threat to him.

Grant looked for Carveth and saw her getting to her feet near the ditch and hedge where she had fallen in the chaos. She was brushing herself off, but her face was ashen, and her eyes could not hide the fact she had been terrified by what had happened. Grant made the weapon safe and tucked it into his waistband. He looked back at the house where Lisa Trefusis was peering tentatively out of the window. He walked back across the road and signalled for her to come outside.

"Did you see that?" he asked, as she opened the door.

"I heard it," she replied.

"Did you recognise the car or the driver? He was parked outside watching your house."

"No." She shook her head. "I thought he was press. I was expecting the media to have shown up by now," she said, then asked, "Are you okay? You're bleeding."

Grant looked down and saw that he had scuffed his knee, ripping his trousers. There were bloodstains on his shin. Now that he had seen it, he felt it. It smarted and he realised that his landing from the bonnet had been heavier and less athletic than he imagined. Adrenaline had its advantages.

"Come in and I'll patch you up," she said. She looked at DC Carveth and said, "Come on, maid, you need a cup of tea after all that." She left the door open as she disappeared.

Grant took out his phone and nodded for Carveth to go inside. He called Middlemoor police HQ and explained who he was and asked for an incident officer. He got through to a man he was yet to meet – Chief Superintendent Whitmore. He reported what had happened and was told to wait for a forensics officer who would collect the weapon, the bullet casings and any bullets they might find. The senior officer expressed his concern that Grant had returned fire but recognised his experience and latter restraint. He then told Grant that DCI Nangiles had expressed reservations about him, but Whitmore had been part of the negotiation to take Grant on and would sit on any further action until Nangiles felt compelled and confident enough to put his concerns in writing. Grant had ended the call aware that he had an enemy in one camp but a friend in another. He felt confident, because he had been forewarned. And forewarned is forearmed. He would handle DCI Nangiles later.

Inside, DC Carveth had made a cup of coffee for both her and Grant and loaded them both with sugar. It seemed the thing to do with the shock of the shooting, and she sipped her coffee, cradling the cup as if it were a mug of soup on a freezing winter's day. Grant realised nothing like that had happened to her before, and he knew how she would be feeling. He had been involved in shootings before and had been on tactical firearms unit for several years before transferring to CID. As he looked at her, he could see how vulnerable she looked and had to resist putting a comforting arm around her shoulder. The thought of touching her made him ache inside, and he realised that it was too late. He was in love with her. There was no going back, no stifling his emotions. He hadn't felt like this since, well, ever.

Lisa Trefusis had taken some items out of a first aid kit and had arranged them as if she were a triage nurse. Grant sat on the kitchen chair, rolled up his trouser leg and she tipped some TCP onto a wet wipe and dabbed the wound. There was some gravel in the abrasion, and she dug at it with her fingernail and wiped the wound clean.

"Brave boy," she said quietly with a smirk.

Grant smarted but did his best to look as if it were no big deal. He failed, perspiration on his brow and turning a whiter shade of pale. "It's just a scratch," he said.

Lisa Trefusis chuckled and wiped it again with another wet wipe and some more TCP. She dabbed it dry with some kitchen towel and used an oversized plaster. "There," she said, smiling. "We're all out of lollipops."

Grant frowned and rolled down his trouser leg then said, "Thank you." He sipped the coffee. It was cheap supermarket instant and plain granulated white sugar. But it still tasted good after what had just happened.

"You're welcome."

The smile had gone, and Grant realised that she would likely be feeling guilty at the brief respite. Or maybe it was something else.

"Where is she, Lisa?"

"What?"

DC Carveth frowned. She no longer cradled her cup. She watched Grant animatedly. A mixture of intrigue and disbelief.

"Where is Lilly?" Grant asked again, pausing to make eye contact with the woman and study her reaction. "Where is your daughter?"

"I…"

"Your manner just now," he said heavily. "I've been unfortunate enough to be around mothers with missing children. And far worse, too. You forgot yourself, just then. You forgot the act."

"How dare…"

"I fucking dare!" he shouted at her making her flinch. "That underwear isn't

on sale today," he said icily. "The cut is all wrong!"

"What?"

He took out his mobile phone and thumbed up the picture. "We found a pair of girls pants and they have been sent to Exeter for DNA profiling. I sent a photograph of the label and an executive at Marks and Spencer is getting back to me within the hour," he lied. It was on his to do list when he returned to the station. "Don't make this worse for yourself." He paused, shaking his head, his expression turning from rage to one of sympathy. "I have a fifteen-year-old daughter and prior to my divorce, I was a pretty hands-on dad, when I could be. I emptied the washing basket, hot-folded from the dryer. I drew the line at ironing. I even bought my daughter underwear. I got the call one day when I was out. Bring back sanitary towels and a pack of under-wear, as she'd be needing more. There's only three or four years between our girls. Admittedly, at that age three years is like ten, but you get the drift."

"I'm not sure I do."

He showed her the photograph. She raised a hand to her mouth, and all the time Grant watched her closely, watched her eyes and her hands. "The pants in this picture are dowdy and grey, and the washing instructions just don't look right." He paused, thumbing to another picture. "Here, look. There's no eco advice, like wash at thirty degrees. Because global warming wasn't everyone's concern back then. My hunch is they're fifteen or more years old. My hunch is..."

"Stop it!" she screamed, cupping her ears with both hands.

"Where is she?"

"I..."

Grant caught hold of her shoulders and shook her. "Tell me where Lilly is!"

DC Carveth stepped forward and touched Grant on the shoulder. "Boss..." she said quietly. She looked at Lisa Trefusis. "Do those pants belong to Lilly?"

"Of course," she said. "Who else is going to have lost a pair of knickers on the moor? You should be out there looking for her, not suspecting me!"

Grant stood back from her and looked into the woman's eyes. "But I never said they were found on the moor, Mrs Trefusis..."

Chapter Twenty-One

The SOCO team came and went. They photographed the area with a laser mapping system that made the entire crime scene a single 3D image, like using Google Street View. Grant had worked with the system many times, and once viewed on a smartboard or computer, it enabled the user to move between solid structures and change the angles in every way possible. Once the scene of crime officers had run the laser imaging over the entire area, the user could take the view down to the bullet casings on the ground and survey the scene backwards, making the entire area interactive from a laptop or tablet. Grant had used the system before to view everything from a body's last perspective. It didn't tell you anything more than what a detective's eyes would when they surveyed the scene, but it was a permanent walk-through that could be viewed as if in real time, rather than spent doubled over a desk studying 2D photographs. After they had everything they needed, they checked that the pistol was safe, boxed it up and took it away with them after Grant had signed it over. They had been unable to recover any

intact bullets. Both the bullet that had hit the ground and
the one that had gone into the Alfa Romeo's door were far
too mangled to get rifling information, but they would keep
them to take powder residue analysis.

With the gunman's true intent unknown, a cordon was
placed outside the row of five houses and an officer
deployed to keep members of the press at bay, who had now
shown up in the form of three national papers, a few free-
lancers and a local reporter more used to writing pieces on
agricultural shows and road traffic incidents. At the end of
the access road a police-liveried BMW estate car with two
armed officers sat vigil. There was now a search going on for
the car and armed police officers had been strategically
placed to crisscross the county. It was standard practice to
have two ARVs or Armed Response Vehicles patrolling the
A30, as it was the central artery of the county and made
access to all areas more feasible.

Grant had collected himself, drinking most of a strong,
black coffee loaded with sugar. He wanted a big caffeine
and sugar hit to steady his nerves. He thought about the
bottle of rum at home, a moving in present from his neigh-
bour. It was locally distilled and had a pirate with an
eyepatch and the St. Piran flag on the label. He could have
done with a decent pull on that, too. Although he had toyed
throwing it out to avoid old habits.

He had been shot at before. Once by an armed robber
who had peppered his patrol car with lead-shot from a
sawn-off shotgun. And the other time had been by a Yardie
who had given Grant no choice but to return fire with his
Heckler and Koch MP5. The youth had taken two bullets.
Centre body mass. Textbook. He had lived. But Grant had
been suspended pending investigation and spent four
months off the job until the incident had been cleared by

the investigating team of a proxy constabulary. Standard procedure. The youth had reformed and now worked with disadvantaged children from social housing projects and was part of a gang awareness charity. Grant, by contrast, had requested a transfer out of firearms and had been given CID and the undercover operative program. A course of action that had eventually cost him his marriage.

Grant looked at Lisa Trefusis. "Well?"

"It wasn't my idea!"

"What have you done?"

"It was the only way we could get justice," she said, slumping down on the chair next to him. "Now it's gotten out of control..."

"So, Lilly is safe and well?" DC Carveth asked, bemused.

DI Grant's mobile phone vibrated, and he answered it, walking out of the kitchen and into the hall. The thoroughfare was barely as wide as his shoulders, so he veered off into the lounge. The carpet was threadbare and covered with rugs that neither matched the décor nor fitted the floor, leaving a curling wave of fabric that he almost tripped over. There were DVDs stacked in four columns three feet high beside the seventy-two-inch television. Grant had lost count of the number of houses he had been in that were devoid of both money and income, struggled to put a nutritious meal on the table, but always had a state-of-the-art TV six-feet wide and unlimited satellite television package. He listened and verified his identity before the full report was released to him, the forensic scientist keeping it simple, using plain layman's terms and assuring him that the full report would be emailed within the hour.

Grant hung up. He scratched his head, looking around the room. He felt he was playing chess while everybody else around him was playing draughts. So much didn't make sense, but then, there was a modicum of familiarity. Of déjà vu. He hated the feeling. Not being able to put his finger on the nagging doubt.

Back in the kitchen, Lisa Trefusis was in tears and DC Carveth was supplying the woman with tissues. Carveth looked up as Grant entered and pulled a face. He guessed she was no further forward. But he wasn't one to take the softly-softly approach. He snatched the next clean tissue away, screwed it into a ball and tossed it on the floor.

"That was the DNA report. Lilly's DNA was on them. As was DNA from someone else. In fact, there was also a third profile." He paused. "You laundered your daughter's clothes, obviously. We took a sample of your DNA last night for elimination purposes."

"Yes."

"And yet, you're not showing up in the profiling," he said. "I find that strange. In fact, the lead forensic officer on the scenes of crime team said it would be an impossibility, given that the underwear would have been in this house before Lilly wore them." He paused, watching her expression change. It was as close to enlightenment as a person could get. The Actors' Guild wouldn't have many signed up who could have pulled it off as well. "Transference of skin, hair, saliva, nasal mucous – whatever the hell that is – a sneeze, I suppose - are all what he would have suspected to find a person to leave simply taking the clothes out of the dryer and placing in a drawer."

"Oh, god..."

"What role has Andy Beam played?"

"What?"

"Answer the question, Lisa!" Grant snapped. "Beam was in prison at the same time as Daniel Vigus. For two years. Two years with the man both you and Maria Bright accused of rape. Only you didn't. You only made that allegation today. And Carrie-Ann Dixon admitted lying about her allegation to back up Maria Bright's claim. Vigus referred to you all as three witches, but only two of you were really sexually assaulted by him. So, who was the third?"

Lisa Trefusis bowed her head and sobbed. DC Carveth placed a hand on her shoulder and comforted her.

"Come on, Lisa. We need to know everything," she said. "If you know what has happened to Lilly, then you need to tell us now."

"I'm sorry!" she wailed. "It all got out of hand," she sobbed. "It was Maria's idea; she and Andy said they would handle it. We had to make it look like an abduction and get Vigus rearrested. She said that Andy knew Vigus had faked the DNA that cleared him, and that the police would re-test Vigus if he was accused of another crime..."

"But how was Lilly ever going to point the finger at Vigus?"

Lisa Trefusis sobbed and looked for something to wipe her nose. DC Carveth tore off a length of kitchen towel and handed it to her. She blew her nose and rubbed her eyes. They were sore and tired looking. "We coached her. But Vigus is still walking around, and Lilly is wanting to come back. It's a bloody mess..."

"So, where is she?" Grant asked.

Lisa Trefusis was sobbing uncontrollably. Grant sensed there was an element of relief, of the lie finally catching up. "Andy has a lockup in Penryn. On a boat builder's yard. Near the big fancy car showroom. It's a tatty yard further back towards Penryn. They advertise repairs and reconditioned outboard engines."

Grant nodded and left the room. He took out his phone and noticed another message from Chloe. He cursed, unable to spend the time reading it. He called the incident line and gave his name and rank and warrant card number, then repeated what Lisa Trefusis had told him. Time was of the essence and getting Lilly to safety and the help she would need was the priority. To DI Grant, getting the truth was more important. He walked back into the kitchen. It was starting to get dark outside. He glanced at his watch. Chloe would be here in a few hours.

"Whose DNA are we going to find on that underwear?" he asked gruffly.

Carveth looked at him and pulled a face. She was still comforting the woman's shoulder. "Boss..."

Grant looked at her. He doubted he would have taken it from another officer. Whichever direction the rank went. But he could see that Heather Carveth was sympathetic, genuinely concerned for the woman's state of mind. She also looked about as appealing to him as it was possible for her to be. He shook that thought out of his mind. Focus.

"The pants, Lisa..."

"Oh, god!" She sobbed and wiped her nose with the paper kitchen towel. "Lilly's! Lilly's DNA," she said matter-of-factly. "We just rubbed them on her!" She screwed her face up in disgust at the thought. "And Vigus's. Vigus's DNA for sure. They were the knickers he removed before he raped..." she trailed off, sobbing into the soggy, torn remnants of paper. DC Carveth tore off a good strip and folded it over, before passing it to her.

"Who?" asked Grant. "Who did he rape?"

"I just want to see Lilly..." she said quietly. "When can I see her?"

Grant said, "There are officers on the way to her now."

He checked his phone, but there were no messages. He hated not being in the loop. He turned to her and said, "It will all be alright, she'll be okay." He regretted it almost at once. Rule one. Don't promise anything. Rule two? Never break rule one. "There are officers on the way. Accompanying them will be paramedics and everybody she needs to be safe." He stopped short of adding that social services would naturally take the child away. He doubted that Lisa Trefusis would ever see her daughter again. Whatever foolish games she had been encouraged to partake in, and for whatever gain or sense of justice they thought would be achieved, her loss would be far greater than Maria Bright's or her partner Andy Beam. Grant looked at her intently and asked, "Who else's DNA will be on the clothing, Lisa?"

She shook her head. "I want a solicitor," she said. "I want to talk to a solicitor first. That is my right."

Grant nodded and took out his phone, checked the screen. No news. He looked back at her and said, "Lisa Trefusis, I am arresting you on suspicion of abduction and false imprisonment. You do not have to say anything. But it may harm your defence if you do not mention when questioned something which you later rely on in court. Anything you do say may be given in evidence..."

Chapter Twenty-Two

He pulled the car over on the edge of a small woods near Gulval. He checked the mirrors, then switched off the engine and listened to the silence. The engine was ticking from the heat of such erratic driving and his ears were buzzing from the noise made from the rear window being shot out. The shape of the car, its aerodynamic properties, had created a vortex of air around the rear that had reverberated in a popping noise and had built pressure in his ears. Stopping was a blessed relief.

He was in a quandary. He had located his target merely by chance. Having driven to the missing child's home to place a camera to work on the facial recognition software, Detective Inspector Grant had presented himself as an opportunity. And the man wasn't one to waste an opportunity. But Grant had been alert, and fast and resourceful. What should have been a simple assassination – so easy it would have been merely an execution – had turned out nearly being his own downfall.

He had underestimated his target. And now he was compromised. The target would be able to describe him, recognise him. He had left his prints on the pistol, too. How much of a problem that would be; he couldn't be sure. But it meant that if he was caught for this, or a crime in the future, then he would be on record, and that would be an end of it for him. He cursed and punched the centre of the steering wheel, then looked up as a car drove past. The driver slowed and looked at the rear of the Ford, the window was all but blown out with a smattering of glass at the edges. The safety glass had broken into gem-sized fragments. The man waved at the driver, like he was ok and merely about to assess some damage. The car drove onwards, but the man was left in no doubt that he needed to distance himself from the vehicle as soon as possible. He needed to dump it someplace. He had already left a set of his prints on the gun, so it no longer mattered that his prints and DNA was inside the car as well. But he needed to dump it away from any CCTV cameras, and he needed another vehicle. Simply stealing one in Penzance would start a trail that was too close to the target. He took out his smartphone and opened Google Maps. He found the train station and traced the line to Truro. If he could leave the vehicle on the edge of Penzance and walk across the town, along the seafront, then he could get on a train for Truro and hire a vehicle with his fake ID. Vehicle hire places were always located near the larger train stations. A quick search and he could see that Truro was no exception. It would put time and distance between himself and the shooting at Gulruan. Once he had created some space, he could plan accordingly. But for now, he needed to get out of the area because the Ford would be on a watchlist and the longer he remained with it, the sooner he'd be discovered.

Chapter Twenty-Three

There are no happy endings. That was DI Grant's take on the job, and his take on this case. Hell, it was his take on life as well. Lilly Trefusis had been found safe and well and had soon broken her silence on the plot to frame Vigus for her abduction. She was only eleven-years old and could see the flaws in the venture. She was certainly a bright little girl. Brighter than the incongruously named Maria Bright, and certainly brighter than her own mother. It wasn't a stretch too far to say she was brighter than Andy Beam, either. How the three thought their masquerade would stand up to scrutiny, Grant did not know. But they had gotten their wish, because officers had stopped by Daniel Vigus' cottage and taken a DNA swab and now that it was established that the found underwear was fifteen years old and Vigus was the suspect in a sexual assault case, then they would soon have the answer they had wanted for so long. The underwear was still being held in Exeter, but the profile was sent digitally and could now be checked against Vigus's DNA – taken today and unequivocal proof he did what he was accused of all those years ago.

Only Lisa Trefusis had upheld her right to silence and legal representation and if she did not cooperate soon, then they would not have the name of a victim for the supposed crime, and it will have all been in vain.

Lisa Trefusis was taken to Camborne police station and held in the cells until a DS and a DC working out of Bodmin station came down and set themselves up in an office suite on the second floor. The DS was regarded as one of the best interviewers in the force and was set to become a DI as soon as a position came up. She was a fast-track officer and had got a first in psychology at Bristol University. The DC was along for the ride, but he was apparently tipped for bigger things. They would now have to wait for Lisa Trefusis to take her counsel.

DCI Nangiles wasn't making it home for dinner with his wife and family anytime soon. But he would be fine with that. He had a result. Job done. He was going over the incident report and seeing where he could credit himself further to the case. He was in good spirits, enough to have seemingly forgotten his run in with DI Grant earlier that day. Grant suspected it would have had something to do with the press being tipped off about the boatyard and arriving on the scene mere minutes after the raid. DCI Nangiles had been photographed walking Lilly Trefusis to the ambulance and waiting social workers. It wasn't a photograph that would do his career any harm.

Grant was drinking a coffee and imagining it to have some of that local rum sinking to the bottom. Someone had bought in some pasties and doughnuts, and he had worked his way through one of each, trying to work out when he had last eaten a meal or slept. The food was nothing special – sold off cheap by the bakery at the end of the day. Thankfully the watch, although long into the start of a new shift, would soon be over. The two detectives would continue to question Lisa Trefusis, the CPS barrister was in the building and looking to have her charged with a whole list of offences and DCI Nangiles was making room on his office wall for a commendation.

"A good result," Nangiles said, helping himself to coffee. "No sign of Maria Bright or Andy Beam yet, but it's still early."

"At least Lilly is safe," Grant said rigidly. He would be happier not speaking, nor seeing the man again. But that wasn't likely, or practical.

"No news on the gunman," Nangiles said. "You returned fire with the man's own weapon, I hear."

It was a statement, not a question, so Grant simply said, "Yes."

"Was that wise?"

Grant shrugged. "Once I'd established that he was of no immediate threat to anybody, I stopped shooting."

"I imagine that's not the last we'll hear of it."

"The gunman or the fact I returned fire?"

"Both." DCI Nangiles stirred his coffee and dropped the plastic stirrer into the bin. The Devon and Cornwall Constabulary weren't onboard with single use plastic yet. "No idea who he was?"

"No."

"Nothing following you down from London? No enemies?"

"I wasn't aware I was on a hit list."

"But it's possible."

"I suppose anything's possible."

"Indeed." Nangiles said, then simply smiled, a crocodile's smile, and stalked
off towards his office.

Grant watched him go. He was too tired and too relieved that Lilly was safe and well to say anything to the man. There was no point. Nangiles outranked him, and that was enough. But Grant always looked at the long game. He'd sort out Nangiles in time.

DC Carveth walked into the room. She had two plastic cups half-full of prosecco. The celebration had started early, even though everyone in the room was aware of drink driving. It was standard, though. Half a cup. It had been the same in London and Grant figured it was the same everywhere else.

"Drink?" she asked, holding the flimsy cup out for him.

He took it and shrugged. "One won't hurt," he said and took a sip. He missed her attempt to tap cups, then did his best to toast without the cup folding completely. "Cheers," he said.

"To getting Lilly back safely."

They tapped cups, but it always sounded better with cut crystal.

"I'll drink to that," he said.

She sighed, checked her watch. "I'm knackered. And hungry."

"Have a pasty."

"They're all dried up and cold." She paused. "Fancy some dinner?"

Grant smiled. "Any other night, but I can't," he said with a shrug. "Not that it would be seen as appropriate, anyway."

"It's just dinner, boss." She shrugged. "Rain check, then?" She looked away, embarrassed.

"Sure."

"So, is it a hot date?"

"My daughter," he said.

"Oh, of course. I'd forgotten with all that's gone on."

"She's bailed on her mum and her mum's partner and taken the train without telling them, so it's probably not without its hassles. That said, I'm dying to see her. It's been almost two months."

"Well, enjoy," she said, raising her glass again. She'd made a gambit, been shot down in flames. Grant was surprised she was still here. "Not the hassles, that is."

"Thank you, DC Carveth." Grant looked at her, wanted to call her Heather. Wanted to kiss her. Instead, he said, "But as I said earlier, she's fifteen. It's all hassles. Nothing *but* hassles." And he realised that like every other single, childless person he met, she simply didn't care. But she hid it well.

Carveth smiled, then frowned. "Where's David?"

"Shit!"

"He's still out on the headland playing with his helicopter?" She laughed, then seemed to think better of it. She took out her phone and said, "I'll stand him down."

Grant nodded. Vigus could keep. Lilly was safe. They would soon have her abductors. He looked up when he heard the shout. People had gathered in small groups. Only Grant and Carveth had been a two. Or a couple.

DCI Nangiles stood in the doorway, a piece of paper in his hand. Usually a smart, well-dressed man, he had taken off his jacket and loosened his collar and tie. He waited for the chatter to die down, then when it had he said, "The DNA has come back from the karyotype test on the underwear found on Gulruan Moor. Trace elements of Lilly Trefusis. We knew it would. There were also XX chromosome in the form of dried body fluids of an unidentified female and the one we were hoping for, the XY chromosome of an unidentified male in the form of dried semen.

Two DNA tests and fabric tests indicate that the fifteen-year window that Lisa Trefusis spoke of is likely." He paused. "However, the DNA sample taken from Daniel Vigus is not a match..." There were muted voices around the room and after a few seconds DCI Nangiles said, "Go home, get some sleep and we'll reconvene in the morning." He walked back into his office and the room turned into a hum of chatter. Opinions and hypothesis and bullshit.

Grant put down the drink and said, "Fuck this. I need to go see my daughter..."

Chapter Twenty-Four

Grant watched as Chloe leapt down from the train and trotted across the platform, her phone in one hand and her heavy fake Louis Vuitton bag in the other. She had grown so much these past two months. Her features had changed, mellowed. And she had a gloss and shine to her hair that he had not noticed before. Having finally outgrown an unfortunate greasy and spotty teenage stage, she reminded him more of Deborah than she ever had previously. The thought saddened him. He couldn't go back in time, and towards the end, that would have been the only way to change things and make them right. Deborah had fallen out of love with him, and like all second parties when that happened, he had been a passenger to a destination unplanned for, unwanted and unknown. Nothing he had tried had changed her mind. She had found someone else, too. And that influence, perhaps the strength gained by the knowledge that she had already moved on and there was to be little uncertainty and certainly no fear of being alone, had bolstered her resolve. The couple who had made this wonderful girl before him, were just a footnote in each other's history. He had reacted the only way he knew how, a voyage of self-destruction. Drinking, reckless and promiscuous sex and gambling. And then he had crossed the line and his actions had ruined an undercover operation and cost a young woman her life. The man at the head of the organisation that he had been gathering intelligence on was still at large, still free and still untouchable. Grant had vowed vengeance one day, and knew it was a dish best served cold. He would avenge her, his career and his relationship in one go. And he would bring down Roper and the rest of the arms dealer scum around him, the untouchable champagne criminals with influences reaching far into Westminster and government alike.

Chloe flew at him when she got close enough. She leapt up and wrapped her legs around him, but Grant struggled to hold onto his balance, and he hugged her close, almost toppling backwards. She did the same, holding onto the phone, but dropping the faux leather bag onto the platform. Neither said anything for a while, simply lived in the moment. Grant breathed her in, her smell no different to the baby he would hug and hold and rock to sleep all those years ago.

"God, I've missed you, Little Lamb..."

"Dad! You haven't called me that for years!"

He smiled, hugged her more tightly. If that were possible. Chloe used to cry like a baaing lamb. She'd been his Little Lamb ever since.

"And what's with the Dad, thing?"

"Sorry *Daddy*, just trying something new."

"Well, don't."

"Okay, but do me a favour?"

"What?"

"Don't ever call me Little Lamb in front of anyone else, okay?" she giggled.

"Deal." He released his grip, and she unfolded herself, long limbs settling back on the platform, and she stood to his chin. He was six-foot, so she had taken after him rather than Deborah, and a part of him felt smug that their daughter would have more in common with him, than with his ex-wife. "I haven't got long," he said, regretting it at once when he saw her face drop. "A little girl was missing, but she's been found," he said, playing down his part. "But there could soon be vigilantes taking it out on the suspect soon."

"Good," she said.

"What happened to innocent until proven guilty?"

Chloe grinned and said, "You always said that the main suspect is always guilty, it's just a matter of proving it, that's all."

"I did?"

"Yes." She paused, beaming a smile at him. "But you also said that you'd make time for me anytime I want to come down."

Grant pushed through the door and sidestepped a homeless man near the doorway. He dropped a two-pound-coin into the man's upturned hat and walked on. He never would have thought there would be such a homeless problem in Cornwall, especially in a remote town like Penzance. But the town was at the end of the line. Every day many dodged the train fare and rode it as far as it went. In some cases, London councils had even provided a one-way ticket to alleviate homelessness in the nation's capital. "I think I said that, thinking that I'd have more than half a day's notice."

She shrugged. "Well, you didn't set out any terms or conditions when you said it."

"Touché."

"So, it's not cool for me to stay?"

Grant put an arm around her shoulders and pulled her near when they reached the car. "Of course, you can stay but I will be in and out. And I haven't heard back from your mother yet..."

"She changed her phone," said Chloe. "Simon bought her a new one and she couldn't switch over the number, apparently. I said that she could, and he went mental!"

"What?" he asked, both angered that Chloe be exposed to such a thing and that Deborah should change her number without telling him. He was still Chloe's father after all, and as such felt he deserved to have the lines of communication held open. Alarm bells had started to ring in his mind. It sounded as if Simon was trying to control Deborah, and that practice often started with phones or internet access.

"He threw a hissy fit and tossed her old phone at the wall. Smashed it into pieces!"

"Does he do that often?" He asked, then added, "Not phones, that is, just throwing stuff about?"

"No. Not really. But he's been really snappy lately. Mum said he's got business worries."

"Good," Grant paused, then added, "That he doesn't do it often, not that he's having business problems."

"Okay, Daddy, once more with feeling," she laughed.

"I'm sorry, but he really is a colossal dickhead."

"Daddy!"

Grant became serious again and said, "He doesn't give you any problems, does he?"

"In what way?" she asked. She was looking out of the window now and Grant could see her reflection in the glass. The lights of Penzance backlighting her face in the darkness.

"Shouting at you, being over familiar, hitting you…"

"No," she said sharply. "I'd kick his ass if he did! But you *are* right. He *is* a colossal dickhead. And he certainly doesn't want me around, that's for sure."

"You shouldn't swear."

"Then don't swear in front of me."

"My bad…"

"And especially don't say that!"

"Sorry, that's my turn trying something new."

"Well don't, it was painful to hear."

"Noted."

"He doesn't leave me alone, though."

"How so?"

"Constant nagging," she sighed. "Do this, do that, do the other…"

"Like asking you to tidy your room?"

"Yes."

"Stack the dishes, the dirty plates?"

"Right."

"Pick up your clothes?"

"It's like you're a fly on the wall."

Grant smiled. "Sounds pretty standard adulting. I mean, boring and still a colossal dickhead, but standard…"

Until now, Grant had been hammering up the A30 at eighty miles per hour. He pulled off at a slip road and after a few hundred metres skirting a bleak housing estate, he was in the country once more with not a straight stretch of road in sight. The road was narrow but with white lines and tall hedges, although at times there still wasn't room for two cars.

"Wow, you really are out in the sticks," she said. "This is miles away from Penzance…"

"Take the train to Truro or Redruth, next time." Grant

pulled the Alfa Romeo off the road and started down a bumpy track.

"There won't be a next time," said Chloe. "Unless it's when I come back from visiting Mum and picking up the rest of my stuff. I'm staying with you now."

Grant stopped the car and looked at her. He placed his hand on her knee and said, "It's not up to me, Chloe. I don't have full custody of you. It's up to the solicitors and the courts."

"I'm almost sixteen!" She paused. "We can work on that. Christ, when I'm sixteen I can join the army and die for my country..."

"With parental consent, which isn't happening anytime soon," he replied adamantly. "Anyway, that's about it. Everything else in life starts at eighteen. That's when you can vote and drink."

"I can have sex at sixteen!"

"Whoa, don't even go there...!"

She sighed, rolling her eyes like he was behind the times. "But I can leave home, with or without consent, I checked."

"You haven't, have you?"

"What?"

Grant hesitated awkwardly. He fidgeted and said, "The sex thing..."

"None of your damned business!" She turned and looked out of the window. It was as black as pitch and it had started to rain, the droplets trickling down the glass. She watched one of them, tracing it with her finger as it ran down the pane. "And, no," she said quietly. "I haven't."

"Sorry for asking," said Grant. "We don't need the whole protection talk, do we?"

"Mum was way ahead of you, so no."

He shrugged. Another thing he had missed, although he couldn't imagine wanting to be part of that one. He patted her knee, more out of relief than anything else, and then drove onwards. After fifty metres the lane widened, and five detached houses fanned out through one-hundred and eighty degrees. There were three dull street lamps casting an orange hue across the parking and turning area. "Here we are," he announced.

"Quite smart," Chloe said enthusiastically. "Shame about the goat track getting in."

"Yeah, apparently the developers won't sort out the lane until they've completely finished the development, and the two houses on the left are still under construction inside. Nobody's been here for weeks. I'm not sure if the money has run out. I only have mine on a six-month let, so it doesn't matter much to me." He shrugged. "It's nice and quiet."

"Or isolated."

"I'm barely ever this way," he replied. He was going to add that would be the reason that her staying long term would be a problem, but he'd save it for now. "Hungry?"

"Starving."

"That might be a problem. We'll get a takeaway," he said. "I didn't want to pick you up and stop straight off at a supermarket." He opened his door and reached in the back for Chloe's bag. They walked in together, the dull orange light barely enough to see by. Chloe jumped and screamed as a dog leaped out from the bushes and started barking. She cowered behind Grant, who laughed and bent down to pet the animal on the head. "That's Bollocks," he said.

"It's not, he scared me!" she snapped defiantly.

"No, the dog is called Bollocks." He paused. "Well, probably not, but that's the name I gave him."

"Why..." she asked, then watched as the dog turned around and made a fuss of Grant. "Oh, don't worry, I get it."

"Quite something, aren't they?" Grant laughed. "And he's a bulldog as well. So yes, they do stick out like a bulldog's bollocks..."

"Daddy!" she laughed. It had been the first time they had shared adult humour and Grant could see she seemed so much more grown up than before he'd moved down to Cornwall. It pained him to have missed out on another chapter of her life. "Is he yours?"

Grant shrugged as he opened the door. "He showed up a month or so ago. He was cold and wet and hadn't eaten in days. I tossed him a few scraps and he's stopped by ever since."

"But someone could be missing him!"

Grant ushered her in. The dog sat and looked up at him. "Oh, for heaven's sake..." Grant called the dog in, and he trotted over the threshold. "Just for tonight," he said. "He usually has my pizza crusts and hangs around for a bit, but I've never had him inside overnight." The dog padded in and as Grant switched on the lights, it looked about the open-planned area approvingly and headed for the kitchen.

"He's so adorable!" Chloe exclaimed. She whipped a tea towel from the draining board and started to dry the dog off. The dog moaned with pleasure, its broad snout in the air and a smirk on its face. He eyed Grant smugly. The cat that had got the cream. Or the bulldog that got a rub-down in the warm.

"That's hygienic..."

"He's hungry," she said, ignoring his comment. "Are you hungry, Boll..." She looked up at her father and said, "Seriously, I can't call him that!"

"What then?" asked Grant, but he smiled and added,

"But given the two gifts that bad boy has, anything else will be a come down."

"Tackle?"

Grant laughed and Chloe laughed in relief, the new-found adult humour boundary was something that only they had shared. "Okay, Tackle it is..."

Chapter Twenty-Five

He had hired a Ford C Max from the Hertz office at Truro train station. He had chosen a family MPV to remain invisible and had removed the hire car stickers before leaving the carpark. He had the AK47 assault rifle and the spare magazines stashed in a large sports bag in the boot. Losing the pistol was an inconvenience and consequently, his strategy would have to change. But he had been caught off guard by the target, and at least just having the rifle meant that he did not have to get up close and personal with who he now knew was a worthy adversary.

The contact had angered him, humiliated him. But he had learned from it. And now he would use it to his advantage. Grant was a man of action. He would rush towards danger rather than retreat. That much had been clear. So, he would find a way to make the man an easy target. That was the secret to a successful hit. He would not fail again.

It was getting late, so he had found a Premier Inn and checked in for the night, but he had booked and paid for two nights. Standard operating procedure. His life was one of laying false trails, and the practice had kept him alive so far. He was fortunate enough to have access to the best Swiss forgers and had multiple passports from various EU countries along with cloned credit cards which he was yet to use. Each card would be used once and then discarded. Cash withdrawals could net him up to five-hundred pounds a day when he was in a pinch. He had paid handsomely for the Russian produced cards. The Russians were the best in the business, intercepting social media accounts for much of the information needed to create the cards. They had made an artform out of the practice. Many of the forgers had worked for the FSB or SVR, some for the KGB before reunification. They were artists, having fooled the CIA and MI6 for years.

He had set up his iPad using the Wi-Fi to scan the facial recognition cameras using the app. He had seen the target enter and leave the Penzance police station, then an hour later the target had once again entered the Camborne station and left forty minutes later. He had looked at the logistics and decided to let the target move freely. He would never have travelled to Camborne in time, and the police presence was too large. As a main station, there would be armed response officers on site. Or certainly nearby. There would be CCTV and traffic cameras in the area, and it was centrally located in the county, meaning that the only way out again would be by the sixty or so miles of the A30. No, he would not be making a hit in that town. But he would have a starting point and that would give him the time to formulate a plan and find a more suitable killing ground. The chance meeting at Gulruan had thrown up too many variables. He would not be ill-prepared again.

Chapter Twenty-Six

"This really is a nice pad." Chloe admired the high-ceilings and roughly hewn timber beams. There were generous portions of glass and matt stainless steel, too. Smoked glass made up an entire wall, and Grant had told her there were glimpses of the sea to be had, but now that it was dark it acted like a giant black mirror. "Oh, I like this! They must be paying you a fortune!"

"Not nearly enough," he said. He had made them both some coffee. *That was new*, he thought. Chloe had been drinking squash the last time he had seen her, but she was now hanging out with her friends at *Costa* and *Starbucks* and drinking frappuccinos and mochas accompanied with giant cookies. He didn't know how kids could afford it. In his day it would have been a thick shake and a small fries from *Burger King*. "No, it's a short-term let. It was in my price range because of the fact it was a building site when I took up the lease, and the lane is a car wrecker."

"Mum wants the car."

"I know."

"Are you going to give it to her?"

"Not yet."

"Why?"

Grant shrugged. "She has a car. Simon bought one for her."

"She likes the Alfa."

"Perhaps Simon should have bought her one, then..."

"She says the deposit for the Alfa Romeo was hers."

Grant imagined Deborah and Simon talking about him openly in front of Chloe. The thought saddened him, his character assassinated in his daughter's presence. He had hoped they would have been more discreet, more respectful, but he knew that wouldn't have been the case. Simon would want to douse Grant's flames for his own to burn brighter. He took a sip of coffee then put the cup down. "I figure I swapped it for the house and everything else I left without."

Chloe held up her hands. "Hey, don't shoot the messenger!" she feigned exasperation. "I know. She should let it go. You need a car to get about. Especially down here."

"Okay, enough about mum. I don't want to do this."

"Do what? We're just talking."

"I don't want you in the middle like some go-between." He paused. "I never wanted that for you."

"Well, I always was," she replied dejectedly.

"And for that, I apologise." He placed a hand on her shoulder. "But I promise never to say anything bad about your mum, and you have to promise to get out from between us. You're not in the middle anymore."

Chloe shrugged. "Alright. Now, what's for dinner?"

Grant pulled a face. "Takeaway."

"Cool, I've got the *Deliveroo* app," she said, taking out her phone.

He smiled. "Not down here, you haven't."

"Oh."

"Something to consider before you move?"

"No, I'll cope."

"We'll talk in the morning."

"You don't want me here?" She looked at him indignantly, then softened and sipped some of her coffee. He got the impression she didn't like it much. Peer pressure, he suspected.

Grant regarded her for a moment. He realised that she had a lot of her mother in her. Hot headed and ready for a fight. But he always knew she had some of him in there, too. Stoic and pragmatic. Grant was a tactician. He saw the bigger picture. But he had a line and people only crossed it once. He imagined Chloe would turn out the same. Hopefully she would have inherited both his and Deborah's better character traits.

"Of course, I want you here. Nothing would be better," he said. "But your mum has full custody and I have residential rights every other weekend. I stand a good chance of being arrested when she discovers you're here. Hopefully she'll see it for what it is. Our gorgeous daughter having inherited a few too many of her genes..."

"She'd love you saying that," she said, rolling her eyes.

They both laughed and Grant took a Chinese takeaway menu out of the kitchen drawer. He tossed it onto the breakfast bar and said, "It will be good to have some company. I can finally try Menu B..."

"Idiot!" She browsed the menu, screwed up her face and said, "Yeah, that sounds okay. Can I have a shower?"

"Sure. But there's a jacuzzi bath in the second bathroom."

"Second bathroom?" She smiled and picked up her backpack, swinging it over her shoulder as she headed for the open staircase. "Can I have a beer?"

"No."

Grant watched her take the stairs two at a time. She reminded him of Deborah as she walked. She'd not only grown but matured in her movements. She still had the little girl sparkle, but he could see it was ebbing away. He wished he'd never taken the undercover assignments. Wished he'd seen the warning signs facing his marriage in time. Grant knew you couldn't turn back the clock. And he knew you could rarely fix what had been broken, but it didn't stop him lamenting what had been lost.

He dialled the Chinese restaurant and placed his order. He was given a forty-minute delivery time but took it with a pinch of salt, or a Chinese sized pinch of monosodium glutamate. It was nothing for the restaurant to take an hour and a half, but it was the only one in the area that would deliver this far out and everything else required collection. He smiled at Chloe's eagerness to use an app. He was sure the county was catching up, but it probably never would. It was too largely spaced with not enough of a hub to offer the same things a large city could.

Grant reached for the bottle of locally distilled rum and cracked the seal. He took out a tumbler and poured two fingers worth. He had taken to drinking during his time undercover. *Just one to steady his nerves...* He had become too reliant on it, and it had taken hold of him. When he had come down to Cornwall last year to recuperate after an injury sustained during a terrorist attack, he had been dry and struggling. Now he found that he functioned better if he allowed himself a drink, but tried to control the urge for more. It sounded good in his head, but he knew that it was not working. He was making excuses and the slippery slope was just under his toes. In the past there had always been an excuse. Infiltrating a gang or a network, getting under the target's skin, getting close to their friends, learning the signs, gathering the intelligence, reporting his findings back to a handler by way of dead drop or a face to face meeting played hell on his nerves.

After he had transferred to counter-terrorism, the weight of decisions weighed harder and he was soon out of control. His recuperation last year in Cornwall hadn't gone as planned, and after he had been reprimanded and reassigned, he had thrown himself once more into his work.

When he had started his affair with John Roper's wife, he had done so as a rebound from both his marriage, and his feeling towards a woman who he had started to fall for in Cornwall, and who had been brutally murdered. However, seeking solace in the warm embrace of someone at the very centre of his target's organisation had at first been a challenge. As if sleeping with her was the confirmation and consolidation of his craft. The ultimate accolade. And then he had started to care for her, start to fall in love. And then he had seen her lying dead on the bathroom floor and his whole world had fallen apart once more.

The vibrating phone on the countertop jogged his thoughts. He watched the device move slowly towards the edge of the counter and the screen light up intermittently. The caller ID read Professor Lucy Milarini. Another could have, would have, should have. But she had been happily married. He wondered what slant her findings would have on Vigus. Presently, the girl in his missing person's case was safe, if not well, and his main suspect's DNA had not shown up as a positive match. The relevance of Daniel Vigus was looking to be a footnote.

"Hi Lucy, thanks for getting back to me."

"Hi, Grant."

"So, what news have you got for me?"

There was a pause. Ominous in the silence. "It's not great, to be fair..."

"A man makes a mock-up of his mother in bed and relieves himself all over it? You surprise me. I'm not thinking this was going to be a wholesome, loving family like *The Waltons*..."

Lucy laughed. Grant could tell she was taking a sip of wine; the rim clipped against her teeth and she swallowed a gulp. "Well, it's a classic case of Oedipus complex."

"For the layman with poor GCSE results, if you please."

"Sigmund Freud. Do you know who that is?"

"Okay, somewhere between poor GCSEs and a couple of shitty A levels. Austrian psychiatrist and the guy who relates everything back to sex."

"Well, you need to further research Inspector, but yes. But the town he was born in is now in the Czech Republic. Příbor was once in part of the Austrian Empire, but that receded. He was the first true psychoanalyst and encouraged the practice we see today of the classic couch and patient format talking through emotive states to dig to the root of a problem. One of his classic theories was the Greek story of Oedipus. The best-known version of the story is that Oedipus was a mythical Greek king of Thebes. A tragic hero in Greek mythology, Oedipus accidentally fulfilled a prophecy that he would end up killing his father and marrying his mother, thereby bringing disaster to his city and family. Oedipus was born to King Laius and Queen Jocasta. Laius wished to thwart the prophecy, so he sent a shepherd-servant to leave Oedipus to die on a mountainside. However, the shepherd took pity on the baby and passed him to another shepherd who gave Oedipus to King Polybus and Queen Merope to raise as their own. Oedipus learned from the oracle at Delphi of the prophecy that he would end up killing his father and marrying his mother but, unaware of his true parentage, believed he was fated to murder Polybus and marry Merope, so left for Thebes. On his way he met an older man and killed him in a quarrel. Continuing the journey to Thebes, he found that the king of the city, Laius, had been recently killed, and that the city was at the mercy of the Sphinx. Oedipus answered the monster's riddle correctly, defeating it and winning the throne of the dead king – and the hand in marriage of the king's widow, who was also, unbeknownst to him, his mother Jocasta."

"God, there's something about a woman who uses *unbeknownst* in conversation. You haven't left David yet, have you?"

"No."

"Didn't think so."

"And I'm not planning to."

"Well, he's a lucky little shit, then."

"He is, isn't he?" She laughed again, then said, "You didn't let me know anything about this guy, and I understand why. So, I can honestly say if this man hasn't offended sexually, then it's just a matter of time."

"Why so sure?"

"Well, the sexual desire required for such a fantasy is so acute, so horrific to what I would determine as 'normal' people, although we try desperately hard to avoid the term, that the manifestation to reality comes by way of breaking one's inhibitions. You see, men... and women, too... will have depraved fantasies. But generally, after peaking the fantasy, climaxing sexually, if you will, then there follows a definite shame. That shame would have most deviants on the spectrum of depravity cleaning up after themselves." She paused. "Take a man masturbating to regular pornography. Afterwards it would be *normal*, if I were to use that term again, to switch off the TV or close the website, delete the history, get out the Kleenex and go to the bathroom. Many people self-loath after such acts. People who abstain from pornographic use, break a habit that has become an addiction, concentrate on a stalled relationship and stop masturbating, almost always end up happier, more well-adjusted versions of their former self."

"I'll have to remember that."

"Oh, Grant, I don't believe for a second there isn't a beautiful vivacious young woman somewhere you haven't got your eye on."

"Thanks," replied Grant, thinking of DC Heather Carveth. He shook her out of his head, then asked, "Beautiful and vivacious sounds a compliment, but why did you say young? I'm not a cradle snatcher..."

"No, Grant, but you fit a profile that would have me thinking at least five to ten years younger than yourself," she said. "That's why it would never work with us," then added. "That and the fact I'm in love with my husband."

"Great..."

"I'll talk more about your profile when next we meet."

"Unbeknownst just got side lined. When next we meet?"

"I'm sorry, darling, but I'm not dumbing down my diction or vocabulary, even for you, sweetie."

Grant laughed. "So, the fact my suspect basically had no shame means he has crossed a socially and morally acceptable line?"

"I would say it's likely."

Grant sunk the rest of the rum and poured another two fingers. He screwed the cap back on with one hand and pushed the bottle away. Enough. He picked up the glass and gave it a swirl as he thought about the image on the bed. The photographs of the awful-looking child in varying stages of awkwardness, the all-encompassing burn ever present, almost dominating the scenes. "I think he has," he said. "Historically. Young girls of twelve or thirteen. Only, as adamant as the victims or complainants are, he had begrudging alibis at the time. I was convinced his DNA would be on a sample of clothing found this morning, but it turned out to be old clothing planted to incriminate him. Except, it had the opposite effect. It cleared him."

Lucy Milarini was quiet for a moment, then said, "What of this man's family?"

"He has none. His mother died recently and there's never been any mention of the man's father," he said. "But if he's not showing up with DNA..."

"You can't beat DNA," she replied. "But there are other ways to beat the system."

"The suspect was recently pardoned. He did a ten year stretch incriminated on DNA, but the force was shown to have broken procedure in its collection and application. The suspect did a private DNA test, which was later corroborated by the Welsh police service, where he had been convicted of the crime. He will soon be basking in the sun with a couple hundred grand and a clean slate."

"I'd like to know more about his parents. If I were to do a thorough psychoanalysis of this man, then I would want to start with his early life and parental relationships. I think that's where you should start your investigation, too." She paused. "Generally, if we're fucked up, it's because of our parents..." she said lightly.

"I heard some anecdotal background on his father today. I'll get it down and email you." Grant looked to see

Chloe at the top of the stairs. She was flushed from the heat of the bath and had changed into jogging bottoms and a Metallica T-shirt. That was new, too. He had seen them play Wembley thirty years ago. He watched her, still drying her hair with a towel. He hoped he and Deborah hadn't fucked her up too much. "Thanks, Lucy. But I've got to get going."

"A beautiful, vivacious, young woman?"

Grant laughed. "You have no idea," he said. "What do we owe you, Devon and Cornwall Police Service, that is?"

"As it stands, it's on me," Lucy replied. "But if you want a full report, a professional verdict that you can take to court, then they can pay up like everyone else. Five grand should do it. Ten if you want me to appear in court."

"Ten grand?" Grant asked incredulously. "Are you sure you won't leave David for me?"

"Quite sure, Grant. You're a bad man. Charming and lovely, and fundamentally on the right side of the law, but a bad man nonetheless and bad men don't make for good relationships. Great sex and fun moments, but not marriage material."

"You've been talking to my ex?"

"No. But I rest my case."

"Great. I feel so good about myself now," he replied sardonically, but he knew she was right. He hadn't been cut out for marriage. "Alright, I'll keep it between you and me for now," he replied. "And thanks again, I owe you one."

"I'll look forward to it," she said warmly and ended the call.

Grant shook his head. Reading Lucy Milarini was like starting a book upside down and working your way from the back page. He looked up as Tackle, aka Bollocks, went berserk and started barking at the door. A moment later, the doorbell sounded, and for the first time since the shooting, Grant felt vulnerable. He had far from shrugged the incident off, but Lilly Trefusis had been his only concern until now. He still hadn't been able to work out if the gunman had been after Lisa Trefusis or if he and Carveth had been the intended targets. Whether the man had been a chance nutjob, or whether he had been interrupted committing another crime and acted defensively, he did not know. He nodded for Chloe to come over and took a large kitchen knife off the magnetic rack.

"Dad?" Chloe asked, a mixture of curiousness and concern in her voice.

"It's okay," Grant said, but he didn't seem to convince her, much less himself. He walked to the door, kept to the side and attached the chain. He kept the knife out of sight and cracked the door ajar. "Hi," he said to the regular driver. He closed the door in the man's face, rested the knife on the dresser and unlocked the latch. He took the bag off him. Grant had prepaid on the telephone, but he dug a couple of pounds out of his pocket and tipped the driver before thanking him and closing the door.

"What the hell?" Chloe asked as he returned to the breakfast bar and started emptying the packages and containers out of the bag. "Do you always answer the door like that? What are you so scared of?"

"I had a close call today, just made me a bit jumpy, that's all."

She nodded sagely. "Mum said you were shot at once."

"Twice," he corrected her, but thought, *so much for listening, Deborah...* He didn't add that today made three. And then he remembered being shot at in a tunnel by a man with a shotgun hellbent on saving his own skin. Four times. Christ...

Chloe hugged him but broke away as he took out a poorly tied bag of prawn crackers. She grabbed one and looked for something to dip it in.

"I love being here with you, daddy," she beamed. "This pretty much rocks."

Grant looked at her and smiled. It certainly did.

Chapter Twenty-Seven

G rant studied the report for a second time. And for a second time, he shook his head. It simply didn't make sense. But it did. DCI Nangiles had read it out to the watch last night, or the salient facts. He'd wanted a nice tidy wrap up, but Grant knew that seldom, if ever happened. Every investigation took some collateral on the way. After a while, it tended to be the officers that had become too close, who hadn't deflected all they should have. Their emotion, sobriety and conscience were the true collateral damage to the most taxing investigations.

There had been no further news on the gunman, either. No sign of the vehicle – and with the shot-out rear window it would be highly likely he would have dumped it – and as Grant had not had the chance to make a note of the number plate, there was only a make, model and colour to go on. Not even a sub model to narrow the gap. The man had not appeared on any CCTV footage, either. The man was a ghost, and that was what worried Grant the most.

"What's wrong, boss?" asked Carveth. "We'll get the

gunman," she said, as if reading his mind. "And Lilly is safe, this could have been another Madeleine McCann situation after all is said and done."

Grant shook his head. "I never thought it would be. You asked yesterday if I thought it reminded me of that case and I said it reminded me of another case. I was thinking that the distinct demographic and the lack of answers reminded me of the Shannon Matthews case."

"The girl who was kidnapped by her own family members up north?"

"Yes. Following the high-profile press coverage and campaigns to find Madeleine McCann, and the publicity the case had, Shannon Matthews was kidnapped from her home in Dewsbury, West Yorkshire. She was just nine years old. Shannon's mother, Karen Matthews and her partner's uncle, Michael Donovan hatched a plan that would see them raise money through the publicity surrounding the case. Shannon was going to be found by Donovan at a later date and they would cream money off the top of any fund people donated to."

"Wasn't the mother's partner involved as well?"

"No, Craig Meehan wasn't involved in the plan. He wasn't even considered clever enough by the other two to be part of it. But during the investigation he was found to have a huge amount of child pornography on his computer and was arrested, charged and went to prison as a result." Grant paused. "The thing is these half-wits didn't have the sense to see that the deception would be uncovered as soon as they released Shannon. And these jokers out at Gulruan are the same."

"Well, that's the truth."

"But whereas Shannon Matthews was taken to generate

money, Lilly Trefusis was taken to highlight Daniel Vigus as a sex offender. So, if he hadn't done anything to Lilly, because we know that she was taken by Maria Bright and her partner Andy Beam, then these women must be pretty bloody adamant that Vigus did what he did all those years ago." Grant handed her the report. "Here, read it."

"But it's not him..." she said, shaking her head. "What are we doing reading it?"

"But it is." Grant paused. "We just aren't seeing it. The girls were certain at the time. Vigus said there were three little witches, but Maria Bright and Lisa Trefusis makes two. Carrie-Ann Dixon admitted to us that she lied to back up her friend 's allegation. I knew she was lying. I could tell. But by that same token, I knew the other two women were telling the truth. I've been a police officer for more than twenty years and I know a lie and the truth when I see it. And I mean *see*, not *hear*. I know the tells, the body language. The eyes, the touching of the face, the looking up or down depending on the time needed to create a plausible story. It has stood me in good stead over the years, because my entire career has been built upon it. I'm a DI, but I've been a DCI previously and was asked to go for superintendent. I made a mistake and got bumped down the ranks. But I like it at this level. It keeps me in the field and away from a permanent desk." He paused. "Those women are still adamant all these years later. Daniel Vigus did things to them. Unspeakable things. And yet he was cleared. He wasn't a well-liked man, but still people came forward and cleared him. He was drinking in the local pub at the same time as he was accused. Later, upon release for a similar offence, he provides a DNA sample and is cleared. How?"

"Could he have had somebody else provide the

sample?" Carveth shook her head. "But no, that's not possible. Vigus' DNA is a match, as close as you would expect, to his mother's."

"But his mother's DNA was never taken. And that can only happen if her body is exhumed..."

"Jesus Christ, boss!" Carveth looked at him intently and said, "The DCI will never go for it. Not in light of the negative DNA test."

Grant stood up and looked out at the sea. It was a raging beast today and cast great spumes of white water thirty feet into the air as it hit the seafront wall. Pedestrians wrestling with umbrellas walked the promenade and took the cascade of seawater in their stride. He looked back at Carveth and said, "When I saw Vigus and looked around his cottage, I was struck by how different he looked in the photographs. Yes, the horrid-looking boy was there, with that grotesque burn, but he went through so many physical changes, I never truly had the sense anyone would ever know the boy, much less like him. He looked the same, but different..." Grant frowned. He was distant, but when he looked back at DC Carveth, he seemed enlightened. "Come on, Carveth."

"Where are we going?"

"To Vigus' cottage. There's something I want to see again." He stood up and headed for the door, then stood aside to allow PC Tamsin Gould past with both of her hands spread around three coffees in plastic cups. To add rigidity, she had placed each cup inside another. "Ah, the woman of the moment! Well done with your find, yesterday."

She shrugged. "It didn't tie anything to the suspect though, Sir."

Grant shrugged. "It's been a great help."

"In what way?"

"Well, it forced a confession out of Lisa Trefusis, and it cleared an innocent man..."

"I doubt that," she scoffed.

"Well, I still maintain it was a vital find." He paused. "You're not helping the environment with that little lot," he chided.

"But I drive a hybrid," she said swiftly. "And coming from the man with a decade-old Alfa Romeo. How much engine does one man need?"

"Touché, constable." He grinned. "What's on the roster for you today?"

She hesitated, the coffee starting to burn through the double layers of plastic. "Briefing in ten minutes, I think I'm on community policing and crime prevention with Neighbourhood Watch leaders." She looked for somewhere to set the cups down.

"Great. Declare yourself unavailable and meet DC Carveth and myself out the front in a support vehicle in ten minutes," he said.

PC Gould nodded and scurried off with the hot cups. Grant looked at DC Carveth, who seemed to view PC Tamsin Gould with ambivalence. She was frowning when she asked, "Has your car been acquainted with another hedge? I noticed some nice dents and scratches last night."

DI Grant did not remark. He had found her reaction to PC Gould interesting. The easy to and fro between them had sparked something in her. Grant wasn't surprised. He found himself more comfortable around women. There was no alpha male rubbish to contend with, no cock measuring, as he called it. He had counted many women as his best friends, but it had occasionally gone past the platonic boundaries, which had presented a unique set of problems. But if he wasn't so blinded by his feelings towards Heather Carveth, he could have sworn she felt the same way about him. She certainly hadn't liked the exchange between himself and PC Tamsin Gould. He headed for the door and said, "When you're ready, DC Carveth."

Chapter Twenty-Eight

Grant drove in his Alfa Romeo with DC Carveth alongside him. PC Tamsin Gould followed in a police liveried Vauxhall Astra with a blues and twos lightbar on the roof. But there was no need to light them up just yet.

"Remind me why we need PC Plod?"

"Oh, the career divide between beat officers and CID..." He paused. "Are you not a fan of PC Gould?"

She shrugged. "I don't really know her, but she reminds me of someone who lacks any passion towards the job. And *job* is the best word for how she views it. It's a profession or vocation for most of us."

"There's people like that in every job."

"I suppose."

"So, she's not particularly career driven or looking for promotion. The world needs those people, too. They grease the cogs."

"Are we cogs?" she asked.

"Well, I am. You're just a lowly detective constable. We detective inspectors see you detective constables as grease."

"With respect, fuck you, Sir."

Grant laughed. "And as usual, anybody starting a sentence *with respect* doesn't ever intend on giving any."

"You asked for it."

"Undoubtedly." Grant felt his phone vibrate and fished it out of his jacket pocket, struggling to read as he steered.

"That's six penalty points and a two hundred pound fine."

"Feisty."

"Because I'm a woman? You'd say I was being a prick if I was a man." She paused. "Seriously, though, you're going to kill us if you try that. Just pull over and I'll drive."

Grant rolled his eyes and slowed the car, pulling into a wider section of road with a worn verge. He read the text from Chloe and sighed. She had taken Tackle for a walk on the headland and was aiming to be back around lunchtime if he ever felt like stocking the fridge with some food. He had to get more organised. He typed out a quick message telling her there was forty pounds in the hall dresser drawer if she needed anything from the shop in the village, and said he'd try to get back there for some lunch. Personally, he didn't hold out much hope. He then noticed the text from Deborah. Not good. Not good at all. Just something else for him to worry about. She had given him a deadline to call before she called the police and her solicitor. How had it come to this? In his defence, he did not know she had changed her number, but now that he had it, he simply wrote – *Busy on a case, will call later. Please don't do anything rash – I didn't know she was coming down. Chloe wanted to be here and won't take well to you punishing me – give her a day or two and I'll drop her back xxx* He cursed himself for adding the kisses. Force of habit. But he'd sent it before he had realised. He put the phone back in his pocket and pulled back out into the road.

"Problems?" asked Carveth. "If you don't mind me asking?"

Grant sighed. "Teenage daughters and estranged wives."

"I think I read a novel with that title."

"Then I pity the author."

Carveth smiled. "What's the problem with your daughter?"

"She came down on the train last night. Now I'm breaking the custody agreement. My wife..." He paused, shaking his head. "Or ex-wife as she is now, is just angry that I haven't died yet and as crazy as it sounds, I'd like my daughter to stay for a while and get to know her again. It wasn't an amicable divorce, let's just say that."

"Why is that crazy?"

Grant shrugged. "I live on my own, work too many hours and frankly, I wasn't the greatest father when I had a family. I suppose I always thought I'd get a little less busy, take a transfer to a less taxing department when the chance arose. Before I knew it, my daughter was almost grown, and a wedge had grown between my wife and me."

Carveth smiled. She placed a hand on his knee, and he started to recoil, but relaxed. She noticed his reaction, but she didn't move her hand. "Well, living on your own isn't much fun and with your daughter on the scene, maybe you can lighten up a little with work. You haven't got to be working as many hours as you do for the more mundane cases. And perhaps this is your chance to get the father thing right, finally. Trust me, teenage girls need their fathers. And they need a good role model, otherwise they won't look for it in a man." She took her hand away but as she did so, she patted his thigh. "You need to discover Cornwall and what it has to offer," she said. "I bet you haven't even tried surfing yet, have you?"

"No, of course not!"

"Well, you should. And I bet you haven't walked on Bodmin Moor or Cubert Common, or taken a boat along the Helford River, or visited the National Trust country houses." She paused. "Wait until the summer and you can do a trip to the Isles of Scilly or go to the Minack Theatre..."

"What the hell's that?"

"Really? Well, you're in for a treat. It's an open performance, like an amphitheatre, right on the cliffs near Land's End. You sit on the granite steps or seats with a picnic or a glass of wine and the sun is setting while you watch a production. It's glorious. There's so much to do down here, it's about time you started living the lifestyle. What better way to bond with your daughter?"

"But I don't have full custody," he said.

She shrugged. "Then let's start on getting you that. I know a brilliant barrister. We dated for a while, but we're still good friends. Family friends, I suppose, so there's no getting away from him." She smiled. "I'll have a word and pass on your number if you like?"

Grant thought for a moment. He thought about Nick, his solicitor. He had been a nice chap with thirty years' experience, but a lousy lawyer. Never filed on time, turned up late to court dates and Grant felt he was always on the back-foot when he needed someone he could trust. Deborah's lawyer had been a hotshot woman of about thirty and had kicked the legal dinosaur's arse at every mediation and hearing. Perhaps it was time he had another go at getting more time with Chloe. He had lost almost everything he owned, but none of that really mattered. What was important was to have more access to Chloe before she reached college age and took off on her own accord. He nodded, "Okay, Heather, I'd appreciate that."

"*Heather*, I'm flattered. So, do I call you by your first name?"

"No."

"Do I get to know it?"

"No."

"Oh."

"Grant will do," he said with a shrug. "Or Boss..."

"I'd better get a promotion, then," she said. "Close the gap a little. I prefer first names."

"You'll never close the gap enough to know my first name," Grant said with a smile. They rounded the corner and Vigus' cottage loomed into view, the light mood leaving him, almost sucked from inside the car altogether. Beyond the dark cottage, the sea was rough, and the headland was windswept and desolate. Three-inch high tufts of seagrass and short clumps of heather were all that grew, except for a barrier of gorse that separated the lower reaches of the headland from the fields further inland. Quite why anybody would choose to live out here was anybody's guess, but as Grant drew nearer, he reflected that for such a severe and cruel looking woman as Mavis Vigus, and her grotesquely disfigured son, then it would have been just about perfect. He thought the cottage to be like the proverbial Pandora's Box, where untold evil and cruelty had been unleashed upon an unsuspecting world, only he doubted that hope had remained inside. As far as he could tell, nothing good remained and he doubted the house had known anything but evil, and he would see that Vigus paid for what he had done.

Grant pulled over and parked the car in the open space.

He wondered why nobody seemed to use the area to park for coastal walks, but then again, you'd have to know the area and he figured the locals knew, and that's why they stayed away.

PC Tamsin Gould was already at his window. He lowered it a touch, the wind howling through the gap. "Why are we here, Sir?" she asked, her eyes on the cottage.

"I wanted a uniformed presence when I speak to Vigus."

She frowned. "But the DNA wasn't a match."

"I know."

She looked puzzled. "He's still a suspect?" she asked. "How?"

"Because of what I believe he's done in the past," he said. "And the fact that the DNA on the underwear found on Gulruan Moor cements that."

DC Carveth interrupted. "But how? The DNA didn't match."

"But whoever was behind it, Lisa Trefusis or Maria Bright, they were convinced whatever was on the underwear would be a DNA match. Utterly convinced." He paused. "And now I want to find out why."

Chapter Twenty-Nine

Grant stepped around the loose rocks and stones and climbed the steps. He stood on the top step, his head brushing the door overhang, and hammered the door with his fist. He had always found it elicited a response when the door shook enough for the lock to rattle and the hinges to strain. The person inside was never too sure whether the door was being knocked or kicked down, subsequently nobody Grant had ever knocked on had waited for him to become bored and walk away.

Vigus answered, but he did so with his iPhone filming and in Grant's face.

"This is police harassment, DI Grant!"

Grant snatched the phone from him and tossed it fifty metres away onto the rocky ground. Vigus was about to protest, when Grant said, "I haven't even started, yet."

"The news said the girl has been found, so why are you here?" He looked at DC Carveth, then hesitated as he looked at PC Tamsin Gould.

Grant watched him. Vigus seemed to drink the woman in, a sordid observation of her curvy hips, trim waist and ample breasts. When he reached her face, he frowned, then looked back at DI Grant. "Why is she here?"

"It's called training. And sometimes it pays to have a uniformed officer's presence when making house calls."

"And that's it?"

"Is *what* it?"

"You're just making a house call?"

"There are people angry enough to harm you, Vigus."

"That's mister Vigus to you..." He interrupted. "I'm sure you shouldn't be using my surname like that. It implies contempt or over familiarity."

"It does?"

"You know it does."

Grant shoved him out of the way and stepped over the threshold. "Well, right now, we're concerned for your safety so we're performing a security check and evaluation."

"You're not coming in!"

"Too late. Anyway, if something should happen to a person wrongly caught up in suspicions over recent, and historical events, then the police service could be held accountable." Grant paused. "And we wouldn't want that, would we?" He looked at DC Carveth, who seemed unsure what to do next. "Stay with Mister Vigus, please. PC Gould, please accompany me..."

Vigus went to follow, but Carveth shoved him out of the way and positioned herself in the doorway. "You heard what the inspector said."

Grant took the stairs on all fours, then straightened up, his head skimming the low ceiling. He took out his phone and photographed the pictures he had studied the day before. Stepped back and walked into the main bedroom. The disturbing sight of the stuffed nightdress and pillows was still there. He took out a pair of latex gloves and a DNA swab kit.

"Oh my god!" PC Gould looked at the bed, her mouth agape.

"Sick son of a bitch, isn't he?"

She said nothing but nodded tentatively.

Grant scraped the swab around the nightdress and pillow and placed it into the bag and sealed it up. He slipped it into his pocket and headed past PC Gould and back down the stairs. Vigus was seething, but he hadn't tried to get past DC Carveth a second time.

"I would like to take a DNA sample from you, Mister Vigus."

He shook his head. "And if I refuse?"

"That's your privilege," replied Grant. "But refusal never looks good."

"But it's my human right."

"So, it's a no?"

"I'm taking the matter up with my solicitor." Vigus paused, his face locked in an expression of arrogance. "Besides, the little girl has been found. And I believe I was cleared of all wrongdoing for the crime of which sentence was served. And that leaves unsubstantiated allegations that the Devon and Cornwall police, or the crime prosecution service, did not feel were worth taking to court."

Grant nodded. "Yeah, I hear all that. But it doesn't change a damned thing with me. You're still a sick bastard, *Mister* Vigus and I'll see that something sticks this time."

"That does sound rather like you'll make something stick, whether I am guilty or not. And I'm sure an officer of your length of service, and highly dubious service record will be able to do that. The fact that I'm innocent won't stop you. All the more reason for me to speak to my solicitor.

And you'll pay for that fucking phone." He turned to DC Heather Carveth and said, "I'd like to make a complaint. You witnessed it."

"Sorry, I must have missed that. What's this about a phone?"

"Typical," he muttered. He looked at PC Tamsin Gould, but then looked away. He could see the lay of the land and wasn't going three for three.

"We'll be going, now," Grant announced. "And it's noted you refused a DNA sample to eliminate you from my enquiries."

"Yes. And it's noted you searched my house without a warrant again, destroyed my property and ignored my refusal to allow you access."

Grant opened the front door and said, "Well, make a complaint. The number's nine-nine-nine." He paused and looked back at him. "Better still, come with me now back to the station and lodge your complaint now. While you're there, you can provide that DNA sample to the custody sergeant. Just to clear yourself of recent allegations."

"And what would you have in your possession to test it against? It was fifteen years ago!"

"Oh, you wouldn't know," said Grant. "We have underwear that one of the accusers kept. Ashamed and unsure what to do with it." He studied Vigus, his body language and eyes. He smiled, then stepped outside.

Chapter Thirty

The clouds had scudded away to reveal a vast blue sky and a rare glimpse of cold winter sun. With it, the wind had dropped, and the sea had calmed considerably – temporarily subdued - but again threatening to rage at a moment's notice. The heaviness had lifted and with it the promise of better things to come. Grant looked at the sea. The sudden calmness seemed like a metaphor. He turned and looked at PC Tamsin Gould, she looked back at him, struggled to hold his stare.

She sat down on a large granite boulder and cast her eyes to the horizon. "You know, don't you..." She had turned her back on the cottage. The darkness of Vigus' home and all the darkness that laid within behind her.

Grant perched beside her. "I suspected."

"How?"

Grant looked at her and said, "You're a promising copper. Nipping out to the shop when you're on family liaison duty didn't seem to be a mistake that you'd be likely to make." He paused, standing beside her. The low-lying sun enough to squint by as they stared out to sea. Already the horizon was starting to cloud over again, a mackerel effect starting to block out the sun. "Neither you nor Lisa Trefusis seemed able to decide whether you needed tea, milk or sugar. When I came in to talk to you in the kitchen, I could see there was already enough on the counter and you hadn't needed to go out at all. Before that, when she turned up down here with her angry mob and shouting the odds, you would have known she had left and didn't call it in. How long does a trip to the Spar shop in Gulruan take? It's measured in minutes. Less than ten, I reckon. You arrived back shortly after I did."

"And you knew then?"

"Shortly afterwards."

"It was the pair of knickers on the moor, wasn't it?"

"Too convenient."

"I didn't set out to deceive, it snowballed. I planted them, but the bloody search party looked everywhere but where they had been placed. I had to swing back around and get them." She bowed her head. "And I didn't know they were planning to fake Lilly's abduction. That was on Maria and Andy. They sort of bulldozed Lisa into it. Then they came to me, because of..."

DC Carveth stepped closer and wrapped an arm around her. "It's okay," she said soothingly. She glanced at Grant and frowned, like he was being too harsh.

"By then, I just wanted to get a conclusion. I didn't know what they planned to do to Lilly. I would never have agreed to help, but I got roped in to get Vigus mixed up in it. Maria said he would pay for what he did, and it wasn't like he didn't do it. We all knew..." She sobbed, wiped her eyes and said, "But I really had no idea they were going to fake Lilly's abduction. I honestly didn't know."

"How did you come to have the clothing?"

She shrugged. "After it happened, I got myself together at a disused public toilet that had long been abandoned and grown over. The roof was almost completely fallen in but covered with ivy. We all used it as a camp... drank, smoked, lit fires and told stories there..." She sobbed. "I went there afterwards, tried to clean myself up..."

DC Heather Carveth continued to soothe her shoulder. "It's okay," she said softly.

"I tossed my knickers behind some rubble and threw some rocks on top of them to hide them. I never went back there. Never went to Gulruan Moor again, until yesterday's search. I couldn't cope with it, never told my parents. Or anybody else. I only told Lisa Trefusis after it happened to her, and then she told Maria about me when it happened to her."

Grant knew he was perhaps being harsh, coaxing her along, but painful as it was for her, his questions needed answering. He also knew that judging from her account, and the timeline, had she reported it then there was a good chance that Vigus wouldn't have been free to attack the other girls. The benefit of hindsight. He took a breath none-theless and asked softly, "What did Vigus do to you?"

"He raped me."

Carveth rubbed her shoulder. "Oh my god! That must have been so hard for you back there with Vigus..." She glared at Grant. "And you knew that, boss? How could you make her go in there with that monster?"

"No, it's okay..." She sobbed. Carveth dug out a tissue and handed it to her. Gould wiped her eyes and blew her nose, and Carveth still glared at DI Grant. "It didn't feel as bad as I thought it would. I don't know why." She paused. "Perhaps it's the fact so much time has passed, or that he's so pathetic."

Carveth looked at Grant and said, "So, what have we got here, Sir? Tamsin didn't know about the abduction..."

"But she knew after it happened that it was a hoax," he replied. "And she falsified evidence."

"Come on!"

Grant interrupted her. "She knew that a little girl wasn't in danger when everyone else thought she was, she knew resources were at full stretch, she knew that evidence was being used to frame a suspect for a crime he did not commit..."

"But it was for a crime, multiple crimes he already committed!" she snapped at him.

"But the DNA doesn't fit!" Grant shouted back.

PC Gould held up her hands. "Enough!" She shook her head. "I get it! I fucked up! I know my career is done, and I know I will face prison for what I did." She went to stand up but dropped to her knees, losing control. She looked up at him as she sobbed. "But fifteen years ago, that man raped me, and I know he raped Lisa Trefusis and Maria Bright, too!"

Grant bent down and pulled her gently to her feet. He hugged her close, then released her and shepherded her back to the cars. He led her to the passenger door of the police car and helped her into the passenger seat and closed the door.

"You're kidding, right?" DC Carveth fumed.

"Heather, I'm not kidding. I'm thinking."

"About what?"

"About how the hell I can make this right!" He looked over at the house. The clouds had come back and the light had dimmed, the cottage had a gothic appearance – dark and foreboding. "Take Tamsin back, don't let her talk to anybody, get her signed out and tell her to self-certify herself sick for a week. Say's it's thrush or a urinary infection or something. Guys like DCI Nangiles will back right off with that."

Carveth nodded. She looked a little dejected, embarrassed she had doubted him. "Boss..."

"Forget it," he said. "Just get her home and make sure she's okay."

"Where are you going?"

Grant shrugged. "I need to make a call to someone at Middlemoor first. Cut DCI Nangiles out of the loop."

"Do you think that's wise?"

"Nope, but wisdom rarely leads to direct action."

She nodded, but she already knew that DI Grant rarely played by the book. She was just going to have to get used to it. "And then what?"

Grant looked back at the cottage. Dark and foreboding against the bleak backdrop of the rocky cliffs and sea beyond. "I'm going home to hug my daughter," he said. "Just to pretend, for a short while, that evil doesn't exist and doesn't stand a chance of touching us."

Chapter Thirty-One

Grant could hear Tackle, AKA Bollocks barking as he pulled up outside the house. The rest of the site was empty, and he considered whether the possibility that the project had stalled for financial reasons could get him a few months extra rental. Especially if Chloe could stay more.

He swung the Alfa Romeo around and parked facing out. A habit from his undercover days. It always paid to get out of trouble faster than you got into it. Tackle bounded out and cocked his leg on the bonnet, exposing his giant baked potatoes. Grant got out and watched as Chloe rounded the path and smiled at him.

"Mum called; she's properly pissed off with you."

Grant seriously doubted the possibility of her staying more. He had succumbed to a daydream and they were the worst to wake up from. "I feel consistency is important these days. Imagine if she started getting on with me, now that we're apart. How warped would that be?"

"She wants me on the first train back to London after the weekend."

"Result!" Grant beamed. "And she won't have me arrested?"

"No."

"Well, *that's* progress."

"But I don't want to go back."

"And I don't want you to go back, but like you said, you're almost sixteen and all bets are off after that. If I say I want you to come and stay with me, and you say you want to spend more time down here with me, then there really isn't much a judge can do. And your mum will see that, too. " He paused, wrapped an arm around her shoulder. That was the first time he had said *your mum*, like there was a distinct disassociation with her, like they were no longer a team, the family he always thought they would be. He would have always simply said, *mum*. The thought made him sad, but he couldn't afford to wallow. He had given over too much time lamenting what had changed beyond reach. Besides, he had made some poor choices, but she was the one who had forgotten which bed she should have been sleeping in. He gave Chloe the long overdue hug he promised himself he would at Gulruan headland. The thoughts of what evil men would do to young girls making him feel insignificant as Chloe's protector. "Now, *that's* progress. Play the long game. See if we can get some movement on visitation over the next few months and we can make some plans. But together, as parents, not just you and me in a secret pact."

"I love you, daddy." She smiled, then looked past him. "Holy crap! How long does that dog pee for?" she burst out laughing.

"Cheaper than a carwash..." Grant watched the patchy and mangy-looking bulldog. His three grounded legs were shaking from the weight and his cocked leg was wavering at the effort. "Come on," he said. "Doesn't look like he's finishing anytime soon." He reached into the car and pulled out a large bag stuffed full of groceries, then placed his other arm around her shoulders and walked her inside. "I got some food," he said. "Co-op's finest. Pizza, ready prepared salad and garlic bread. Oh, and a whole load of sweets, crisps and fizzy pop."

"Sound's good to me."

"And ice cream."

"Perfect. Anything for breakfast, this morning was a struggle," she smiled. There was a clawing at the door and the dog started to bark. "I'll let him in," she said.

"You'll give that bloody mutt ideas," he replied, then added, "Sorry, I just have coffee in the mornings."

"That's healthy!" she called behind her, letting in the dog and watching him trot inside like he owned the place.

"Keeps me in the same sized trousers..." he said glibly. "But I got bread, ham, cheese, jam and cereal. Seeing as I have a guest. Oh, and Nutella, I know you love that stuff."

"Not anymore. It kills orangutans."

Grant raised an eyebrow. Another thing he'd missed. She had practically eaten it with a spoon every time a new jar magically turned up in the cupboard. He shrugged. "Who the hell would give an orangutan Nutella?" he chided.

"Daddy! It's the palm oil production. They cut down all the trees."

Grant smiled. "Well, they shouldn't give orangutans chainsaws..."

"The farmers cut down the trees!" She laughed. "That's such a *dad* joke!"

"Oh," he said dumbly. He had missed winding her up. In fact, he'd missed everything.

"Are you back for the day?" She took the bag off him and started unpacking the groceries. "I'm starving, shall we have a sandwich?"

"Yes, ham and cheese for me," he replied. "Oh, and no, I'm not back for the day."

"Oh," she said, dejectedly.

"There's just a lot on, sorry."

"I could come with you," she said breezily, taking out the loaf and packets of ham and cheese. "Got any mayo?"

"No, sorry."

"Anything moist?"

"HP?"

She turned her nose up in disgust. "Do you *ever* eat here?"

"Not much," he said.

"So, if I came with you, I could wait in the car, or at the police station if I have to. When you finish, we could go to Nando's for dinner afterwards."

Grant smiled. "Not down here you won't."

"Seriously?" She rolled her eyes. "Okay, whatever they have down in Penzance. I'm not fussy. McDonald's, even. But at least we can spend some time together."

Grant watched her make the sandwiches. He'd missed being with her more than she could ever know. He glanced at his watch. He couldn't see the harm in her tagging along with him. Like she said, she could remain in the car. "Alright," he relented. "But you stay in the car if I tell you to."

Chloe beamed. "Yes, sir, detective chief inspector, sir!"

"Detective inspector," he corrected her. "I got put on the naughty step again."

She laughed and they ate their sandwiches and Grant showed her the view out to sea as they ate. There were fields and a distant farm, but the sea was visible in the distance. After their hurried lunch, Grant announced it was time to go and reiterated she would have to remain in the car or at the station if anything developed. At this point, Grant would have let the dog out, but Chloe seemed to have adopted him, so he just hoped he would be ok on his own and not damage the house or chew up his shoes, but the fact that Chloe was so taken with the animal almost made the risk worth it.

Grant showed Chloe the coast road from Portreath to Gwithian and it afforded them great views over the tossed white water across the bay to St. Ives. At Hayle, Grant took the A30 single lane towards Penzance and after a quick detour a few hundred metres to Mount's Bay carpark, where she could take in St. Michael's Mount – the medieval castle and church built on an island just offshore – they arrived at Penzance police station shortly afterwards.

"Stay..."

"In the car?" she interjected. "Deal."

"I won't be long."

"I'll browse the net on my phone."

"Good luck with the signal."

Grant closed the door on her and jogged up the steps. He bumped into DC Jones, who looked subdued and appeared unable to hold Grant's stare. "What's wrong, David?"

"DCI Nangiles has taken me off the case and given me an official warning for using non-official surveillance equipment." He paused. "The software had a glitch and that was why it lost Vigus for a while. It's my own fault; I was too wrapped up in my own abilities."

"Nonsense," said Grant. "And don't worry, I'll smooth it over for you. There's a high-ranking officer in Exeter who I might be able to have a word with. I haven't alienated him, just yet," he said, thinking about Chief Superintendent Whitmore and their earlier telephone conversation regarding Nangiles' complaint about him and the fact the chief wouldn't be taking it any further. "Once the bigwigs see what you have, they may put you in the driver's seat developing it for official deployment."

"Thank you, Sir," said Jones, his mood seeming to have brightened.

Grant left him and walked through to the incident room, where officers were starting to bustle, an air of tension engulfing the room. There wasn't really a development left to have, except for the location of Maria Bright and Andy Beam, and Lisa Trefusis had spilled most of what she had known, it was just a matter of the interviewing officers from Bodmin to get her to do it in the most appropriate order to get a conviction.

DCI Nangiles walked in and pinned a picture of Beam on the whiteboard. He looked around the room, and the chatter died down and fell to silence. "Andrew Peter Beam, known as Andy, aged thirty-five. Found dead thirty-minutes ago in Unity Woods. Looks like suicide. Uniform are in place, SOCO are on route and DI Grant..." He looked up and stared at him. "Now that you're finally back from what-ever leave of absence you've taken, you take control of the crime scene. Maria Bright is still missing and should be considered a suspect."

"Sir, with respect, I think Maria Bright should be considered at risk, and will quite possibly be the next victim."

"What makes you so sure?" DCI Nangiles interrupted.

"Daniel Vigus."

"Is in the bloody clear!" He snapped. "The DNA did

not match, and it is indisputable." He paused, shaking his head. "Vigus is a shitty little pervert, but we have nothing on him. There's no smoke without fire, and he'll get what's coming to him when he slips up. Forget him and move on with finding out how Beam died, and whether Maria Bright had anything to do with it."

Chapter Thirty-Two

"Are you seeing my dad?" Chloe asked, staring out of her window and watching the mudflats of Hayle rush past.

"No!" DC Carveth said quickly.

"But you like him, don't you?"

"I..."

"It's okay, I won't tell him."

"Good," she said. She pulled out as the road widened to two carriageways, but it was only a short overtaking lane, so she pressed the throttle down and took the plain Vauxhall Insignia up to eighty. She knew she'd be ok with that – she expected half the police force to be heading to Unity Woods, but she still didn't know where that was, just that it was near St. Day. Grant had asked her to drive Chloe home while he set up at Unity Woods, then she would meet him there. He had apologised and promised to buy her a drink for her taxi service. She reflected that with DI Grant, she could be easily bought. She glanced at Chloe and said, "What makes you say that?"

Chloe smiled. "He likes you; I can see that."

Heather Carveth chuckled, but she knew the fifteen-year-old could see right through her. "How can you tell?"

"He kind of loses himself in you, when you talk. He's listening, and dad doesn't listen unless he really has too. He's always churning something over in his mind." She paused. "It's how he used to look at mum, before..."

"Tough, isn't it? My parents separated when I was eighteen. I remember thinking, *so what, you've got me out of childhood and just call it quits?* It didn't seem fair, like my entire childhood was a lie. I looked back at all the lovely memories I had on special occasions and wondered whether they'd just been faking it. I ended up wishing they'd separated earlier, rather than staying together. It would have been better somehow."

"I know, right?" Chloe turned in her seat and looked at her animatedly. "But mum was the one to call it quits. Dad had a lot on, a lot of pressure. He wasn't easy to live with, and he wasn't there for months at a time after his stupid undercover work, but he set a deadline on it, this one particular case. After that, he was going to be done, take any posting and concentrate on mum and me. Only my mum couldn't wait. So, I'm at home with this dickhead that helped wreck my family, and my mum who should have known better." She paused, shaking her head. "And I just know mum wants dad back, knows she's made a terrible mistake. She isn't happy."

"Really?" Carveth shook her head. That complicated matters further, but it was already complicated. "Do you think your dad would go back to her?"

Chloe shook her head. "I think there's a lot of water flowed under that bridge. Besides, he's big on loyalty." She paused. "If you cross him, you're on the list. Simple as that. He won't forgive mum and play happy families, no way."

Carveth nodded, made a mental note of what she had said. She could see that this would be true by the way Grant looked at DCI Nangiles. She had seen that other people had noticed, too. The chances are it wouldn't end well for Grant. In a place like Cornwall, like many rural and remote locations, career survival meant knowing which allegiances mattered and which battles were worth fighting and which ones were better to walk away from.

"It's a small pond down here," said Carveth. "I hope he can settle in."

"Is there someone he doesn't get on with?" asked Chloe. "A higher ranking officer?"

Carveth frowned. "I'm not sure I should be having this conversation."

"Oh, you shouldn't, but who am I going to tell?"

"Your dad, for one."

"No. I won't."

"I have your word?"

"I'm a Grant," she said. "I won't break your trust."

Carveth shrugged. "There is one officer, a DCI."

Chloe smiled. "He's punched out much higher than that," she said, smiling. "It was a chief superintendent that got him transferred." She paused. "Mum said that anybody else would have been kicked off the force, but dad has done a lot of things, made a few friends, but basically he has an incredible record."

"Really?" Carveth smiled. She recognised a daughter idolising her father. She had done the same until he had let her down. Walked away from his family. "What like?"

"He met the Queen once. He got the George Cross medal for bravery."

"Wow," Carveth replied, genuinely impressed. "That's pretty cool." She slowed the car down and frowned as she negotiated a grass triangle at the end of the road, then got her bearings and turned left. She had misjudged the angle and the car bounced on the grass. She smiled, embarrassed at her driving, then asked, "Is it this lane?"

Chloe nodded and Carveth drove slowly, the car bouncing and scraping, nonetheless.

"Thanks," said Chloe, opening the door as they stopped.

"I'm coming in," Carveth told her. "My orders were to take you home, show you inside."

"Dad's, eh?" Chloe got out. "Okay, you can meet Tackle."

"Tackle?"

"Our dog."

"Oh." She frowned. "What kind of name is Tackle?"

"You'll see. Dad called him Bollocks, but he got a hasty name change when I showed up."

"Right..." Carveth followed Chloe down the path and stood back as she opened the door. Tackle bounded out, almost knocking Chloe off her feet. He barked once at them, then trotted across the grass and cocked his leg on a granite stone feature. "Oh, Lord!" exclaimed Carveth. "I get it now."

"They're mesmerising, aren't they?" Chloe giggled.

"How long has your dad had him?"

"Officially? Since last night, I guess. He's been tossing him scraps for a month after he showed up one night. I think dad thought he was like Six Dinner Sid; you know the cat in the story who had all the homes in the street. But he started hanging around for longer. Dad let him in last night because I've always wanted a dog." She paused, hearing a crunch of gravel. She imagined Tackle was still peeing. "I hope dad doesn't report him lost, I think he's good company for him."

"Your dad for Tackle, or the dog for your dad?" Carveth chuckled.

Chloe didn't respond. She looked past Heather Carveth, her face frozen in fear. Carveth was aware of a shadow, blocking out the light from the open door. She turned around slowly, catching her breath when she saw the man in the doorway, the assault rifle held casually in his right hand, the barrel pointing at the floor.

Chapter Thirty-Three

Carveth raised her hands slowly and stepped in front of Chloe, shielding her more to block Chloe's view than provide protection. If they were going to be slain by a hail of bullets, she was damned if the girl would see it coming. "Please..." she said quietly.

"You are close to Detective Inspector Grant," said the man.

His accent was a curious mix of Slavic, German and French with a subtle twang of American – a feature often unwittingly cultivated in international schools. Carveth kept her eyes on the gun, which the man had raised and now cradled in both hands, aimed from the hip with the barrel frighteningly close to them.

"Please..." Carveth repeated. "Please don't shoot..."

"You!" He craned his neck to look at Chloe behind her and aimed the rifle higher. "You are young. You kissed him at the police precinct. He is your father, yes?"

Chloe frowned at the word precinct. But she got the gist and nodded all the same. She was sobbing, her hands held up to her mouth, doing her best to keep it together.

"Where is he?" the man asked.

"You tried to shoot us at Gulvaddon," Carveth said. "Why?"

"I will ask the questions!" he raged, then shouted, "Where is he?"

"I am a police officer..."

"I know! I followed you from Penzance police precinct!"

"Just put down the gun and..."

The man raised the assault rifle's muzzle to the ceiling and opened fire with a short burst spraying plaster and debris down on their heads. Both Chloe and Carveth screamed and the man shouted, "Shut up!"

Carveth's ears were ringing, and she had barely heard the man's shout, but two seconds later she heard the man's wail as Tackle clenched the man's calf from behind and shook violently from side to side. He let go of the assault rifle with his right hand and desperately struck at the dog with his fist, but Tackle was short and heavy and fast and he soon had the man off balance as he growled and dug his teeth in harder. The dog's claws scraped on the polished wooden floorboards and he started to lose traction. The man squatted and caught hold of the scruff of the dog's neck, but the dog quickly released its grip and snapped at his forearm instead. He wailed again, but this time he growled back, psyching himself up and controlling his aggression as he released the rifle completely and jabbed his fingers into the dog's eyes. Tackle yelped and let go and the man made a dive for the rifle, but Carveth – momentarily transfixed on the battle – rushed forward and kicked the weapon across the room where it skidded off with a clatter into an open cloakroom-come-alcove at the side of the vestibule. She dodged back, caught hold of Chloe by her hand and raced across the open space towards the door. The man was crawling across the floor, his hands and leg bloody from his encounter with the bulldog. Tackle was shaking his head, his eye irritating him, but he seemed to forget the pain and went for the man again, this time closing his jaws around the man's crotch. The man was in raptures of pain now, howling like an animal himself and desperately reaching for the weapon. He was far closer to it than Carveth, so she charged for the door and bundled Chloe ahead of her.

They ran for the car and Carveth fumbled with the keys and dropped them. They bounced and clattered and landed underneath. She dropped to her knees and reached, scraping and clawing in the mud. The weapon fired again and even outside the volley of gunshots was almost deafening. Chloe screamed and Carveth froze for an instant, then clawed until her fingers latched onto the key fob and the large yellow tag fitted to the pool cars. She thought she had unlocked but Chloe was frantically pulling on the passenger door handle. One click to unlock the driver's side; two clicks to unlock the entire car. Chloe screamed that she couldn't get in, but Carveth was already starting the engine and pulling away. She slammed on the brakes and pressed half a dozen different switches on the dash until she found the right switch and unlocked the rest of the car and Chloe swung the door open and jumped in. There was another burst of gunfire and both women flinched as Carveth floored the accelerator and the tyres slewed on the muddy ground.

"Wait! Stop!" Chloe screamed.

Carveth looked towards the house to see Tackle heading towards them at full pelt, his great loose jowls almost moving in slow motion as he covered the ground in giant leaps.

"I can't!" Carveth screamed.

"You have to!" Chloe shouted and opened the door. She held her arms open for Tackle, then saw the man stumbling out of the house clutching the rifle. She screamed and the car lunged forwards as Carveth made her choice. Tackle was mere feet away and the man was gaining. "Wait!" Chloe shouted, then leaned back in and hoisted up the handbrake.

The car slowed and struggled as Carveth kept her foot on the accelerator and the rear wheels locked up and dug in. Tackle bounded in, leaping into Chloe's lap as Carveth released the handbrake and the car shot forwards towards the lane. Gunfire erupted behind them and the nearside rear quarter window shattered, and the offside passenger window blew out. They both screamed, but as they entered the safety of the lane, Carveth breathed a deep sigh and looked across at Chloe.

"You could have bloody killed us!" she snapped. She looked at Tackle, slobbering and panting on Chloe's muddy lap. "I hope that bloody mutt is worth it..." Chloe started to sob, but Carveth gripped her thigh to comfort her. She felt like crying, too. It was pure adrenalin, and when it spiked, she knew it needed to ebb away and that usually meant a flurry of emotions. Although, she would have to admit, she had never experienced a rush like that before. "It's okay, Chloe. It's okay..." She stared ahead, her heart sinking as she saw a Ford C-Max blocking the end of the lane.

"Oh no!" Chloe screamed.

Carveth slammed the vehicle into reverse and floored the accelerator. "Hang on!" she shouted.

She reversed the car back down the lane at speed. She misjudged a little and the car scraped down the hedge, taking the passenger wing mirror off, where it dangled by the electrical wire and clattered against the door. She could see the man in the rear-view mirror. He had stopped running and was bringing the weapon up to his shoulder. He fired a few rounds, and the rear windscreen spider-webbed. She could no longer see, but as she glanced in her own wing mirror, she could see that he had turned around and was sprinting for his life back down the lane to the parking area. Carveth grit her teeth, intent on running him over, but he got clear just in time as the Vauxhall Insignia hurtled backwards, its engine whining in protest. Carveth swung the steering wheel, but kept the vehicle in reverse, weaving and correcting until she headed back into the lane in reverse. She had her foot to the floor and struggled to navigate with just the one mirror remaining, buffeting the hedge on both sides.

"What are you doing?" Chloe shouted.

"We can't ram that car with our bumper, or we'll take too much damage to the engine and get stuck!"

"Oh shit, he's back!" Chloe shouted. "And he's aiming at us!" She watched, almost transfixed as the man stopped running and settled into a strong stance to aim the weapon. "Drive!"

Carveth remained steadfast on the accelerator. The vehicle starting to lurch from side to side again under such speed in reverse gear, pushed back in line by each hedge as she failed to correct the steering in time. The man fired, the muzzle flash clearly visible, and then the man disappeared from their view as she half steered, was half buffeted around the lane's only bend.

"Yes!" Chloe squealed.

"Hold on!" Carveth shouted and a second later the rear bumper cannoned into the side of the parked car and all the airbags inflated in what sounded like a single gunshot within the cabin. The Vauxhall slowed, skidded and ground to a halt in the middle of the road. The Ford was jammed against the hedge opposite them, and a group of cyclists had pulled up just in time. One of the cyclists was dismounting as Carveth engaged first gear and turned the vehicle in the road. Her window had shattered in the impact and she elbowed the glass into the road. "Get down the hill!" she shouted at the cyclists. "There's a gunman firing at us!"

It seemed to dawn on the cyclist that it was plausible, they would have heard the gunshots after all. The man got back on his bicycle and his companions were already powering down the hill towards the village of Portreath. Carveth knew the steep hill, and they would be close to car speeds soon enough, if not already.

Carveth waited for them to climb the rest of the hill and turned left for Pool, before she reached for her mobile phone and handed it to Chloe. "Get that onto Bluetooth and dial nine-nine-nine. It's time to call the calvary..."

Chapter Thirty-Four

Andy Beam had hung himself. There was no great mystery to it. The man had been involved in a scheme to raise money on the back of Lilly Trefusis' abduction and whether it was a hoax or not, he obviously couldn't see a way out. To be found out would give him serious prison time, and he already knew what that was like.

Grant watched the man being cut down. SOCO had left him dangling in place until a senior investigating officer had arrived at the scene. Fortunately, Unity Woods, situated near Chacewater, was a quiet place and only used by a few dog walkers. Grown on old abandoned mine workings, there were both capped and hidden mine shafts and the ruins of pumping houses - or what people mistakenly called tin mines - dotted all over the woods. The mines were in fact underground and the classic building of a two-storey stone-built house with a giant chimney stack on the side was what was used to pump the mines of seep water.

Beam had served in Parkhurst. The same prison on the Isle of Wight as Daniel Vigus. For two years. But that would have been plenty enough time for him to know him. And presumably Maria Bright would have visited. Grant already had a hunch about Vigus, the historical allegations and now Andy Beam's death only consolidated that hunch. But he couldn't voice it yet. But, as he watched the man lowered and placed in an open cadaver bag, he couldn't help thinking about Vigus' trip to Pool and the DIY store. DC Heather Carveth had spoken with the cashier and taken the receipt that Vigus had left. A shovel, a pick and some heavy-duty rope...

Grant walked over to the forensic scientist, nodded a greeting.

"Apart from being pretty athletic to reach the lower branches to use as a platform, it looks like a straightforward suicide by hanging," said the forensic scientist, still jotting his findings into a notebook.

"Is the rope new?"

"Oh, yes. Brand new and previously unused, I'd say."

Grant looked up at the length of rope hanging from the tree. The cut end of the rope had started to fray and was waving in the wind. "Are you just leaving that there?"

"I can't reach it."

"But it's evidence."

"Not when it's a suicide."

"It's not in good taste."

The forensic scientist shrugged. "We don't need it, and I can't reach it."

"The knot might give us a clue."

"Like what?"

Grant frowned. "Well, what type of knot it was, first. Andy Beam worked at a boatyard in Penryn. If it's a crappy granny knot, it would point to him not being the one to have tied it."

The forensic officer thought for a moment, then said, "I suppose..."

"Get a ladder and get it down, carefully." Grant looked at the ground and said, "There are a lot of scuff marks here. Old footprints will have debris in the treads. If you can get casts of two individual pairs and match one of them with the victim, then the other might well be a perpetrator. How close did the person who discovered him get?"

"Twenty feet."

"Then there is a good chance that scuffed area will have some evidence."

"It looks pretty straightforward to me."

"Because you're already trying to see it like that. I don't believe this was suicide, so I'm looking past it. I'm not meeting you in the middle here. Either do what I've asked or take your arse out of here and I'll request someone else."

"Look, we're not all yokels down here..."

"Then stop fucking acting like one." Grant paused. "Look, I know you're as good as anybody else, but right now, I suspect foul play and I need more than just a case closed suicide because it looks that way."

"But DCI Nangiles..."

"Isn't here..." Grant interrupted. "Look at the scene. Look at the rope and when you get back to the lab, go over the body with a fine-toothed comb. Then call me." He took out a card and handed it to him. He'd seen enough of the crime scene. He wasn't convinced Beam would have been able to judge the length of the rope and make the climb. It was just a little too perfect. He'd seen bodies swinging in the woods before. And he'd seen how far from a clean death it would have been. Hanging worked as an execution. Hands tethered, the drop calculated, the rope measured, the coiled knot at the neck thick enough to dislodge the vertebrae when the rope pulled tight – it was a quick death. But Grant had seen nothing like that. Not ever. Grant had seen poorly tied knots, not enough drop, feet scuffing the earth and hands that had clawed desperately at a synched slip knot that merely strangled the person for a slow and undignified death. Alone in the woods.

Grant walked back towards the uniformed officers who were talking to the person who discovered the body. He stopped to check a message on his phone. It was an email in response to the call he made on the clifftop at Vigus' cottage. He reread it, then clicked on the link provided and typed out a short message then copied the sender and the new recipient into it and sent it. Nothing ventured, nothing gained. But he had a feeling his relationship with DCI Nangiles would soon be taking a turn for the worse.

Grant nodded at the two uniformed officers. He didn't recognise either of them, so he showed his warrant card and introduced himself before speaking to the witness.

"I'm DI Grant, can I ask you a few questions?"

The woman nodded. She was still obviously shaken and was cradling a cup of tea and held a retractable lead that was on full extension with a yellow Labrador sniffing where other dogs had left their mark along a length of sheep netting interspersed with posts every eight feet of so. Grant had seen a catering van parked in a nearby layby on the way and guessed one of the uniformed officers had gone out to fetch some tea for her. He knew the officers would not be in a hurry to leave. While they were keeping people away here, they were probably missing out on something like an RTC that meant altogether more grisly work. A cup of tea and a long sit was to be made the most of in the middle of a twelve-hour shift.

"Did you see anybody else in the woods?"

"No." She paused, concentrating hard. It was an easy enough question, but in Grant's experience witnesses often tried to be helpful and let the person asking the questions know they were being sincere and trying their hardest to recall the facts. "No, it was just me and Jessie."

"Jessie?" Grant asked, then shrugged. "I take it Jessie is your Lab?"

"Yes, going on five," she said.

Grant smiled, unsure what the dog's age had to do with anything, but he could see that the woman was nervous. "You parked here, in the parking area and walked down the track to the woods." He paused. "Nobody else on the way?"

"No. Not a soul."

"And no cars when you arrived here?"

She shook her head. "No," she replied, then added, "Oh, wait... yes, a vehicle swung out and turned left back towards Redruth. I had to wait for oncoming traffic before I could pull across the road and park."

"Can you remember the make of the vehicle?"

"No. Just a big off-roader type. Big and boxy."

"Colour?"

"Green."

"Can you remember any of its number plate?"

"No. I don't think I even looked. Just noticed the size and colour."

"And the driver, or any passengers?"

"No," she replied. "But the driver was sort of, oh, I don't know..."

"What?" Grant prompted. "Skin colour? White, brown, black...?" He didn't go into the skin colour codes referred to as the Phoenix Codes I/C 1 to 6. Most people didn't have a clue how it worked.

"Well, that's it, you see?" She frowned. "When he was

looking right, down the road towards Chacewater I could have sworn he was white, but then when he swung out and drove away and I was left waiting in the crown of the road, he seemed darker somehow..."

"What, like Asian?"

"Sort of," she said. "Or maybe his collar was tucked up?"

Grant's heart started to pound against the wall of his chest. He looked at her earnestly and said, "Could it have perhaps been a burn...?"

Chapter Thirty-Five

Grant got the call as he sat back down behind the steering wheel. DCI Nangiles. He considered not answering, but only briefly. He still had a job to do.

"Where are you?" Nangiles asked curtly.

"Still at Unity Woods," he replied. "About to leave. The woman who discovered the body has identified the same colour vehicle as Vigus and thinks she saw a man with a burn to his face behind the wheel."

"Just bloody drop it!" Nangiles snapped. "SOCO said it was suicide, plain and simple."

"They're doing some further checks..."

"I've not called about that, anyway. Just listen. There was an incident involving DC Carveth and your daughter..."

Grant sunk deep into the seat of the Alfa Romeo. His heart started to race, and he felt his stomach tense. "What?"

"They're okay," he said sincerely, which surprised Grant. "That shooting yesterday... well, there must be a connection..."

"Spit it out for Christ's sake!"

"A man shot up your house, DC Carveth got your daughter out and they made it safely to Camborne police station. Carveth totalled one of the pool cars getting to safety, but both are okay. SOCO and armed officers are heading for your address and the chopper is inbound to search the area with thermal imaging, just in case the gunman is trying to hole up until it all dies down."

"Are they still at the station?"

"Yes." Nangiles paused. "This is a big deal, DI Grant. DC Carveth said the man had what looked like an AK47. That's not commonplace down here. In fact, I've never heard of shootings involving anything else but shotguns and the odd black-market pistol. The last shooting I recall was a double murder near Truro about twelve or thirteen years ago when I was a uniformed sergeant. That was with a point-two-two hunting rifle. An AK47 is something else entirely..."

"Well, I've seen a few," Grant replied tersely.

"I don't doubt it. But I want you to stay there. I have an armed response unit en route, and they will shadow you back."

"It's okay, I'm close, just a couple miles to the dual carriageway and then I'll be there in ten minutes."

"No. Sit tight. That's an order. They'll be there any minute." He paused. "And then we'll need a talk. Simply you being down here would appear to be a risk to my officers."

Grant ended the call. DCI Nangiles had an agenda and DI Grant wasn't a fit for him. So that was how the man would play it. Grant cursed and dialled Chloe's number. Straight to voicemail. He left a short message asking if she was alright and told her he loved her. Next, he dialled DC

Carveth. Unsurprisingly it went to voicemail, too. He assumed they were in a blackspot. Cornwall seemed to have more than a few.

The BMW X5 arrived with flashing lights, but no siren. Blues; no twos. One of the officers stepped out and approached the car. Grant looked at the man. Six foot plus, wearing body armour and carrying not one, but two Glock 17 pistols. One in a holster across his chest, the other on a leg holster. Both fitted with coiled lanyards which he knew to be made with a titanium core to make it difficult to be snatched from his possession. But it would have to be a brave or foolish person to try. He also carried a taser in another holster and cradled a Heckler & Koch G36 assault rifle with a twenty-round clear plastic magazine. He top and tailed with military boots and a police baseball style cap. He made for an impressive, if not intimidating figure. Britain may not routinely arm its police officers, but when it did, there was no messing about. The man looked ready to storm an embassy.

"DI Grant?"

"I am."

"ID, please, Sir..." Grant took out his warrant card and opened it for the man to see. "We're to escort you back to Camborne police station. I'll ride up front with you in your car, Sir."

Grant nodded and the officer walked around the Alfa Romeo and struggled into the passenger seat. He racked the seat all the way back and positioned the rifle as best he could, given that it was attached to him by a short webbing strap that kept it at his shoulder. Grant himself had found them cumbersome, although when he had been part of an armed response unit, he had been issued with a 9mm MP5, about half the mass of the more powerful G36. The threat from suicide bombers had called for more powerful hardware that would get the job done in just one or two shots.

The drive back to Camborne was uneventful. The armed officer walked Grant to the door then went back to sit with his colleague in the BMW. Grant watched them as he walked inside, but the vehicle did not move again, and Grant assumed they would be taking up a static position until he was on the move. He didn't like Nangiles, but he did appreciate the protection. However, the cynic in him soon thought that the man would have merely been covering the bases. Factor in an officer needing round-the-clock protection and that would soon make that officer's position untenable. And the more he thought about it, the more he thought it to be true. These men hadn't been assigned to protect him; they were there to unwittingly usher him out. DCI Nangiles was desperate enough to use resources, place officers in harm's way and draw attention to Grant as part of a ploy to get him moved on. And for the life of him, apart from an obvious personality clash that happened in every workplace the world over, Grant could not think what he had done to deserve such a response.

"Grant!" Carveth waved at him as she approached.

"Heather are you okay?" he asked, rushing towards her. He didn't know why, but he hugged her, and she hugged him firmly back. She smelled good, like jasmine and felt warm as well. He pulled away from her and hated having to. "Where's Chloe?"

"Come with me, she's in the family room." Carveth released her grip on him and led the way down the corridor and up a flight of stairs.

"What the hell happened?"

Carveth stopped and turned around. "Jesus, it was terrifying. Look, you're going to want to see Chloe first, and she's fine by the way, but I'll get us some coffee and meet you in there and tell you what happened." She backtracked and headed for the vending machines on the lower floor.

Grant found the door ahead of him and on the right. He knocked for some reason he could not justify, then opened the door a crack and peered in. Chloe was curled up on a yellow sofa with Tackle lolling on his back while she rubbed his chest and tummy. His lips and gums hung loose like slices of ham and his loose tongue was so long that it was almost as impressive as his balls. Chloe looked up as Grant opened the door and stepped inside. She rushed over to him, the dog almost falling off the sofa, and wrapped her arms around him.

Neither said anything for close to a minute, and then Chloe said, "Daddy, I was so scared..."

"Of course, you were," he said softly. He stroked the back of her head and down her long hair. For a moment he was taken back to when she had been four or five years old and unable to sleep for nightmares. He closed his eyes, reliving the moment, savouring the memories of innocence and love before their family had fractured apart. "It's okay, Little Lamb..." He felt her hug him even harder, but she let go entirely and stepped away when Carveth entered carrying three cups of coffee on an upturned clipboard she had repurposed as a tea tray.

"We're on our second cups," said Carveth.

Grant took a cup and sat on the sofa beside Chloe. Tackle slid off slowly and flopped on the floor with a grunt or a fart. "Take me through what happened," he said.

"It was the same guy who shot at us at Gulruan," said Carveth. "He was watching at Penzance station and saw you kiss Chloe goodbye. He asked her if she was your daughter."

"Wait, you got shot at?" Chloe asked incredulously. "Why didn't you say?"

"I didn't want to worry you."

"So, you just assumed it would be safe at your home?"

"The girl has a point," said Carveth.

"I thought it was a random act," he protested. "But now, it looks like someone is after me." He pictured his former lover on the bathroom floor. Her body still and cold. "And I've got a good idea who..." He paused. "I'm pretty self-aware, and I didn't see anybody when I left the station."

"Perhaps he set up a camera," said Carveth. "A camera on a vehicle's dashboard or something like that." She took out her phone and spoke for a moment, outlining what she wanted. Grant noticed she was polite and respectful and asked rather than ordered. She ended the call and said, "That was the Penzance desk sergeant. He's going to get some constables to do a sweep outside and see if they can find anything." She paused, then continued as she put her phone back in her pocket. "There are armed response units out looking for the car. It was obviously still drivable, but he won't be able to blend in with it. It's completely smashed in on both sides, where I hit it and where it was shoved across the road and hit the hedge. The PNC check has already confirmed it as a hire car from Hertz in Truro, because somebody phoned it in on the coastal road. They thought it odd that someone would drive such a damaged vehicle and supposed they'd been involved in an accident or hit and run." She paused. "A vehicle has been reported stolen from a carpark in the dunes at Gwithian. That's a highly rare occurrence, so the smart money would be on that being our man. It was a red Ford Focus..." She read out the number plate from her notepad between sipping coffee. "It was a surfer's car. Most surfers use key safes that padlock to a tow bar or wheel spoke these days, but this guy was old school and tucked the keys up under a wheel arch. I dated a surfer once, and he and his friends were pretty casual about that."

"I didn't have you down as a surfer chick," Grant commented. He was already jealous of a strapping hill walker, a barrister who was also a close family friend, and now a surfer. He wondered briefly if a forty something detective inspector with a history of insubordination, a personal life in tatters, a near-constant drinking problem and a contract on his head would make that list.

Carveth smiled. "Nor did I. And nor did they once I voiced thinking about training as a police officer. That kind of killed it dead right there." Grant frowned and she added to clarify, "Half of them are on pot."

"And the other half?" Chloe chipped in.

"Something stronger, or they know someone who is." She paused. "It's all a bit different now though, I suppose. The bubble burst and everybody surfs now. It's less of a culture and more of an outdoor pursuit with a healthy image. Lots of photos and hashtags on Instagram. Not a lot of knowledge of the ocean or how to treat it."

"I can't wait to try it," said Chloe excitedly.

"I'm driving you back to London," he told her. "Right away and no protests."

"But..."

"No buts!" Grant shook his head. "I'm up to my neck in an investigation and someone is trying to kill me! And he almost killed you!" He put an arm around her shoulder comfortingly. "I can't let anything happen to you. When this is over, I'll get some time off and you can come and visit me again. We'll try surfing and try even harder not to have somebody shoot at you with an automatic weapon..." He smiled.

"Okay, but Heather has said we could stay with her," said Chloe. "For tonight at least."

Grant looked at DC Carveth and raised an eyebrow. "You said that?"

"It's no big deal, boss. There's plenty of room and what are you going to do, drive all the way up to London tonight and then what? Find a hotel? You're needed here. I suspect DCI Nangiles will post an armed support unit nearby, and station an armed officer with Chloe tomorrow. He allocated those armed officers to you today without hesitation."

"So that he can say my position is a drain on resources and my position will become untenable."

"Do you think so?" Carveth asked, incredulous. "That's quite a stretch."

Grant stood up and ushered her towards him. She frowned and stood up, followed Grant to the door. "What about rumours?"

"What rumours? There aren't any rumours."

"Exactly," replied Grant. "But there soon will be if I stay at your place."

"It's not just you, it's Chloe and that bloody freakishly endowed dog of yours, too." She smiled. "It's just helping out a colleague and giving a young girl some comfortable time with her father, rather than a cell here, or a shitty hotel nearby with two armed officers outside the door."

Grant looked at Chloe stroking the dog. She was beaming, and that surprised him. The girl seemed to take the incident in her stride. But Grant knew the mind was a complex entity and the fear and shock and anguish would come to her eventually. As it did in the dead of night in his own dreams and nightmares. He looked back at Carveth and nodded. "Thank you, Heather. I... we, both really appreciate it."

Chapter Thirty-Six

He had stolen a car from a carpark near the beach. It hadn't been difficult – he had watched the young man stash the keys under the wheel arch, gather his leash and tuck the surfboard under his arm and jog into the dunes. Once the man had disappeared over the crest of sand and seagrass, he had simply taken the keys, transferred the sports bag containing the AK47 and driven away. He had then used his mobile to search the internet for a 24 hour pharmacy and found what he was looking for nearby at a small retail park at Hayle. He walked with a limp, the dog's bite tearing his scrotum and inner thigh, and his right hand had been badly bitten, along with his wrist and forearm.

He loaded up with paracetamol and ibuprofen, hydrogen peroxide, cotton balls, a can of spray coagulant, tape and a selection of plasters and dressings. He lived a hard life and had made these runs before. He had never failed in his tasks but had done so twice in two days. He needed to hole up somewhere, tend to his wounds, reload the assault rifle and finish this once and for all.

Chapter Thirty-Seven

Mavis Agnes Vigus had been buried at Gulval Church, along with various members of the Lyle and Vigus families over the years. A small 12th century church with views out to Longrock and Mount's Bay, it was both quaint and picturesque apart from a hideous green shed tacked onto the side. Grant reflected - as he passed the grave of a man called John Daniel, who had a large skull & crossbones chiselled into the masonry – that somebody, most likely a committee, had little foresight in the detrimental effect on such a beautiful churchyard. Other than that, Grant thought it one of the most picturesque churchyards he'd seen. And he'd never seen the grave of a real pirate before, so that was a bonus.

After ordering an Indian takeaway and sending down a plate each to his two-man armed response team parked outside, they had spent the evening in DC Carveth's upper floor converted town house apartment in Falmouth playing Scrabble and Monopoly. Grant had won the scrabble but had been bankrupted to the point of begrudgingly writing IOU's, while Chloe and Heather Carveth had ganged up in some sort of conglomerate sisterhood against him. Chloe had taken Tackle into the spare room with her and Grant and Heather had sat back and discussed the case and anonymous assassin. Grant had stayed on mineral water and lime while heather had started and finished a bottle of red wine all by her self. Grant had later taken the large sofa with a comfortable fleece blanket and Heather had gone to her room. In the morning, Tackle had spent ten minutes contaminating the tiny gravelled outside area to the rear of the property and Heather had nipped out in her Mini for McDonald's breakfasts. The armed response officers were due a shift change and handed over after eating bacon rolls and hash browns. Chloe remained with Tackle at the flat with one of the officers posted in the vehicle outside while Heather checked in at the station and Grant drove to Gulval Church accompanied by the other officer, who remained in the vehicle. Grant found the armed officer to be distracting from his work. So much of his time was spent mentally working through events and recalling conversations, that to have the presence of somebody else was akin to damming the flow of water. He simply couldn't think matters through. The walk among the gravestones was freeing his mind up once more, and he was getting closer to seeing the picture of Daniel Vigus and the events that had unfolded more clearly.

The forensics team had erected a tent over Mavis Vigus' grave, and the technicians had enlisted the local grave digging duo to excavate the earth by hand. Grave digging was a skill and required more stamina than the forensic technicians could muster, and they would have known that from old. The two grave diggers were now leaning against the church smoking cigarettes and talking animatedly about what the forensics officers were doing. Even over the hills and moors from Gulruan to Penzance, Daniel Vigus had a reputation and the two men, sleeves rolled up and muddy from their arduous work, were deep in speculation about why the woman should be removed from her final resting place.

Grant approached the tent, caught the eye of a technician who then nodded a greeting and led him inside. Grant sipped some coffee from his go cup. He found the taste and aroma helped dissipate what he would smell next. Barely four weeks since her burial the body would be breaking down and the rotting muscles and organs would be decaying quickly. Bodies were rarely embalmed these days - unless an open casket funeral was required. The technician handed Grant a tube of peppermint oil and he applied some under his nose to repel the odour and then under his bottom lip to eliminate the taste when he breathed. He sipped the last of his coffee and the assault of peppermint on his senses ruined the flavour but told him it was working as it should.

Inside the tent a technician was removing the coffin lid. It was a simple, relatively unfinished coffin. No paint or lacquer and no ornate brass handles. Probably much like the simple coffin the pirate would have been buried in three hundred years before. Grant saw the forensic scientist preparing her DNA kit. Like the technician she wore a full white coverall suit with a hood and had a blue face mask. Grant could only tell she was a woman from the way the baggy suit hung around her breasts and hips, and the shape of her delicate eyebrows. Grant knew she would not have worn makeup or mascara because of the risks of contaminating any evidence.

"I'm Rebecca Shaw," she said and handed him a card. She washed her hands with alcohol gel and put on a pair of blue latex gloves. "The number is on there; I never seem to be at my desk these days. Middlemoor sent the brief. A quick in and out with a graveside DNA sample. I will take hair samples and a scraping from the ear canal as saliva will now be minimal. I will take fingernail clippings, too. But because of the keratinized cells in the nails this procedure will take longer than a simple cell swab and will have to go to Exeter." She paused. "Am I seeing to that as well, or are you taking care of it. I will add, I'm extremely busy..."

Grant shook his head. He'd learned enough over the years to cover himself. He wasn't going to be alone with DNA evidence which could later prove vital in a trial. "Sorry, but I want a clear and concise handling with this. You take the sample, you present it and you sign it off," he said with a shrug of his shoulders. "I don't want anything for egocentric defence barristers to create doubt in my case."

"Fuck it, okay," she said begrudgingly. "Well, that's me for the day then..."

Grant said nothing. She was earning enough for her time and skills. The technician had finished prising the lid off the coffin and looked to the forensic scientist to give him the go ahead, which she did with a curt wave of the hand. Grant stepped around the pile of loose earth and peered inside. He almost laughed but caught himself in time. He'd developed a terrible black humour over the years. Sometimes it was all that got him through his day. Mavis Vigus had obviously left a request to be buried in her wedding dress, only fifty-years on, it hadn't been the best fit. He felt a little foolish at his response and was glad he had checked himself in time, because the old woman looked like all resting bodies he'd seen – sad but at peace - and he thought back to the cottage on the cliff that emanated evil and foreboding. Although she rested peacefully, this woman had created Daniel Vigus and, in his book, that made her at least partly responsible for the man's actions. Or was it a case of nature verses nurture? Were some people just born evil? Grant stepped aside, even with the peppermint oil he could smell the decomposition.

The forensic scientist ordered the technician to change his gloves, and when he had done so, she started to collect the samples, seal them in the plastic tubes and write directly on the pre-fixed labels, but also again on the lids. She handed the tubes to the technician, who walked them over one by one to the case she had previously prepared. Clipped, swabbed, snipped and scraped and they were done. The forensic scientist took a picture of the body and again of the technician refastening the lid to the coffin. She called in the two grave diggers and Mavis Vigus was committed to the earth once more. The technician started to pack away the equipment and Grant stepped outside the tent into a relatively warm and sunny morning. He watched a vicar walk the path towards them carrying a bible. By the time he reached them, the folding frame tent was down and being stowed into a large bag. The two grave diggers had their shovels and waited for the vicar, who stood at the foot of the grave and shook his head distastefully.

"I buried her less than a month ago," he said disdainfully. "Let us hope poor Mavis can now rest for eternity." He looked at DI Grant and said, "I believe this was *your* doing?"

Grant nodded. "It will aid our investigation, yes."

"Then I do hope it will be worth it. The great sanctity of being laid to rest is that it be respected. Did you know that conquering forces would regularly return to dig up and scatter the remains of the enemies they once vanquished?"

"I do know, yes."

"Really?"

"Yes. I read. Or watch the Discovery Channel, at the very least."

"Don't be flippant, my son." He nodded to the two grave diggers and they dropped their cigarettes on the ground and started to fill the earth in. "Well, seeing as you had no qualms about disturbing poor Mavis, you can stand there and show some bloody respect while I perform her service once more..." He opened the bible and started to read from Ecclesiastes 3:1-4. "To everything there is a season, and a time to every purpose under the heaven: A time to be born, and a time to die; a time to plant, and a time to pluck up that which is planted; A time to kill, and a time to heal; a time to break down, and a time to build up; A time to weep, and a time to laugh; a time to mourn, and a time to dance..."

Chapter Thirty-Eight

Grant walked into the Penzance police station with his armed officer following. The man peeled off and took a seat near the door. Grant was buzzed through and met Carveth on the way in. She glared at him, as if trying to tell him something, but DCI Nangiles stepped out of an office behind her and made right for him.

"What the fucking hell have you done?" he raged. "You requested a Home Office body exhumation without going through me?"

Grant shrugged. "I thought you'd say no."

Carveth gasped. A sort of intake of breath, but hastily designed to cover her laugh. She failed and Nangiles glared at her. She tried to turn it into a coughing fit, unconvincing though it was.

Nangiles turned to Grant, stepped closer and said, "What the hell are you hoping to find?"

"It's a hunch," replied Grant.

Nangiles stepped even closer, his face right up to Grant. "Your witness bullshit yesterday was exactly that. Daniel

Vigus was at the Hunter's Arms. He sat alone at a table from eleven to three. He read the paper and worked his way through half a dozen pints. Even had an altercation with one of the locals. What do you say to that?"

"I say, take a step back, because you're in my face..."

"Oh, hard man, are we?" Nangiles edged even closer, if it were at all possible and Grant shoved him in the chest, right up against the wall. "Grant...!"

Grant held up a finger to stop him talking. "Don't push me," he said. "And don't try to keep blocking me, either." He took a step backwards, putting a few feet between them. "What about the rope and the footprints in the woods? I bet there was someone else involved."

DCI Nangiles straightened his tie. He had turned pale when Grant shoved him, but the colour was slowly returning to his face. But this time, he kept his distance. "There was. But as the witnesses in the pub will corroborate, it wasn't Vigus at the scene." He smiled. "So, you're barking up the wrong tree, DI Grant. As much as I want him to be, Vigus isn't your man." He turned and walked past DC Carveth, then hesitated at the doorway. "Oh, and DI Grant... Your personal situation isn't exactly workable, is it? I mean, shacking up with a junior detective who is on the hunt for a promotion is one thing, but how long do you think I can maintain two specially trained armed officers? Maybe you should think about a transfer, or perhaps taking a sabbatical. I'll have a word with Middlemoor later and see what we can work out."

"But it wasn't suicide," said Grant. "So, that tells me two things, the first is that I was right about that. That Andy Beam's death was something wholly more sinister. A murder, even..."

"And the other thing?" DCI Nangiles hovered in the doorway unable to hide his impatience.

"Well, that tells me you're not man enough to accept that you were wrong, and that you still haven't got the balls to do so." He turned his back on him and winked at Carveth. He heard the door slam a moment later and smiled at her.

"What a bastard!" said Carveth. "Insinuating that about me." She paused. "I think *I'm* the one who wants a bloody transfer."

Grant shrugged. "Don't worry about him. He's just full of piss and wind."

"I can't believe you got an exhumation without running it by him first," she smiled. "You don't like a smooth ride, do you."

"I don't like people taking shortcuts because of budget restraints or looking for a fast, convenient result," Grant replied. "And I don't like being pushed."

"Well, I've noticed that." She paused. "And I think DCI Nangiles knows that, too."

Grant shrugged. "I may not be here long enough for it to make any difference," he said. "There's this gunman problem for a start."

"You think it's personal?"

"Absolutely. The man is a hired gun. I've never crossed paths with him before. And if I had, whatever it was wasn't significant enough for this." He paused. "But my last under-cover assignment went south." He left out the fact he had been sleeping with the target's wife. No good would come from that admission. "And I think the target has taken a contract out on me."

"It needs taking seriously, investigating as it would with

any other victim. Not as a random act, but as a premeditated crime."

"And the difference is?"

"Reactionary has officers out looking for a vehicle, using photofits, looking for witnesses, making an appeal and generally casting a wide net." She paused. "As a premeditated crime, someone needs to interview you and find out your suspicions and work backwards to your last assignment."

"Just testing," he said. "Remind me you're ready for the sergeant's exam when the time comes around."

She smiled and nodded. "I'll be sure to," she said. "Your old team and team leader will have to be involved. This is a problem originating in London, not Cornwall."

"Great. That could be a problem."

"Why?"

"My team hate me for blowing the operation and I punched my team leader. Three times."

"You hit him on three occasions and still kept your job?"

"No, I punched him once, then twice more on just the one occasion. Like a combination."

"Oh shit!" She shook her head. "Why?"

"Well, once I hit him, I just thought *what the hell...*"

"No, I meant why did you hit him in the first place?"

"I messed up. He rubbed my nose in it, relished the power. I just saw red."

She shook her head and headed for the door to the second floor. "When the sergeant's exam comes around..." she said, looking back and smiling. "Maybe you shouldn't be my reference." She paused. "Do you know something? For someone who played chess in college, you don't seem to make the most strategic moves."

Grant looked at her and said, "What?"

She let go of the door, then stepped aside and allowed two uniformed officers to get past her. "You said after you visited Vigus' cottage that you couldn't stop thinking about a chess match." She frowned. "You said it felt significant. Anyway, you can't investigate a threat to your own life. You're too close," she said, then added, "I'm going upstairs to see if there's any progress on finding the gunman, and what the long-term plan is for your *problem*."

"No," he said sharply. "Get two uniformed officers and DCI Nangiles. Tell them to meet me out front sharpish." He shook his head, cursing under his breath. "I should have listened to my little voice..."

"Your what?"

"My little voice." He paused. "The voice in my head."

"You're hearing voices now?"

"Just go and get them. And hurry!"

Chapter Thirty-Nine

Grant hadn't given DCI Nangiles much choice. He had made it clear he was going to search Vigus' cottage, and that he believed there to be a threat to life. That was all he needed. A warrant secured an officer the right to search and seize property and possessions during an investigation, but it wasn't needed if there was the suspicion of a threat to life. What became a problem was when a search such as the one he had planned yielded nothing. That was when lawyers and legal action generally followed. Usually it could be countered and won, but there had been occasions in Grant's career when it had not. He knew he couldn't afford another scenario like that.

DCI Nangiles only had to attend in order to cover himself. If he went with Grant's hunch and it didn't pan out, then he had ammunition in his arsenal to continue his political attack on him. If Grant was right, then he could swoop in, play the rank card and ride the wave of success. If he remained at the station, then he couldn't be part of anything. He hadn't yet spoken, but he had exuded an air of smugness for the entire journey, short though it was, to Gulruan and the headland beyond.

Carveth rode in the back. She had settled back in her seat and was along for the ride. She didn't know what Grant had planned, wasn't entirely sure he did, either. Both armed response officers followed behind in the BMW X5. Nangiles hadn't seen the need for more uniformed officers to accompany them, and ever aware of resources and budget, he had stood them down. It was clear he thought this was going to be a waste of both time and energy.

"You seriously think Maria Bright has been taken by Vigus?" DCI Nangiles finally broke the silence. "In my opinion, she should still be considered a suspect. We haven't been able to get her prints or DNA profile yet. It's obvious she's severing the weakest link in her plot and now Andy Beam can't tell us anything. I imagine she will blame him entirely for everything that has happened."

Grant slowed the Alfa Romeo and swung across the rocky ground. The sky was darkening with heavy rain clouds and the sea had taken on a silvery slick of calm with a mirror finish. The sea could change beyond belief overnight. Fishing boats dotted the horizon. Grant thought that it looked like a storm was brewing and the boats were heading back to port in St. Ives. Vigus' cottage looked dark and ominous. He looked at the Land Rover Discovery. Green, just as the woman at Unity Woods had confirmed. Grant knew he was taking a leap of faith, but he was in it now. There was no going back. He parked the car, took out his phone and got out. He dialled Rebecca Shaw's mobile number and waited. She was surprised he was hurrying her, and she didn't hide the fact. But he got what he wanted, then asked her for something else. He wanted the DNA profile compared to the second party on the rope that had killed Andy Beam. They weren't a match. He then asked for something else, and she did not try to hide her surprise. She said it would take some time, but she'd be right on it and ring him back as soon as she had a result. He thanked her and ended the call.

"Ready?" DCI Nangiles asked sarcastically.

Grant walked towards the cottage without answering. Nangiles was a detective, hopefully he'd work out the answer all on his own. DC Carveth followed and jogged over to Grant.

"What's the plan?" she asked. "I've got to admit, I'm pretty confused. What prompted this?"

"You did."

"How?"

"You reminded me of that game of chess I once had at university and that was what had been nagging me from the first time I met Vigus." He stopped at the door, took a breath and hammered his fist against it. He didn't let up.

Vigus answered the door. He ran a hand through his greasy hair and shook his head. "Detective Inspector Grant," he said slowly. "To what do I owe this pleasure? Perhaps you have bought me a new phone?"

"I'm surprised you didn't make a complaint."

"I still might."

"I'd welcome that, because I can seize your phone records and see your internet browsing history."

Vigus shook his head. "I'm sure you won't find anything. If you really thought you would, then you could have checked the records already. You don't need my phone for that," he said confidently. "You won't find anything on my phone bill, just like you won't find anything here."

"I have reason to believe there is a threat to life here,

that threat being you. I have the right to enter your property and check."

"I'm calling my solicitor."

"Got a new phone already?" Grant paused, peering past him. "There's no landline registered in your name or for this address."

Vigus stared at Grant and shrugged. "I'm still not letting you in..."

Grant shoved him in the solar plexus with the heel of his hand and the man fell to the floor, winded and heaving for breath that would not come. His face turned white and he panted like a dog in a car on a hot day. Grant stepped over him and nodded for Carveth and DCI Nangiles to follow. "Asps out and stay alert, we're not alone here." Grant snapped out the retractable baton and headed for the stairs. Carveth unslung her shoulder bag and dropped it on the floor. She snapped out her asp and followed Grant up the stairs. He had already reached the landing and tore into the first bedroom. He caught hold of the bedframe and heaved it onto its side sending the grubby bedding onto the floor. There was no sign of the sick roll of pillows and stained nightdress. The photograph had gone, too. Carveth shouted that the bathroom was clear, and Grant opened the wardrobe door. He looked up for a loft hatch but there was nothing there. He joined Carveth in the second bedroom and opened the wardrobe. Nothing. Carveth got on her hands and knees and looked under the bed but got up quickly. Again, no loft hatch in this room, either. On the landing there was one, and Grant stood on tiptoes and opened the hatch. He took out a pencil torch and placed it between his teeth, then jumped and dangled for a moment before grunting through a complete pull-up. He shuffled his arms around to either side of him and pressed himself up into the gloom. Carveth grabbed his foot and positioned it onto her shoulder. The extra purchase helped him inside.

The torch beam cut through the darkness. There were boxes around the hatch, but nothing where a person could be hidden. He shouted for Carveth to stand clear and lowered himself to the floor.

"That just leaves downstairs," said Carveth hopefully.

Grant nodded. He half ran, half slid down the tight spiral staircase and peered into the lounge-come-breakfast room. A range cooker, which he assumed would heat the building, a television so old it was practically a radio and three threadbare wing-backed chairs facing it. Grant checked a built-in cupboard, a sinking feeling in his chest.

"Sir! Quickly!" Carveth shouted.

Grant headed into the kitchen and saw Carveth on her knees beside DCI Nangiles who was lying flat on his back. She was clutching a bloody wound and dialling on her mobile phone. She cursed the one bar signal and tried to hold the phone higher. Nangiles had been stabbed and he couldn't breathe. The wound was large, and he was bleeding out. Grant noticed bubbles in the blood. No wonder the man hadn't screamed, his lung had been severely punctured.

Grant dropped onto his knees and snatched Carveth's shoulder bag off the floor. She frowned, looked about to protest, but continued with her call. Grant tore through her bag and retrieved a tampon. Heather Carveth looked at him, her expression somewhere between humiliation and bewilderment. Grant took out his wallet and snatched out a credit card and a condom. He returned Carveth's look with a shrug, then opened the tampon and removed Carveth's hand from the wound. He jammed the tampon into the wound and left the string dangling. Nangiles flinched, arched his back in pain, but still made no sound, other than a wet gargle. He was almost pure white, now. Grant then opened the condom packet, put the credit card inside the condom and tied it after getting all the air out. He placed the card in its sterile wrapper against the wound and at once it was airtight. Nangiles took his first proper breath and the colour started to return to his features. The wound stopped bleeding and Nangiles's chest was working like a bellows.

"Where is he?" Grant asked him.

Nangiles pointed at the fire hearth, his hand shaking. "Under there," he rasped.

Grant went to the hearth and ripped it up. It was hinged but weighed at least eighty pounds. He peered down into a dark hole chiselled into the rock. It was just about wide enough for him. Vigus would have had room to clap. Grant turned to Carveth and said, "Get Nangiles to press on that as hard as he can. Go and get the armed officers. Put one on this end and go with the other to the mine." He shook his head, unable to get his words out fast enough. "The pumphouse over there!" He nodded his head towards the first of Wheal Pittance's line of pump houses, then dropped down into the pitch black, the hearth slamming shut above him.

Chapter Forty

Grant had the pencil torch, but in his haste, he had forgotten the asp where he had placed it beside the hatch opening. He was on his hands and knees and placed the torch in his mouth as he crawled. He was not keen on enclosed spaces. He had been locked in a cupboard as a prank by his older brother's friends when he was nine, and the fear had remained with him. An hour of high jinks had shaped his life and left him with a phobia. He dealt with it easily enough on a day to day basis – he simply stayed away from confined spaces. But today wasn't one of those days.

His hands shook and he found it difficult to breathe as he edged forwards. In his mind he was scrabbling at a terrific pace, but he was in fact edging nervously forwards. He was close to discovering the secret, close to confirming his suspicions and nagging doubts. He stopped and breathed, steadied himself and willed himself onwards. Everybody was somebody's son or daughter. He had always told himself that, and it helped when things got tough, because he imagined someone doing everything that they possibly could to help Chloe. He was doing this for Maria Bright, her family. He was doing this for Lisa Trefusis, her daughter Lilly who had been unwittingly caught up in the effects, like the ripples from a stone cast in the water, all these years later. And he was doing this for PC Tamsin Gould. Raped all those years ago, too afraid to tell her terrible secret. He thought of Andy Beam. A man of limited intelligence who served time with Vigus, and if Grant was right, then Vigus would have wanted the man silenced as quickly as possible after his release. The man would know too much, and that was what Grant was counting on as motive for his murder.

Grant found the strength to press on. He shuffled more quickly, his head scraping the rough stone ceiling and forcing him to duck and hunch his shoulders. He could see light ahead. Dim, artificial light and panicked voices. There was a scream of protest and the sound of a struggle. Grant crawled for all he was worth and could see several pairs of legs moving ahead of him. At the end of the tunnel, he saw a lump hammer and a crowbar. He switched off the torch and pressed onwards. Picking up the lump hammer, he swung hard and cracked Vigus on the ankle bone. The man screamed and dropped to the floor and enabled Maria Bright to fend off her other attacker with her hands and feet. She had been bound with rope, and it looked the same type that had been noosed around Andy Beam's neck. The rope had been cut, but as Grant struggled out of the tunnel and into the cavern, he could see the strands had been frayed. As his eyes grew accustomed to the light, he saw that Maria's mouth was bleeding and raw and he knew then that she had chewed through her bindings. He stood before the other man, the likeness eerily similar. Almost like twins. The same gaunt features, the same height and weight. And the same burn. A grotesque blemish on the entire cheek. The same shape and depth of burn. It would have been easily recreated and Grant imagined the young boy being pinned down as Mavis Vigus pressed the red-hot iron, heated on the range in the cottage, down onto his soft, unyielding flesh. Recreating the accident which had shaped Vigus' identity so profoundly. He imagined the screams and the other boy watching. His twin being created in front of his eyes. Would he have been terrified as he witnessed such a heinous sight? Grant certainly thought so. But he feared the young Vigus was by then immune to feeling and emotion.

Grant clenched the lump hammer and watched the man with the knife. It was all about timing. Running away was the best defence against a knife, but he did not have that option. He readied himself, knowing that he needed to control the blade. But the other man would think only of the knife and would forget to watch for the rugby punt to the balls. Grant was ready to kick as the man advanced, but the cavern was thrown into daylight and a strobe torch played in the man's face, the light dancing around the cavern's walls like blue-white disco lights.

"Armed police officer! Put the weapon down! I am authorised to shoot!"

Grant hadn't heard that tagged on the end before, but it was a nice touch. Vigus was still on his side, cradling his shattered ankle, when the other man tossed down the knife and was ordered to climb up the metal ladder.

The cavern was clearly a living area. There was a cot bed, prima stove, magazines and boxes of tinned food with pots and pans hanging from old fashioned iron nails hammered into cracks in the rock. It had been lived in for years, but Grant could see a cell had been recently constructed. A three by three recess hewn out of the rock with bars fashioned from old mine shaft capping. Poor Maria Bright, whatever her involvement in the charade of missing Lilly Trefusis, would have been unable to do anything but stand or squat in her cell. Grant could see her sagging in relief, and he put his arm around her and helped her to the ladder. She was half pulled, half climbed up the ladder herself. Grant kicked the knife out of the way and pulled Vigus to his feet, then pressed him against the rock wall.

"I imagine a long sentence is on the cards for you," he said. "By the way. I saw mummy today..."

"What?" Vigus grimaced. He was seething and the white of his right eye was highlighted against the contrast of the facial burn. "You exhumed her? What for?"

"To confirm that her DNA wasn't a plausible relationship match to the semen samples we now have in our possession from an attack fifteen years ago. And that the same samples of DNA taken from that historical sexual assault don't match the DNA found on the length of rope that was used to hang a man in Unity Woods. So, we've got one of you freaks for rape and the other freak for murder..." Grant swung him to the ladder, and he howled in pain as his ankle bore his weight on the uneven ground.

By the time both men had been handcuffed and read their rights the ambulance had arrived, but a paramedic was already loading DCI Nangiles inside the Cornwall Air Ambulance. The red and white helicopter had landed on the flat ground nearby and its rotors were turning as the pilot waited for the word to go. Grant requisitioned the ambulance to take Maria Bright to hospital for assessment, where two CID members of the special victims' unit would work gently with her to talk not only about what had happened, but what had transpired all those years ago. Grant reflected that to get a prosecution against her rapist, he would have to encourage PC Tamsin Gould to come forward and recount her story, and that in doing so it would all unravel that she had agreed to be part of the ill-conceived plan. He vowed to protect her as much as he could, do everything within his power to fight for her job, but he would not let that stand in the way of seeing that both of these men paid for their crimes. He wasn't prepared to compromise on that, so at the end of it, PC Gould may well lose her job and go to prison for perverting the course of justice, but her rapist would indeed pay for his crime.

Grant watched the helicopter rise and bank northeast towards Truro. He took out his ringing mobile phone and watched a police van bumping its way over the stony ground. He saw from the phone's display that it was Rebecca Shaw, the forensic scientist, so he leaned on the bonnet of the car, the adrenalin subsiding. He answered her call and listened, watching both armed response officers escort the two men to the van and the awaiting uniformed officers. Grant had asked for the two men to be transported separately, and with one man in the van, the armed officers marched the other to the BMW X5. He could see the man limping and realised it was Vigus. He made a note to get the police surgeon to check over the man's ankle. The man would need to visit hospital, he wasn't going to compromise his case by denying him medical attention, but he didn't want the man anywhere near Maria Bright, either. He would just have to wait his turn. Grant thanked Rebecca Shaw, slipped his phone back in his pocket and looked at Carveth.

"That was the forensic scientist. The samples I scraped from Vigus' mother's nightdress were a match for him." He paused. "It's a pretty fucked up family."

Carveth perched on the bonnet beside him and shook her head. "Okay," she said. "Run it by me, because I haven't the foggiest idea how we're even here..." She paused. "What was with the memories of the game of chess?"

Grant watched the police van and the BMW X5 turn a wide circle on the rough ground and set off up the track. They were alone. Looking out to sea and the squall which had started to lash the horizon. He wondered whether it would pass and if the boats got to St. Ives in time. They would have to remain at the scene until SOCO arrived, but it seemed fitting to have the place to themselves. To savour the victory.

Grant smiled at Carveth and said, "I couldn't get the feeling of familiarity out of my head. It started with the photos of Vigus upstairs in the cottage. I must have subliminally looked at them and started to think of Vigus as two different people. It was subtle, or at times it was less so. Vigus went through many transformations... weight gain, weight loss, height and hair style changes. All of them natural, but in some of the photos his features changed a great deal. It was like watching two children growing up, which was exactly what it was. My eye was always drawn to the hideous burn." He paused. "In university I entered a chess tournament that pulled from other universities and lasted over three days..."

"Wow, snooze fest."

Grant smiled. "I enjoy the strategy of the game. Anyway, these games can go on a bit, and then you play the winner of the next round and so on. By day three I was mentally drained. I made mistakes and ended up coming fifth. I was pleased, considering the calibre of the competitors, but I was in awe of the mental capacity of the last few, especially the young man who eventually won. But he didn't. He was found out. Two chess protégé brothers, not twins but amazingly similar in features and hair colour entered and won. Basically, one would rest up while the other played and so forth. To create a singular similarity, to draw peoples' eyes, they both wore a pair of horned rimmed spectacles with a piece of sticky tape on the hinge of the frame. I doubt they were even broken, but your eye was drawn like some sort of conjuring trick and that was enough. They were caught leaving after the presentation... so I came fourth in the end," he smiled. "But it was the burn of Vigus' that always drew my eye. The way he was conveniently cleared of the rape of the girl in Wales after serving out his sentence made me think of the possibility of there being two of them. But they couldn't be twins, or even half-brothers for that matter. The one with negative DNA simply stepped forward and cleared the other. Maria Bright, Lisa Trefusis and Tamsin Gould were so certain that Vigus had raped them, that it just didn't seem conceivable that he could be innocent. When PC Tamsin Gould met Vigus, you'll remember she didn't feel as bad as she thought she would, that was because it wasn't the right man. Her brain had subliminally discounted him. Her emotions told her to feel different, though."

"So, what about the burn?"

"You remember those two boozers in the Jolly Smuggler pub? The smaller, older man said that it looked like the burn had happened all over again. All blistered and sore. How likely would it have been for Vigus to have had the same accident twice? Mavis Vigus simply replicated it. My guess is it was time to let her other boy out into the world and begin the charade?"

"But who was the other boy?" Carveth shook her head, perplexed.

"I think it was her husband's child. When his lover showed up with a child, he went off with the woman. People just assumed he went Padstow way, I suspect up there, the woman's friends and relatives thought she'd started a new life down here." Grant shrugged. "Many people didn't even have a phone back then. In areas like Gulruan. Like your ex said of the area, *Strawdog*s country. We take all the communication and social media platforms for granted now," he said, then added, "I think the secret will lie on the headland. Underneath the ground around the cottage of the first of the Wheal Penance pumping houses. Remember what the man said about the numbers not stacking up? It's a fair assumption that Daniel Vigus wasn't Harvey Vigus' child. Like a sailor's lot. Maybe she just turned to the arms of another man on those lonely nights. Her life didn't sound to be a bed of roses."

"So, the older boy belonged to Mavis and an unknown father, and the one she moulded into her son's *twin* was Harvey Vigus' and the woman he was seeing in Padstow?"

Grant nodded. "Whether it was a fit of rage, or premeditated, we'll never know. But I'm confident Mavis Vigus killed them both and kept the child. Maybe Harvey Vigus rubbed her nose in it and she flipped out? But I bet Harvey Vigus' DNA is a match to one of those sick bastards."

"But we haven't got a sample of Harvey Vigus' DNA."

"No. But we can work backwards from the woman. She's likely to have family, however distant, in the Padstow area. Someone who knows she went missing. What, thirty-five to forty years ago? Simply disappeared. They might have written her off as finding a new life and not looking back, but the moment we put out a search and ask the right questions, someone will put two and two together." He cast a hand across the cliffs, the mine and the ocean. "But their bodies could be anywhere," he said solemnly. "That man at the Jolly Smuggler said someone should have dropped Vigus down a mine shaft years ago. The county is practically honeycombed from mine workings. As for the sea? Someone with the right knowhow could scatter the remains and feed the crabs."

Carveth turned up her nose in disgust. "It doesn't bear thinking about," she said. "And with Andy Beam serving time in Parkhurst with Vigus for two years, they wouldn't have known if he had twigged the differences between the two men. I suppose that was their motive for killing him and then Maria Bright needed to be silenced, also."

"But they thought they'd have their fun with her first." Grant stood up and stretched. "It nagged me about how Vigus defeated DC Jones' drone gadget as well. The man is a genius. But he created it to work on facial recognition and body language. The software does what it is programmed to do. The burn wasn't enough. Not if the jawline, cheekbones, brow and body movement is incrementally different from its subject sample. Vigus gave us the slip in St. Ives and again on the headland. Because it wasn't really Vigus, but his mother's project twin. By the time Beam was killed in Unity Woods, Jones had been stood down and DCI Nangiles had read him the riot act regarding the use of unsanctioned equipment and software. We had been warned off by Nangiles because of the negative DNA connection. No match. By then, the two men could come and go as they pleased."

Carveth shook her head incredulously. "It was all there, you just connected the dots."

"I was slow with the rocks around the cottage. I damned-near twisted my ankle on my second visit, but just kicked the rock away. I believe the tunnel has been here for years, the cavern near the pump house as well. I think it's where either one of them bolted to when there were people calling. Not that many would have before we turned up. But I'm confident that the cell that we found had been recently dug, and what I tripped on was waste from the digging. They weren't about to chance being seen near the end of the tunnel, so one of them would have brought the waste back and scattered it near the house." He paused, shaking his head incredulously. "And then there were three wing-backed chairs in the breakfast room. Threadbare and worn over the years. Mother in the middle and a freakish mutant twin on either side." He shook his head at the thought. "I imagine the cavern was part of the workings of the pump house, I have no idea, need to learn more about the construction of such things. But they recently dug out that cell for Maria, and I believe they planned something similar for Tamsin Gould and Lisa Trefusis, too. Perhaps when the heat died down with Lilly Trefusis." Grant paused, waving a hand across the moonscape of the old mine workings. "They scattered the loose rocks from the excavation all around, rather than place them in a pile. One of them got sloppy when they dumped a bucket load near their own doorstep."

"They should have dropped the rocks down one of the many mine shafts," Heather Carveth said with a smile. "What about Lisa Trefusis and reuniting her with Lilly?"

Grant shrugged. "Well, from experience, I doubt they ever will be," he said solemnly. "Social Services would never allow it. No, I think poor Lilly Trefusis will be relocated in a programme and Lisa will rue the day she ever went along with such a ridiculous scheme."

"Or the day one of the Vigus men raped her and started this chain of events," she said pointedly. "But I believe she's already been punished enough. Every day for the past fifteen years."

Chapter Forty-One

S cene of crime officers, otherwise known as SOCO, arrived and sealed off the cottage and pump house. It was crucial to speak to both men, so Grant called Chloe and told her he would be late. He gave her his debit card number and told her to get busy with whatever she wanted from a takeaway. As he ended the call, he reflected how he would struggle with her staying with him while he was working. The thought made him sad. Whatever snatched moments he had taken with her during the past few days, he had loved every minute of it. But he couldn't foresee helping her through her exams or providing her with emotional support with friendships or relationships when she needed it. Teenage girls fell out with their friends or peer groups all the time. How could he be there with support, anecdotes or just popcorn and a hug on the sofa when he was out all hours searching for a missing person or staring at a body washed up on a remote beach?

Carveth climbed into the passenger seat beside him and put away her phone. "DCI Nangiles is in a stable condition and is being prepped for surgery. Maria Bright has been taken to the West Cornwall Hospital. We've got a female officer and a counsellor with her now. She claims to have been raped by both men and has undergone an examination and DNA testing. She's also been whipped extensively on her back..."

"For Christ's sake..."

"There is extensive damage to some of her teeth caused by chewing through her rope bindings," she said, her voice shaky. The speed of events and adrenalin was what carried you through. When the dust settled, the body and emotion adjusted. "I know she used Lisa and Lilly Trefusis and Tamsin Gould to try and force a conviction, possibly gain financially from any subsequent fundraising, but she didn't deserve any of this..."

"Of course not. And I doubt she knows her lover is dead, either." Grant paused. "Get word out that the news will need breaking properly. No ham-fisted drops into the conversation." He started the Alfa Romeo as Carveth took out her phone and dialled.

Grant drove over the rutted track and was relieved when he reached the tarmacked cliff road that made a loose loop around the headland. There were concrete ruins along the edge of the road, and he could see that at one time there had been a barrier across the road. The barrier was now gone, but the posts either side remained. Carveth had finished her call and he said, "Was this place used for something else?"

"The RAF requisitioned the headland and used it as a listening and observation post during the war. I think the Royal Navy operated a lookout here as well. It wasn't a base, as such, but they had anti-aircraft guns up here. I don't think it saw any action, though."

Grant nodded. The ruins reminded him of pill boxes.

He supposed a sentry would be posted with a rifle and operate the barrier. It would provide them with some cover, but he doubted it would survive an attack from German paratroopers. He carried on driving around the corner, then stopped when he saw the small, red hatchback parked across the road. He frowned. It must have only just parked. The police van and the two armed officers in the BMW X5 had only just passed through.

The gunfire erupted and the windscreen shattered instantly, showering them with gem-sized fragments of glass. Grant slammed the gearbox into reverse and floored the accelerator, the engine whining against the din of the gunfire and Carveth's screams beside him. It was only when he reached the concrete ruins, that he realised he was reversing into the gunfire and that the rear windscreen was shattered also. And then the gunfire stopped altogether. Grant knew that whoever was firing was changing over to a new magazine. For a moment he froze. Head back for the headland, where they would be cut off, or drive for the car and barge it out of the way and try to escape to the road beyond? But he knew that if he struck the vehicle with his front bumper the impact would almost certainly destroy his radiator and they would make it no further than a few hundred metres. The gunfire erupted again. This time in short bursts and it forced his hand. He slammed the car into first and accelerated towards the car.

"We'll take too much damage!" Carveth screamed. She should know, she had made every effort to barge the ambush intended for her and Chloe with the rear bumper.

"If we get away onto the headland, he'll pick us off for sure!" Grant had deduced that the weapon would be the AK47 that Carveth had reported. The man could get comfortable at five hundred metres and pick them off at his leisure. "Brace yourself against the airbag!" he warned her.

Grant aimed for the front quarter of the hatchback. He reasoned he may cause enough damage to the engine for the man to be stranded. Carveth had her phone out and was halfway through dialling 999. Ironic, but it was the quickest way to report what was happening and get some help. She looked up a split second before the impact.

The Alfa Romeo had the weight and momentum advantage over the stationary vehicle, but the impact was significant and after they had ploughed through, the hatchback spun almost one-hundred and eighty degrees, and the Alfa Romeo slewed to a halt in the verge. The airbags had activated, and they had both been flung back in their seats. Grant was shocked and winded, but he clawed at the airbag and looked across at Carveth, who was shaking her head and rubbing her ringing ears. The small amount of explosive used to inflate the airbags had sounded like a gunshot inside the confines of the vehicle and they had resin on their faces. Carveth seemed less affected – she had only experienced it yesterday – but the sound of gunfire behind them, and the bullets peppering the rear bumper and boot lid shocked them into action. Grant restarted the Alfa Romeo and selected first gear. As he accelerated away and the boot lid flipped up and blocked his rearview. He checked his wing mirrors and could see the man pursuing with the AK47 cradled in both arms. As Grant had feared, there was steam escaping the vehicle's crumpled bonnet and the dashboard was an array of red and orange lights. He floored the accelerator and took the car up to forty-five miles per hour, then spun the steering wheel and pulled hard on the handbrake. The car slewed and bumped to a halt. It wasn't a perfect handbrake turn because modern traction and stability control had long put pay to that, but the vehicle was now broadside to the man.

"Lie down across the seats!" Grant shouted at her.

Grant didn't see if she did, but he got out of the car and ducked for cover as the man opened fire with a short burst. Grant made it to the boot of the Alfa Romeo and fumbled for the shotgun he had confiscated from Lisa Trefusis' cousin, John Crocker. He scrabbled inside for the cartridges, which had come loose from the pocket recess he'd stored them in. Although he was firearms trained, Grant had only ever used a double-barrelled shotgun once before on a stag weekend where they organised clay pigeon shooting. Those guns had been over and under designs whereas this one was a more traditional side-by-side. Grant glanced over the boot lid and could see the man had slowed to a walk and was changing over the magazine again. He was close enough to recognise as the same man who had fired upon them outside Lisa Trefusis' house two days ago. Grant worked the lever to open the action and put two of the oo buckshot cartridges into the barrel chambers and snapped the weapon shut. He could see the safety was the same simple forward-push design as the guns on the stag do, and he made the weapon ready as a matter of course. There were no hammers, but the weapon had two triggers and he figured one would be for each barrel. He ducked as low as he could and made his way back to the front of the car, where Carveth was outstretched on her front, her eyes closed and desperately calling the incident in. She seemed to have accepted she was going to die, but she would keep reporting what had happened until the time came. She knew she wasn't making it out of there alive.

Grant watched the man tilt the magazine back in place. He had trained with the same weapon once in a familiarity exercise, and had found it to be the most ridiculously awkward magazine change, so different from the Met's tried and tested choice of Western-made weapons. The man still had to charge the cocking lever, but Grant couldn't afford to give him the opportunity. Without shouting a warning, Grant stood up, shouldered the shotgun and fired. The man went down and skidded backwards a foot on his back. The shots had peppered the man's left side. Grant could already see that from the bloody red holes, he had clipped him with only three of the lead balls. He stepped around the bonnet of the Alfa Romeo , still aiming. The man struggled onto his side and got the weapon cocked. He struggled with one hand to raise the weapon. There was no time to get closer, no time to question him. Grant had one shot, one chance remaining for both Carveth and himself. There was simply too much distance between them. At twenty metres, with the AK47 rising slowly towards him, Grant aimed and fired dead centre and the man slumped into a crumpled heap and lay still.

Grant realised he was still aiming at the body, even though the shotgun was empty. He lowered it and returned to the car. He'd been around enough bodies to know whether one was going to pose further risk, or need medical help, and the man wasn't in either category. He dropped the weapon into the boot of the car. He wasn't going to be holding a gun when the armed response unit turned up, and he could already hear approaching sirens in the distance. He went to the driver's door, where Carveth was looking up at him, tears in her eyes and the colour returning to her cheeks.

"You got him?" she frowned. "How in god's name..."

"Community relations," replied Grant. "Lisa Trefusis' cousin turned up with murder in mind and I confiscated his shotgun and told him to cool off and pick it up next week. I forgot all about it until the boot sprung up. I'm in for a world of shit, now. Confiscating a shotgun and forgetting to check it in? Then using it to kill someone..."

"A man who shot at us before, tried to kill Chloe and myself and then tried again just now?" Carveth shook her head and clambered out, standing in front of Grant. "If you get in trouble for this, then I'm quitting. I wouldn't want to stay part of a machine that could not look past this." She hugged him closely, and to her surprise, he hugged her back. She looked up at him, into his eyes and then looked away as the first of many police vehicles screeched up and armed officers got out, weapons raised.

Grant and Carveth released their embrace and raised their hands. Grant walked towards the officers slowly and gave his name and rank and started to explain that there was no longer a threat to life and that they should stand down. He thought about the embrace, the feel of her, the smell of her body and perfume. And then it was gone. There was a job to do and he needed to get on with it.

Chapter Forty-Two

"Smooth, isn't it?" Grant poured another measure of the twenty-year old Macallan whisky into the plastic beaker and handed it to DCI Nangiles.

"It's warming the insides nicely," Nangiles agreed. "Not having one?"

Grant shook his head and leaned back in the plastic chair cradling his coffee. "Trying not to..." he replied. He'd drank a great deal after his split with Deborah. He'd partied hard, slept around and none of it had made him happy. He had struggled with drink last year when he had come down to Cornwall to recuperate after an injury. It hadn't been pretty. But he had dealt with it in his own way and felt that he was on top of it now. The bottle of rum he had opened when Chloe had first visited was still half-full, and this was the first of two bottles he had presented to DCI Nangiles in his hospital bed at the Royal Cornwall Hospital in Truro. He'd wrapped the other bottle in paper and suggested he keep it for a special occasion.

Nangiles was sat up in bed, his ribs bandaged and a catheter feeding him intravenous fluids was fitted to the back of his left hand. The IV stand contained two bottles feeding into one tube. Grant didn't know what the fluids were, but he'd heard Nangiles had been in a bad way and had needed a blood transfusion. It was also common knowledge that had Grant not acted both swiftly and as efficiently, then DCI Nangiles would have died of his injuries.

"You had some excitement, I hear?"

Grant nodded. The Crown Prosecution Service had told Grant he would not stand trial for the shooting. The man was a ghost. No fingerprints or DNA on file, not even on Interpol's databases. The shotgun was to be held as evidence. Cases were never really closed, but Grant wasn't too worried. He had a feeling this would stay buried, although he still had to address the fact that a contract had been taken out on him. But he already knew where to look and he knew enough about Roper's organisation to make a start. John Crocker had been given a store credit at Helston Gunsmiths for seven hundred pounds in return for the shotgun. He had not been displeased with the settlement.

"The bastard twisted the knife," Nangiles said quietly. He didn't look Grant in the eye, but he sipped another mouthful of the amber liquid and looked content as it warmed him through. "I barely felt the knife go in, but my body didn't fight back. I fell to the floor and had no control. That was the worst of it. I always imaged I'd fight for my life in that situation, give the other guy a bloody good beating. My body just gave up. Vigus leaned over and twisted the knife as if he had his hand wrapped around a motorcycle throttle. He grinned the whole time as he pulled it out. I even saw my own reflection in his eyes..." He shuddered at the memory. "My wife has money. Family inheritance. What I bring home makes little difference, despite my rank and number of years in service. She's wanting me to give it all up. I haven't decided yet, but she's making a good case."

Grant nodded. "We got off to a bad start. It doesn't have to continue that way."

Nangiles nodded. "Agreed." He sipped some more of the whisky and said, "It doesn't seem worth it right now. The long hours, the red tape, the constant public dissatisfaction in what we do. That knife, that sick bastard..."

Grant had been there. All police officers had. Nangiles had some soul-searching to do. To lighten the mood, he raised his coffee cup and said, "Well, here's to your retirement..."

"I don't know how to thank you," he said.

"Please don't, I hate awkward moments."

"Where did you learn that kind of battlefield paramedicine?"

"On the battlefield," replied Grant. "Or more accurately, the rougher London streets. I've been on them for twenty years. You learn stuff."

"I think I misjudged you," said Nangiles. "I thought you were going to come down here and be the hotshot from the big smoke. What I didn't realise was that you had skills that we could all learn from."

"We all keep learning," said Grant. "I've never worked with an officer or with a team I didn't learn from." He paused. "Perhaps I came down with a bit of a chip on my shoulder. I was all but finished, both in my career and personal life. But someone somewhere remembered I hadn't always been an outcast and got me the position down here." He sipped some more of his coffee and said, "I suppose I thought it was all going to be a bit agricultural fairs and cream teas and the biggest challenge would be finding somebody's lost dog. By the time I realised it was such a huge remit with some real-world, big city problems, I'd given off a bit of arrogance."

"Oh, you're arrogant, alright. You don't work well as part of a team and you resent the chain of command. But you are a brilliant detective and a good man in a crisis."

"Okay, that's enough, drink your fucking drink and get well soon." Grant chuckled and put the empty cardboard cup down on the table. He picked up the file and dropped it onto DCI Nangiles' legs as he stood up. Nangiles moved his legs and flinched. Grant pulled a 'whoops' face and looked awkward. He soon recovered. "A bit of bedtime reading for you. And get ready to nail that son-of-a-bitch in court."

"Oh, I will," he said.

"I've no doubt that he wanted to kill you."

"Me neither," replied Nangiles quietly. He looked up, and changing the subject he asked, "What are you doing now?"

"I'm making this watertight," he said, pointing at the file that Nangiles had opened and had started to scan. "And I want to search the area on Gulruan Headland for the bodies of Harvey Vigus and an unknown woman. My hunch is they're buried nearby. There's something about the coldness Mavis Vigus showed in burning the other boy purposely, as if keeping him hidden up to that point wasn't enough. She would have coached them on what to say, how to act and how to pull off the charade of in fact being one person. She liked the control, and I imagine she would have relished knowing the bodies were buried nearby. In the same way that the two men enjoyed their secret and got off on the deception."

DCI Nangiles nodded. He didn't say that it would be a waste of resources, and Grant knew that finding their remains would only cement a case Nangiles was now heavily invested in. He wanted a conviction, and he would have had enough time flat on his back thinking about it. The bodies could be anywhere, but the more Grant thought about it, the closer he thought they would be.

Grant walked to the door, glanced back at Nangiles and raised a hand.

"Thanks for..."

"Don't," Grant interrupted him.

"... For the whisky..." he nodded, raising the beaker. "Now bugger off and seal the deal."

Grant grinned and left the room.

Chapter Forty-Three

rant had found that getting into a wetsuit required no less than an acre of land in which to move and that the space between his newly repaired Alfa Romeo and the Volkswagen T5 van would not be enough. Even standing at the rear of the car and using the space there presented its hazards as he found himself in the way of other vehicles driving past, the drivers searching desperately for a parking space.

"Couldn't you find anywhere quieter?" Grant asked Heather Carveth, who was parked the other side in her Mini and already suited and booted and putting on a pair of neoprene gloves. "I pictured a quaint cove with just the seagulls for company."

"Safety in numbers," she said. "When you're just a *kook* and starting off." She smiled. "Chloe doesn't seem to be having any problems with her wetsuit."

"Must be those old bones, dad. Perhaps you need cod liver oil for your joints?"

He had noticed Chloe calling him dad in front of Chloe, and daddy when they were alone. He wondered how long before she would drop it completely. Almost certainly before he stopped calling her Little Lamb, which he had started doing just to embarrass her in public. "My joints are just fine. I just seem to have a smaller suit than is required."

"I told you not to eat that large pasty before doing this," said Chloe.

Carveth walked around the car and caught hold of the back of his suit and heaved it up for him to put his arms in. "Come on," she said. "We'll zip up down there."

Perranporth Beach stretched for just over two miles of golden sand on the north Cornish coast between Newquay and St. Agnes, and Grant had been assured by Heather Carveth that the conditions were great for learning today. She had provided them each with a surfboard, what she called a Mal. Wide and long with two painted stripes down the middle. A classic sixties shape which was ideal for learning on.

Chloe had been granted the half-term with Grant. He saw it as a victory, despite the fact Deborah and Simon had gone for a last-minute skiing holiday in Italy. He knew it was more because of the convenience than a breakthrough lobbying for equal custody, but Heather Carveth's barrister friend had given an unheard of free ten minutes of consultation over a drink and said it would set a precedence.

Despite the wetsuit, boots and gloves the sea was freezing cold and Heather insisted they should go under quickly, and she led the way diving under a wave and showing them how to ease a small amount of water under the collar of the wetsuit to help with movement and put a layer of water between the insulated neoprene and their own body heat, which would soon heat up and keep them warm. She showed them how to stand waist deep facing the shore and hold the board, then leap on their stomachs as the right wave broke behind them and paddle for the shore. She showed them how to get up, balance, shuffle their weight on the deck and paddle back after they had wiped out. All the time pointing out they should hold the board tightly to avoid it buffeting into their faces, and to be aware of tripping on the leash. It was a lot to take in, but after riding the first three waves to the shore on their bellies, they were well into the fun-zone, loving every minute of it and had forgotten almost everything she had told them. She encouraged Chloe to stand, and she did for a second before wiping out and resurfacing with a beaming smile and her eyes as alive as Grant had seen them in years. Carveth paddled out the back and sat two-hundred metres out, behind the breaking waves in the line-up. They both watched her catch a green wave, get to her feet smoothly, work her way from top to bottom across the face of the wave and flick off before paddling back out. She had said she hadn't surfed in a while, but Grant found it hard to believe. He could never foresee becoming that good. And he probably wouldn't even try. He was enjoying time with his daughter and it didn't matter how good they got, or if they rode on their bellies in the white water every time, just as long as they enjoyed each other's company and made a million memories like these.

Grant watched Chloe splash about, grab her board excitedly and launch into another wave. She squealed with delight and as he watched her, it was difficult to imagine not living for days like these. He felt it was a new start, a new chapter in his life and one that involved Chloe and not suffering isolation and misery, always feeling he had lost everything worth having. And he knew he would fight with his last breath to protect this.

Chapter Forty-Four
Herengracht Canal, Amsterdam

Spring sunshine warmed the streets and reflected off the canals, bringing life and energy to Amsterdam. The café tables and chairs had been dried from the rain and people were enjoying the warmth of the sun on their faces and the promise of more days like these.

Richardson sipped his cappuccino and watched a pair of swans glide the canal, bobbing in the wake of a tour boat that had motored slowly past a few minutes earlier. "Why couldn't we meet at your offices," he asked, thinking of the two leggy beauties with tanned thighs and exquisite taste in delicate underwear. The last time he had been there, they had given him the urge and desire to browse the windows of the red-light district and find a similar woman to fulfil his fantasies.

"I prefer to meet here," Van Cleef replied. "We met at my office last time and I think a second meet would be tempting fate. I make it my practice to avoid repetition."

"And what about your fears about government agencies using covert surveillance and parabolic microphones?"

Van Cleef smiled. "I have a man above this coffee shop

using a white noise projector. I also had you followed, and I had a team lurking in the shadows to spot anyone on your tail."

Richardson nodded. He had suspected as much, but he hadn't spotted anybody following him and he'd taken the time to practise his own anti-surveillance drills, doubling back, crossing the road several times and even taking a water taxi. The Dutch fixer used ex-special forces soldiers for his security detail, and it obviously paid off. Richardson took a sip of his coffee and broke off a piece of shortbread. "Well, mister Anderson, we obviously have a problem. The mark is still very much alive, and your assassin is very much dead." He paused. "Which leaves my employer dissatisfied. Extremely dissatisfied indeed."

Van Cleef smiled and sipped his espresso. He took two slow, deliberate sips and replaced the cup to the saucer. "My dear man, you can rest assure we will see to this problem. And we will fix it. You are getting ahead of yourself, underestimating the organisation that you have placed both your money and faith in. Once paid, we will endeavour to complete the contract. You can tell mister Roper... assure him, if you will, that the contract is fluid. We will see it through. No matter how many assets it takes, we will see to it that Detective Inspector Grant dies. Of that, you have my word..."

Author's Note

Hi - thanks for reading this far, and I hope you enjoyed the story!

I am currently writing another book, but if you enjoyed this and would like to read more of my stories, then head to www.apbateman.com where you can find out more.

If you have the time to rate this story or leave an Amazon review, then you would make this author extremely happy!

DI Grant will return soon...

A P Bateman

Printed in Great Britain
by Amazon